Lynne Alexander lives in Lancashire where, as well as being a novelist, she teaches creative writing.

ADOLF'S REVENGE

Lynne Alexander

An *Abacus* Book

First published in Great Britain by Abacus 1994

This edition published by Abacus 1995
Copyright © Lynne Alexander 1994

A CIP catalogue record for this book is available from the
British Library.

ISBN 0 349 10624 X

Printed and bound in Great Britain by Clays Ltd, St Ives plc.

Abacus
A Division of
Little, Brown and Company (UK)
Brettenham House
Lancaster Place
London WC2E 7EN

Acknowledgments

My special thanks to Tess Coslett for listening to and liking the writing as it went along. Also to Alison Easton for advising at short notice on the title. To my family of friends for being there. My appreciation to Adrian Cunningham for reminding me of the story of Jael; to Deborah Rogers for her helpful suggestions; to Philippa Harrison for her continued belief in me; and to Richard Beswick for his patience on the way to publication.

PART ONE

Their roaring shall be like a lion.
Isaiah 5:29

One

Will a lion roar in the forest when she has no prey?

The Prince is at my mercy, see how he cowers and trembles like a frog before my slippers.

A blasting and a mildew on your garden! I say unto him.

Oh the day is dark my face is dark and hairy, this is a day of wrath of darkness of thick darkness.

A fishhook on his head!

My name is Dreadful.

'No it isn't,' says my sister Pinball, a thorn even in death. 'Your name is Adolf, which is bad enough.'

'Nothing is bad enough for him,' I say. 'Soon he shall be stubble.'

'Neither root nor branches,' she finishes off.

I refer of course to what the Prince did to Keziah my niece my sister Pinball's child which makes me so mad I could spit.

I do spit. *Thut!* goes an arc of fig juice over the porch railing smack into the trunk of an innocent tree.

Innocent, pih.

The Chick's letter is on my lap. 'Dear Aunt Adolf, are you sitting down?' is how it begins. By now she is forty-two years old, as for me I am as old as garments even the moths leave alone. Yes I am sitting down, my sweet dried fruit, sitting and rocking and drinking lemon tea dunking a Fig Newton, very

3

good for the digestion. 'Did you know,' she wrote me (it must have been soon after she landed, a reverse Pilgrim in his land), 'did you know they call them fig *rolls* over here?' I knew it not but I know it now. The damp end which is in my mouth for sweetness turns just as the one God gave to Ezekial – *Eat! Eat this roll!* – to lamentation and mourning and woe.

Yea, even our Fig Newtons are stale.

Feh.

The letter falls from my fingers. The tongue of a duck goes flap flap even it would say, 'disgust work'.

My dead sister's rocker rocks beside mine.

'It's the end.'

'An abomination.'

'An adulteration.'

'He has taken away her glory.'

'Even her heritage.'

'For ever.'

'And ever.'

'Amein.'

Hey ho, what are we saying? Rocking and bestowing, bestowing and rocking a blessing on the head of our enemy?

Her enemy.

NO NO NO! I discuss with myself I say to myself do something protect your sister's progeny from iniquity. But what can I Do? An ocean boils between us. What can I DO?

What could we DO for ourselves?

Doing, pih.

My sister Annie was having relations with a pinball machine. You don't play pinball with your hands you play with your crotch. A man will do bump and grind tilts but with my sister it was her eight-and-three-quarter-months' belly she was thrusting back and forth, the hottest pinball manipulator this side of the Catskill Mountains which are not real mountains according to Keziah who was trying to get out of her belly at the time. My sister however wasn't interested in things getting *out* but in getting a miniball of silver *in*. Ping! flip! slap! This is how she rode out her labour panting hanging on woe unto him who tried to pull her off.

So Keziah my sister's child was born under a pinball machine. You never saw such a blanketful of chicken flesh, that she could live was a miracle let alone marry a prince. She was too big for an incubator too small for life, my sister was only half cooked herself. I think she tried to do a deal with God when the baby came into the world she be granted the privilege of slipping out of it. No such luck.

My sister held on to the bars of the crib like the prisoner she was lamenting. 'Of what have I taken deliverance, a child or a pullet?' The thing weighed four and a half pounds the thighs you could ring with thumbs and forefingers the skin fell down like bloomers. 'From where could such a thing have come?' Her language was ancient her newborn baby already an elder. Wherever it came from it had landed blue and flapping on the cockly pink shells I crocheted out of wool called angel's breath. Angel, pih, this was a fowl in torment. Pinball pointed between its legs saying, 'A shrivelled knish', which was true if you have ever borne witness to a leftover potato knish in a delicatessen window. 'A real Chicken Little,' I commented, seeing the thing was trying to fly. So when the birth certificate arrived my sister wrote under last name 'Little' and under first 'Keziah' but in private we called her Chicken. Chicken Little.

Chick.

My sister was known as Pinball.

And I am known as Adolf.

I appeal to the heavens but no one looks no one sees no one is at home up there or down here except me and Pinball's rocking ghost.

'Shut off the waterworks,' it says, compassion having departed via the back door of the corpse's heart. I give her rocker a shove. It has upholstered arms mine has bare oak the better for driving home a point. 'The chiseller! The pervert!

The liar! May he rot down unto compost on the bottom layer of hell!'

'He will,' says the post-mortem prophet.

Pinball in life had less get-up-and-go than a dust mop, a dust mop at least dances. A heavy workout was the raising of a wrist the lowering she'd trust to gravity. She could criticize she could say, What did I tell you? but as for Doing there was no Doing. She could rock was what she could Do.

However, Pinball's ghost-self seems to have a surprise up its sleeve – her sleeves were never tight.

'What are you talking about?' I demand information but her peaches wobble away from me, even in death her nightgowns are transparent.

'Ha ha!' she cackles among the trumpets. If she wasn't already dead I'd wring that chicken neck even unto corkscrews.

Keziah my Chick is in trouble an outcast among deceitful moles.

'Look what he did to her!' I shake my fist I see blood fire pillars of smoke, I see visions of Doing. *Bum bum bum* go my chubfists, right left right, on the arms of my rocker. Watch out, Princeling, here I come. You can't do what you did to my niece my sister's chicklet and think you can get away with it!

'Please, Aunt Adolf,' the Chick's own wine comes in wavelets across the Ocean courtesy the Telephone Company.

'What "please"? Why do you give the cheek to him who smiteth you?'

'I don't. He did what he had to do,' she says, her voice crackles like seeds.

'We have a rotten connection.'

'It hurts but I love him for what he did. I hope he's happy.'

'Happy? May he lament like a virgin! May he lie all night in sackcloth!'

Her head shakes long-distance she stills see a Prince Among Men.

'A prince? A bowel movement! All their princes are revolters! Give me his knees! Give me the crunching of bones!'

'Please . . .' She has a wilderness in her throat. 'You don't understand, it was my fault.'

'Your fault?' Can a bird fall in a snare upon the earth where no trap is set? I appeal to the space between the arms of Pinball's rocker. 'What is this crown of thorns your daughter wears on her head for decoration?'

A snort comes forth, the Chick and I are alone in this.

'Listen to me,' I tell her, 'don't let him get away with this!'

'Aunt Adolf, what can I *do*?'

'Do Something! Anything! Do!'

Shout, O daughter of Jerusalem! Stick up for yourself! Lift up your hand against your enemy! O my niece, arise from your griefwork and beat his head to pieces!

'A BALDNESS ON HIS HEAD!' roars the lion who is Me into the telephone piece which has gone disconnected with fear. A spindle from my rocker cracks. Even Pinball is impressed.

'You look like you're about to take off.'

'I am.'

'Where?'

'How should I know? You tell me.' Pinball may not have done anything in life but in death she is a formidable proposition.

'I should have been born a man,' I say.

'Meet him as a man,' says my sister, making a logical progression. 'Make him go down on his knees,' she says.

'How? What shall I Do?'

'Do.'

'What?'

'Something.' *Our persecutors shall not triumph!*

'Umph,' says the echo that is Me.

Look at us. We rock back and forth like unemployed rabbis we smack our own cheeks until they burn we stand at our kitchen sinks with water running off our elbows but what do we Do?

It isn't enough to go on rocking in this Valley of Bones. A madness that has nowhere to go except back and forth back and forth.

'What do you want to Do?' she asks.

'I want Doing I want Revenge I want Cut Off His Giblets! I want roast them with potatoes sprinkle parsley on top! I want feasting I want fat dribbling down my chin! I want tear out his thumbs and his big toes! I want chop him in pieces as for the pot! I want . . .' I raise my fist in the Philistine's direction.

'"Take heed,"' quotes Pinball, '"that ye deal not treacherously against the wife of your youth!"'

And with that she leads me, a vision in interesting nightwear, to the door of my flat which is upstairs from her flat. She points to my refrigerator. 'Open it,' she commands.

'What for?'

'Do what I say.'

So I do.

It contains chicken.

'What now?'

'You know.'

I know.

It is Spoken, let me obey.

I pull the pullet out. I take both its legs in one hand and raise up my arm, this Liberty's torch hath no heat but it sure can swing. Watch out, Princelet. I am a fat triangle I am a top my feet are planted on star-studded linoleum my arm goes round and round my hips which are the width of the world my head also goes round and round yea even unto dizziness.

The skin of the chicken goes round and round.

'Don't stop,' orders my sister.

Around and around.

Two

The Chick met the Prince at Four Eyes an eyeglass place. She was sitting next to him at the fitting bar thigh to thigh elbow to elbow squinting into their personal mirrors with their naked scholars' eyes. Along comes the try-on girl. 'Mr Prince?' she says, holding out a pair of glasses to which the Prince presents his nose for delivery, the frames are bright red plastic. 'There, how does that feel?' He considers. 'Fine I should think.' He pulls down his cheeks like a camel in the Sinai desert but the Chick's giggles disturb his posing for Middle Eastern animal crackers.

'I beg your pardon,' he addresses his remarks to the Chick's mirror, 'is there something you find amusing?' She slides off her stool of a sudden inspired to do a survey of men's metal frames. The important thing is not to look at him. At the water fountain she splashes composure at herself. When she takes her seat again he is getting ready to go. He removes the glasses, holds them out by one skimpy red arm with a vein running through its middle. 'Pity,' he says, 'I had thought them rather fun.' A man big enough to admit of his own foolishness.

Her heart goes out to him, it says, 'please'. He puts the glasses back on in order to interpret this 'please', she closes her eyes in sincerity and self-protection. 'I mean, please don't pay

9

any attention to me, that was very stupid of me. And cruel.'
'No no,' he disallows, 'merely honest. I only wish you'd been
here last week when I chose the frames. The problem is of
course not being able to see oneself.' 'I know I know,' she
knows. 'You have nothing to go on but blurry wishful
thinking.' 'Quite so,' says the agreeable self-deluder. 'However, having ordered them I have no choice but to wear
them.'

'Wait a minute,' says the Chick. 'Let's have another look.' So
she looks and he poses and the more she looks the better he
looks to her in his red glasses. 'Really,' she says revising her
verdict, 'they're not so bad, in fact they're almost . . . cute.' At
which point she suffers another slippage of seriousness. Poor
Prince, what can he do but slide his damaged dignity off his
stool? As for the Chick she is condemned a ridiculer even of
nobility. She hangs on to his tweedy sleeve. 'I'm sorry,' she
says. 'I've been terribly rude. It's nothing personal – just me,
the giggles, I get them. Please try to forget it, OK?'

'I doubt if I shall,' he says, and his camel's legs goeth before
him.

The Chick removed a pair of red plastic glasses from her Black
Watch school satchel, unfolded them, fed the arms through
her braided hair which guarded her two ears like sisal soldiers.
September. A new school term she was sitting on the old porch
love seat which was pushed against the front of the house her
chubsticks dangled her anklets were wide, she was a slow and
careful child. I sat on my rocker and rocked. Where Pinball was
at this time I do not know. I doubt if Pinball knew.

'Don't mind me,' I said, picking up stitches. In other words,
while the Chick studied her books I studied the Chick, *click
click click click*, a nice trick. I was knitting her a sweater, forest
green moss stitch little bumps all over.

I was just about to say, 'Those are nice glasses you're
wearing,' when she turned her head to one side and I saw.

Lo, there was no reflection.

I said nothing.

A little while later she reversed the procedure, she slid the skinny red arms out through her braids and folded them up like a doctor after a consultation. She left to visit a friend. Pinball came banging out on to the porch.

'Did you see?'

'I saw.'

'So what is this glasses development?'

'A development.'

'She doesn't need them.'

'She needs them.'

'There's nothing wrong with her eyes.'

'I know.'

'What do you know?'

'Let me show you something,' I said, and I rootled in her satchel. I held up the red glasses with their arms sticking out like a child in need: 'No glass.' I poked a chubfinger through.

Pinball looked to heaven in the form of the porch roof.

'God will not explain to you,' I said, 'I will.' So I did. 'There is need and need, there is more to seeing than magnification. When she puts them on she can see to Outer Mongolia over the heads of all the little children. When she opens her books she can see the feathers of Indians the sexual parts of flowers the leaves of tea they dumped up there in Boston harbour. All is clarity when looked upon through these lenseless lenses. Therefore,' I concluded, 'they are necessary.'

Hoo ha, a fancy speech. Pinball banged back into the house but she did nothing about the glasses-without-glass so all that fall and all that winter the Chick wore them for studying and for looking at the blackboard and watching TV and she ignored the children who mocked her and went to the head of her class.

Fifteen years later she's wearing glasses with glass. She's living in California she's telling me over the phone how she met the Englishman again.

'The Prince?'

'He's not a prince,' she corrects, 'it's his name.'

The One called Prince.

I let the question of royalty pass. 'You don't happen to remember a time when you wore a certain pair of red glasses yourself?'

'Me? Red glasses?'

'You red glasses.'

So she thinks so she remembers so she confesses. 'Aunt Adolf, do you realize they had no glass in them?'

'I realize.'

'How come you didn't say anything?'

Still I didn't say anything.

'Are you still there?'

'I'm still here.'

'I got them at Woolworth's. They were sunglasses originally only I poked the dark glass out.'

'You poked and then you saw?'

'I poked and then I saw.'

Now her seeing is otherwise. She sees Cinderella and the Prince in matching designer eyewear. She sees feet dancing in furry English house slippers. She sees Happily Every After.

'Did you tell my mother?'

'I told.'

'What does she think?'

Pinball thinks of dancing she thinks of mourning. This I do not tell.

'She said, "Watch out a pair of red glasses is not a sign from the finger of God."'

Three

Annie and Adolf the Skull and Crossbones Girls, had He planted us in the Garden of Eden we would have sniffed out that snake in two shakes of the sneak's tail. It wasn't just our noses it was the radar of waving whiskers beneath the nose. For I was cursed God help me with a moustache.

He didn't. I helped myself.

Welcome to the New World.

It was the Fourth of July a big American holiday. The Chick wanted to go up to the roof of a friend's apartment building to watch fireworks. 'Six storeys,' we considered, 'a long way to fall.' 'Don't worry I won't go near the edge.' Pinball and I looked at each other and rocked, our eyes rocked too. To not know! To not understand the whys and wherefores of a roof! To not be attuned to the voice of the serpent hidden in a crack in its ledge, *Come, come to me, from here you can see to the edge of the world to the origin of all fireworks . . . the whole sky is lit up, come! closer! there! see!* We shook our heads at what would come to pass.

For we knew. From our metatarsals to the runners of our rocking chairs we knew danger: danger dressed up danger dressed down danger in all its forms and fancies. Nor was it imagination. What were the rockets' red glare the bombs bursting in air to us? Independence Day, pih. You stand on

13

another person's dead belly waving with joy the belly feels squishy. 'They're coming they're coming', the maggots wave too. Liberation, hoo ha, handsome Americans, what are you standing on over there? Never mind. *Put your arms around me, baby, hold me tight* ... So Pinball who was a beauty but weak of spirit did as she was told and I yelled from under my moustache What About Me! You hold on too she told me. So I held. 'Get that there monkey off you!' ordered our Liberator. For once in her life Pinball said no to something. *Nein* she spat from between her teeth which were like the flock of sheep in the Song, even shorn and newly washed. So I witnessed.

Afterwards I shoved him so hard in the back of the knees he fell forward all his things sticking into the mud. And then I danced on the roof of his back which was hard and not squishy with maggots. Call this gratitude? he snarled, but even then he was afraid of me. I was six years old. Our mother and father and their mother and father and all the other mothers and fathers and *their* mothers and fathers were in a hole an heap of bodies all those holes in their teeth which were black sheep and unwashed and would never eat again.

Thank you for rescuing us, let's have a party.

Fireworks, hoo ha.

Pinball and I were souvenirs. What did you bring home from the war, soldier? Answer: Two sisters, one a lily of the valley the other a thorn in his side. Why blast me if that kid don't look like that Adolf Hitler himself! Which Adolf Hitler was that, sir? I would have inquired if my English was up to it which it was not.

So we were rescued so we were grateful so Pinball was a war bride so I rode piggyback like a hairy bridal veil.

Our rescuer was an American. He was going home to be a prize fighter. Pinball was his prize I was his price. He was the one who first called me Adolf who dared take that terrible name in vain. At first we could not speak but then we laughed and then it stuck it stuck like a phoney-baloney moustache you can't peel off. Or numbers. Or a certain feel of mud on the soles of your feet. Which may explain why from the time she hit American soil Pinball went barefoot. She also refused to wash her feet she carried the burden the matted memorials underfoot as of two secret graves growing on the ends of her own body.

Or it may not.

What are we doing here? Pinball and I would say to each other and then we would laugh. What else could we do? For it soon came to pass that Solly Little our rescuer our saviour was comely with curly hair and laughing teeth but dumb.

He got his brains beaten out on the battlefield. We'd gotten other things beaten out. Maybe we deserved one another.

Pinball began keeping track. Solly Little went out to work he brought home newspapers. Pinball went to her kitchen drawer she found scissors she clipped she cut. Then she put the flapping scraps into boxes: cigar boxes shoe boxes cookie boxes candy boxes. Reports of accidents natural and otherwise. Plagues blasts calamities catastrophes. Illness of fortune illness of illness, her sad cases spilleth over.

Welcome to Pinball's Disaster Drawer.

One day when the Chick was little the doctor's son who lived on our street was playing hide and seek he hid behind a parked car and the driver got in backed up felt a thud got out to check and there was the little boy, seek until the shadows flee away and unfortunately ye shall find him. Crushed like a soft box. Which teaches you not even doctors are immune to disaster. After that the driver of the car a hunted-looking little man crossed to the other side of the street to get to the end of the block.

But let us return to the Chick who was planning to go to college in California.

Pinball stuck her head out of the screen door. 'Come,' I said, Pinball took her place. We rocked.

'You heard?' I asked.

'I heard,' she said.

'So?'

'So what?'

'She's planning to fly.'

It was bad enough she went into the city by train where we saw her being sucked down on to the tracks by some invisible force or pushed from behind by a visible maniac. But flying! As we rocked we saw flames a spiralling a nosedive blood fire pillars of smoke it was terrible it was hot, Pinball fanned herself with the fly swatter.

'It's all right,' I said, 'she'll get there the plane will land safely I promise I can feel it in my bones a smooth landing.' But Pinball was not reassured. Something was bubbling up I could feel it in my feet. Finally out of the earthworks of her mouth it came – 'Earthquakes.' I felt the ground tremble. 'Floods,' she poured on top of that. I saw a hillside of houses go sliding down into the sea, inside the Chick curled up in an armchair reading one of her Little Golden Books.

'Runaway cable cars,' I began.

'Convertibles,' she offered.

'Perverts,' I said.

'Actors,' she chipped in.

'Adulterers.'

'They are all adulterers,' she embellished.

'The sun.'

'What sun?' For once in her life she looked stupid.

'What "what sun"? Cancer, of course.'

'Of course,' she agreed, adding, 'The Golden Gate Bridge.'

I braked with my feet, now it was my turn. 'What's wrong with the Golden Gate?' She looked at me with pity I saw my mistake I saw in her eyes which were dark as drawers the suicides lining up putting a leg over, the Chick launching herself up and over into the wavy blue water. And yet I balked I resisted I hollered, 'Why should she want to kill herself?' Again that how-can-you-be-so-stupid look. For I knew her mind like it was my mind and it worked like this. One day the Chick would be walking across the Golden Gate Bridge minding her own business admiring the sailboats bobbing on the water when a voice booms in her ear in time to the waves below, 'Jump! jump!' The bridge's erector set arms pull at her she stretches forth her own, take me home.

The next thing we know we're collecting her from the airport in a body bag.

Four

Her feet on my floor. Blue and white saddle shoes clumping on stars. Red green yellow, my linoleum was designed with the sky in mind only more colourful. 'Keziah,' I called her to mark the gravity of the situation, 'sit down, have an Othello from Ebinger's this could be your last chance.' I pushed the box towards her. 'Fresh, yesterday was Arthur's Day.' She lifted the lid she sniffed. A moment of deliciousness also a moment of What do I do? as if she would insult the other five by choosing one of their number.

She reaches in she chooses from the six egg-shaped cakes with pale butter-chocolate filling and darkest chocolate icing just as she used to when she was ten years old, a time when the Othello–Arthur connection was not so easy for her to grasp.

'How come Arthur always brings you Othellos, Aunt Adolf?' she'd ask.

'Because he knows I'm partial to them he gets them from a special bakery only he knows about it.'

'Why does he visit you every week?'

'He's a friend.'

'What do you do all day?'

'We eat Othellos, sometimes he plays with my birds.'

'Do they like him?'

'All except one who likes to draw blood with her beak.'

18

'Which one?'

'The Princess.'

'I wouldn't mind being a princess some day.'

'Is that so.' It was no question.

Out of princesses she grew into scholarly ambitions. 'I've decided to go away to college,' she made her announcement. 'You've decided,' repeated Pinball, her voice was terrible her rocking even worse. Let me explain. The idea of a daughter going away to college would be to most mothers a source of pride but to my sister Pinball it added up to you-can't-do-this-to-me.

Who was the mother? Pinball tried to keep Keziah home from school as a protection against disaster. Whose disaster? Pinball said she was protecting the Chick from no-good but the Chick knew otherwise.

For an example. The Chick said she needed an alarm clock to get her up in time for school. 'Don't worry,' Pinball promised, 'I'll wake you up, when did you ever know me to sleep after six?' The Chick opened her mouth to speak but closed it again. Pinball stayed up reading about the *Titanic* or the tragic life of Robert Schumann. By six o'clock in the morning she was snoring away.

Let me tell you a few things about Pinball. First of all Pinball stank, second of all she rumbled, third she lay on her back with her legs folded open like a virgin with no secrets from the world and fourth she wore no bloomers.

And fifth she was no virgin.

At seven-thirty the Chick woke up and her wailings were great. 'You did it again! You promised to wake me up and you didn't!' Pinball padded like a polar bear skinny under its fur the colour of a bad tooth across the inlaid wooden floor to her front window which was below my window. Here she took note of three yellowy-white flakes falling past her nose from my dust mop and prophesied snow. 'Stay home you'll break a leg.'

But Chicken Little did not. She had to get away from Pinball's secrets she had to get away from Pinball's darkness she had to get away from Pinball's Drawer.

At night she dreamed she got sucked into the Drawer and it was not a nice place to spend the night.

Even when there were six-foot snowdrifts hurricanes tornadoes and other so-called Acts of God she'd wrap up her neck and go. She never got stomach aches imaginary or otherwise, nothing short of an A-bomb could keep her away from those blazing two-storey windows with the meshed glass and the cut-out pumpkins grinning at her, *Come.*

The Chick went. She went to her schoolhouse and vomited. Even as the others were settling themselves behind their desks she'd be up and running to the toilet. But not today. On this day she felt light of heart and free of nausea. She stood up to do a recitation of 'By the shores of Gitche Gumee' but when she got to 'by the shining deep sea waters', it grabbed her she heaved all down the second row splashing several pairs of scalloped anklets.

They said she had a nervous stomach, she said it was the smell of her cream cheese and jelly sandwiches. I say she was paying for her escape from my sister Pinball Annie. Getting out of the house and down the steps was a major achievement, the darkness the Drawer and Pinball's need would pull her back make her heart pound make her stomach churn the muscles in her legs ache like an old woman's. She wanted to run and skip like the other kids but Pinball's feet became her feet. They dragged her down they turned the flat streets into cliff faces. But she kept going, one foot two feet, she got intimate with the cracks in the sidewalk.

True, the closer she got to her not-so-little red schoolhouse her pumpkin of hope and away from Pinball's negative pull the easier it got but not until she could hold on to her sloping maplewood desk with all her chubfingers did she feel safe. Three fingers at a time hooked into a dry inkwell.

Pinball told the Chick a story about how a school super had grabbed a little girl who stayed late for religious instruction, he laid in wait for her took her down to the basement where there were no windows to see into and the pipe arms and boiler bellies which were cooling down for the night seemed to howl, *Be our guest*.

Safety, pih.

Years later the Chick sits in my kitchen with the stars on the floor and the Othello box on the table. She takes nibbles all around. She pulls at the chocolate coating with the shovels of her front teeth she scrapes at layers of chocolate cream and jelly and last of all she stares down into a flatbed of sponge the colour of gall. Dust made fat with fatness.

'Aunt Adolf, may I have a napkin?' I hand her a napkin. These napkins she used to love to draw on with crayons picking out the white-on-white design until the snow scene burst into spring.

'Did you know, Aunt Adolf, that Othello is a character out of Shakespeare?' 'Is that so?' I say, chocolate-cream filling squirting out from between the parting of my ways. 'A moor, a jealous Moor,' she says. I nearly choke the other half of my Othello is perspiring she is crying, three of my canaries have settled in her hair she looks like one of those old paintings holding out her hands saying, 'How can I leave her, Aunt Adolf?' to which I reply, 'Easy. You walk out the front door.' But I was wrong. It was not the front door she left by.

The Chick packed her favourite books into a box, tied it up with string. She also cleaned the dust and roach eggs out of an old suitcase, still a slow and careful child. She left the suitcase open to dry, she would pack it in the morning. And then she went to bed.

Meanwhile Pinball Annie sat up all night drinking from the cup of trembling. By the time dawn came even my birds knew better than to open their mouths.

It was a surprise attack. Awake, my Keziah, she cometh straight from the lion's den! Into the Chick's room she burst roaring grabbing clothes off hangers out of drawers, handfuls armfuls bras socks skirts flying girdles garter belts of young womanhood, into the waiting suitcase. Zip strap buckle, out the window went the whole business, it landed in the alley. After that she turned her fury on the Chick. 'Now you,' she snarled. 'If you're going, Go!'

The Chick went the way of her belongings. She slid herself out the window while my sister the twister ran around trumpeting like an invading horde.

Keziah sat on her box of books a thing cast out, her eyes ran down with rivers. By the time the taxi arrived the skin of her cheeks looked like magazine paper (delicious to nibble when fresh!). She picked herself up she slammed the door on the scene of Pinball's perversity. As for me I hardly had time to tie a kerchief around my head lean out my window and wave to the back of her head, 'Bye-bye, O sprung daughter of Jerusalem!'

Five

The Prophet Ezekial you remember had a vision of fire with brightness all about it. When he realized it was God he fell down on his face. When the Chick saw the red glasses coming at her through a desolation of tear gas she did some fancy footsy-work. A hug and a lunge and they both fell down on their faces, neither of them broke their glasses thanks be. The Prince was caught in the crossfire, an innocent abroad a foreigner a man Not Permitted to Make Trouble Or Else. Yet all around him bodies fell tear gas cannisters hissed. They called it a student demonstration, Pinball called it a war. She rocked she cut and snipped. NATIONAL GUARDSMEN OPEN FIRE ON STUDENTS. Free Speech, hoo ha.

We watched television. We saw them marching, floppy sloppy cuffs beads headbands. We saw hundreds of students occupying a great building on the campus the Chick and the Prince happened to be attending, eight hundred lining the hallways up and down they raised up jello and Chinese food in cartons from a pulley on a first floor balcony, they hugged they danced they made love on the floor in their sleeping bags, Joan Baez sang them to sleep, *Hush, little baby, don't you cry . . .*

And in the morning the president of the University called in the troops and they raised up their billy clubs and the skulls of the students were crushed into forgetting.

23

'You think she's in there?' I asked Pinball.

'Who knows?' Her scissors were very busy.

'They call that a civilized American university campus?'

She shrugged, 'May their wars be relatively enjoyable.'

Jello and chow mein, feh.

The Chick hears the hiss of tear gas she dunks her scarf in a fountain, presence of mind. With this she covers the Prince's mouth and nose, hoists him up by the armpits, and thus entwined they go forth with hacking coughs from the scene of battle otherwise known as a place of higher learning. Waterfalls cascade down her cheeks the burning in her eyes is that of knubbles of raw garlic she has eyes to see but does not except for vague shapes, young people falling about like stumblebums.

That night the Chick telephoned to say she was all right not to worry she'd been jailed and gassed but she was fine now and bailed out, oh and guess what she'd met up again with the Englishman in the red glasses. I said to Pinball maybe we should be grateful to the president for calling in the troops to gas and fire on the students' heads because otherwise Keziah might not have had the chance to rescue the Prince.

For in the beginning I too was blinded by his glory.

Pinball banged out on to the porch. I remembered a story she used to read to me when I was small about a prince who consisted entirely of precious gems. It was written by Rabbi Nachman of Bratslav, even we had our dreams. I called out after her, 'Maybe she'll be lucky maybe God is not so incompetent after all maybe she will strike it rich she will marry the Prince and live happily ever after. Who knows?'

I heard rocking I heard spitting I heard knowing. I heard my sister's voice. 'They lie in wait for blood.'

Six

The Chick was not the only thing that got pushed out the window of Pinball Annie's life. Neighbours had learned to give our porch a wide berth for you never knew to what it would give birth, in other words what manner of things would come flying over it. One day long before the Chick was old enough to even think of going away to college a bed came sailing over the railing.

It was Solly Little's – the Chick's father's – bed. The window it passed through normally needed a stick to prop it open but on this occasion it stayed respectfully open, as indeed who should blame it to see my sister in the role of Samson with a bed on her head. She lifted that spring over her head, yea and it came to rest balanced but wobbling on the porch railing so Pinball stepped out and helped it over. It was at this point the window remembered itself: down it fell a shattering judgement on its sill. Solly on the other hand forgot himself, in other words he hauled off and punched Pinball breaking most of her ribs.

The Chick found her mother on the porch sprawled on a bed of broken glass. Solly stood over her making a sound like gas escaping from a narrow hole. Sorriness, pih. He raised up one of his arms as if to point a finger at God but brought it down to point instead at Pinball: 'One, two, three –' one of his few talents was counting – 'yer OUT.' The Chick rose up and called her mother not blessed. After that she called an ambulance.

A mother is supposed to guarantee a child's safety, she is the protectress the enveloper the umbrella the shoulder the breast the lap. The Chick crept upstairs I held open covers for her. 'Come,' I said, 'stay close Aunt Adolf is here nothing will hurt you your mother will be all right you'll see now close your eyes and sleep', but it was hard for us to close our lids on the picture of her own mother my sister with her ribs taped up. Neither could we get the sound of Solly's gas leak out of our ears.

The other night I saw a TV programme it was about a mother pilot whale and her offspring. *The youngster travels effortlessly pulled along by her slipstream.* And so it was you saw them shimmying and swivelling about, mother and daughter in twin wet-look outfits.

I made a wailing like the dragons and a mourning as the owls.

How could the Pin carry the Chick along in her slipstream when she had no stream and wore no slip and did not know where she was going except around and around her five rooms which joined up in a circle?

Once we went shopping, Pinball and I, so off we went the beautiful war bride of eighteen and her sister the baby mustachioed wonder. She planned to buy us dresses.

Dresses, pih. We never got dresses. On our way to the department store Pinball pulled me over to the side of the building she leaned against it her hand was on her heart her slip was on her ankle bones. 'Annie, you lost your slip!' Hah, I thought this was funny until I saw. I saw shaking I saw sweating I saw the greenness of spring which did not look good on my sister's skin. I kneeled at her feet. One after the other I lifted them up they were heavy as loaves of unleavened bread. I freed them from their ring of slip which I slipped into my pocket.

What slipstream? What stick by me? What nothing to be

afraid of? Everything to be afraid of! You go out with your slip you come home without it! Better not to go out at all!

Which Pinball didn't after her nineteenth birthday.

Otherwise she might have had a brilliant career as a door to door saleslady for the Book of Horrors.

On their wedding night Solly began climbing the walls pulling on the new paint with his nails. 'What are you doing?' she asked him. He raised both his hands like he was praying to Allah-on-the-ceiling. 'Money, dontcha see it? All that money up there I gotta get it.'

They were no richer in the morning. On the second night he poked her in the ribs. 'Annie! There's a man in the kitchen.' So she wrapped her chenille robe around her, her bridegroom tiptoed behind her. There was no man anywhere in the house.

Pinball instructed the Chick in stories which did not appear in her Little Golden Books. It could be argued they provided her with a superior kind of education.

Once upon a time there were sixteen women in a labour ward their screams were legion ... Once upon a time there was an old man bent down to pick up a cigarette butt they shot him in the back ... Once upon a time there was a pack of rats the size of a little girl ... Once upon a time they pushed an old woman into setting concrete she was buried alive ... Once upon a time they took down a fence they pushed a mother and father out, Escape! Escape! they shouted and then they shot ...

Pinball's storytelling showed no mercy when it came to child-rearing, neither did her collarbones.

So now maybe you begin to see why the Chick fell at the feet of a man who denied there was anything in this world to be afraid of.

I will give him something to be afraid of.

As for Solly Little he was a man who could not find his own pyjamas. If you searched the streets of all the towns and cities you could not find a stupider man than Solly, his big joke was, 'Whaddya think I am, stupid? – don't answer that.'

One day the Chick was walking home from school, she met

her father coming from the station he had a newspaper tucked under his arm his eyes were closed. She called his name, *Daddy*, she said, *Daddy*. But he did not hear her for he was fast asleep. She delivered him home. 'He's not safe out on the streets,' said the Chick. 'I know,' said Pinball.

'What are we going to do?'

'Do?'

She was at an age when fathers are supposed to walk tall down streets make their daughters proud. 'How could you?' She meant marry him.

'He saved us,' said Pinball.

That wasn't the only reason. Let me explain. As far back as I can remember marrying made my sister feel sick. 'Just the thought of being a wife makes me want to vomit.' She was seventeen she was leaning between her legs like she might be about to demonstrate. I jumped back so did the other girls. They were dreaming about marriage. Pinball was plotting escape.

When we got to America I said, 'Do you remember how you once told me the thought of marriage made you sick?'

'I remember,' she said.

'But you're marrying Solly...'

'Solly.' She might have been saying 'cardboard'. 'Learn to listen.' She pulled my ear. 'What I said was the thought of being married to a *man* made me sick.' So you see it made good sense for my sister to marry Solly for being married to Solly was as close as she would ever get to not being married at all, it was more like having a child than a husband.

Besides she was pregnant.

So Keziah had a father for a few years yet she didn't have a father. Solly Little was there as far as muscles and heart and several rows of teeth were concerned but the interior of the head was more like a pumpkin filled with seeds and strings, happy Halloween.

He mourned his bed. He did not eat his chicken pot pies. He sat on the front stoop and stared at it with an unfathomable pumpkinish sadness. He spent half a night in Keziah's bed the other half (it was summer) out on his bed. He could have picked it up and brought it back inside but he did not. In the end he went the way of his bed only he didn't come to rest in the front yard. Keziah never saw her father again.

Poor Chick. Poor Solly. (Praise be for Pinball!)

So when you hear about how the Chick fell under the Prince's spell kindly remember this fact, compared with Solly the Prince was God in the flesh.

In some religions I gather they crucify their gods.

Seven

Pinball was right, the son of strangers made as if to deliver her. Said the Prince to our Keziah, 'I'll pick you up around seven, shall I?'

It was the *shall I?* made my moustache quiver.

Oh mouth of pomegranates that spews forth words one upon the other scarlet and transparent causing the ears of a virgin daughter to be polluted with an abundance of enchantments, unto him I say, *Spit blood, Princeling*.

Prince Shall I arrived in a car the colour of sacrifice blood. It had a GB sticker on the back and a canvas top which layed itself back in folds while the round-and-round-where-do-we-go-nobody-knows finger of God circled above. And what shall we throw down on their heads today, rocks? birds? planes? lightning? hailstones? bullets?

Bullets. President Kennedy slumped over sideways in his convertible. The writing on our postcards said, Do not go willingly into the bucket seat of a convertible driven by a seducer especially foreign and gentile.

But the Chick ignored our commandments. One chubleg followed the other she smoothed her skirts which were long with little mirrors. She smoothed the two sides of her hair which spent nights and more nights Scotch-taped to the soft fruit of her cheeks for the style of the day was to have hair

30

smooth as flowing rivers whereas the Chick's was more like an heap of holly, variegated with fire.

The smell of old wood went straight to the tips of her branches and they curled in disobedience.

'Oh dear, is there a smell?' The Prince was interested in taking blame.

'Delicious,' she said, and she watched him as he let the handbrake out put the shift stick into first adjusted his mirror turned the steering wheel and signalled a right turn all at the same time.

'You drive,' she said. She might have been saying, *You walk on water.*

'My father taught me the summer before I went up to Oxford. He had a series of cars, my favourite was a rather broken-down Alvis.'

From what she could remember of him the Chick's father could barely walk in a straight line.

'And your mother?' asked the Prince of Fairness.

'My mother drives a mean rocking chair.'

Hoo, his scholar's eyes laugh behind their red glasses, little does he know.

And now he tells her a story concerning cars and a grandmother. 'I can remember riding in the Alvis with my grandmother, it must have been one of the first cars in England, it kept stopping and starting. We were passing a farm and a chicken ran out. 'Can't stop,' she cried over the pops of the motor and ran straight over the chicken. She got out, marched up to the door carrying the poor creature by its feet, presented it to the farmer's wife saying, "Have it plucked, my good woman, I shall be back for it in half an hour." Of course,' he adds, 'I was rather shocked.'

'Of course,' says his echo, feh.

And now, 'We'll just make a small detour, shall we? To Inspiration Point to watch the sunset.' It is after seven o'clock the Chick's stomach is also in need of inspiration. And I say unto Pinball, 'Their worlds are further apart than miles.'

'It's not too far for you? You're not too hungry?' asks the Prince of Consideration.

'Of course not,' she says through her teeth which are my teeth and therefore filled with gaps for lies to sneak through.

The Prince holds his camera to his face his nose lays itself down sideways he snaps a picture of the sun going down behind the Golden Gate Bridge. The Chick sees another hopeless case hitting the water, *smack*.

Click. 'Isn't it lovely?' he says.

'Mmnn.' Does a question from God admit of denial? Her lips are blue. He walks her to the furthest point of the Point where he points with his finger. 'D'you see that? That's Angel Island where the Japanese prisoner of war camps were.' He teaches knowledge he teaches endurance. She looks she sees a toy model bought for him by his father Lord Hoo Ha and although all his information is correct and his sympathy is great yet the wind waileth and howleth at Keziah like Habakkuk the Prophet.

How long shall I cry out and thou wilt not hear?

Finally he admits of a certain human weakness. He drives her home to his house on stilts in the hills, he puts her to walk ahead of him up a steep staircase where clumsy with emptiness her chubfeet trip. With the pureness of his hands he delivers her to his apartment.

A fishbowl on the skyline. The Prince and the Chick swim around each other while in the distance the Golden Gate winks and blinks. He introduces her to his cat Henry a love-starved animal with blocked sinuses who drools with stroking. She takes him in her arms he slobbers into the folds of the sweater I knitted for her, seed stitch with cables.

'Do sit down,' invites the Prince of Generosity. And now, 'Would you like a Pimm's?'

'A what?'

'Ah,' says the Oz, disappearing behind a curtain. And lo! he reappears he hands her a frozen cloudy glass with a darkish reddish liquid and a slice of lime riding its rim and two mint leaves reclining on the surface. 'A very Oxford drink,' he explains. 'Especially of undergraduates. Drank it in punts whilst carrying out our inane peccadilloes.'

The Chick sits on a low sofa, the Prince is a pine tree hanging over her. Pimm's? punts? peccadilloes? *whilst*? Her ears are lined like a nest. 'I've never tasted anything like it,' she says. That, my Chick, is because all we ever gave you was a glass of red Kiddush wine once in a blue moon.

He gave her a piece of that too.

'Stilton, try it,' he recommends. And with the cheese cometh the pear. And after that cometh the coffee and after that the sweet which requireth unwrapping.

Keziah, my sweet.

'They shall offer to their idols sweet savour,' says my sister.

'And when they do watch out!' say I.

He kneels before her, a man in the throes of an after-dinner experience, he nudges her arms out of the way he consumes her between the legs like delicatessen.

'What does he think she is, a potato knish?' I smite the arm of my rocker.

'Woe to him that spoilest and thou wast not spoiled.' Pinball rocks like Jeremiah under house arrest.

The Prince comes up for breath, may he go under two more times and never come up.

'Mmmnn.'

But wait it gets worse for now the Chick changes places with him. She drops to her knees she works on the zipper of his Levi's one notch at a time a slow and careful child, down down until the fruit of his manhood is pointing at her. Lo! and she lays herself down under his laden bough her mouth open like a baby bird's.

'No! No! A thousand times don't do it!' I stomp with my feet.

'Thou shalt not suck the milk of the gentile!'

I fly upstairs to my birds my thirty birds released yea as I would my Chick from the danglings of His Fruithood. And as the thirty yellow bodies of my birds fly round and round the mountain of gall that is me also goes round and round until it falls to the floor its forehead decorated with loose canary movements. Pinball is beside me.

'Feh is his fruit,' I complain. She lifts the hem of my housedress and wipes my forehead.

Meanwhile there is another lifting up as the Prince takes the Chick by her hand and delivers her to his bedspread. Above them is a great skylight as of the eye of God peering down.

'I promise not to hurt you.' And the uncircumcised dog lays her down on the bed with the stars overhead and he makes bare her leg and uncovers her thigh and he spreads his furriness upon her.

'May the stars lose their shining over him.'

'May he pee on a live rail,' spits more to the point Pinball.

Eight

The next thing we know he's standing in front of us. On meeting a Prince our people used to say, 'Who hast given of His glory to flesh and blood'. I said to him, 'You like potato knishes?'

'I don't believe I've ever tried one.'

'He doesn't believe,' said Pinball. I said, 'Hoo.' We knew what we knew.

'Excuse me,' said the Chick, 'but when you two are finished with your private joke here maybe I could introduce you to my friend.' They teach advanced sarcasm at the University of Berkeley.

'Introduce,' I said.

She gave a bow like they taught her at the Casa del Rey dancing school which closed down due to Señorita Margolis of the black bun and the fishnet stockings slipping a jar of Spanish olives into her carryall. 'Aunt Adolf, Mama, I'd like you to meet my friend Geoffrey Anthony Osborne Prince.'

The lamb who was named sat in silence.

'That's a lot of information to take in all at once,' said the planter of stings in lambs' tails.

I reached forth my hand, I called him Geoff. He gurgled after the fashion of newborn babes.

'Actually it's Osborne. Over there,' he explained, 'it's a

custom in certain families to use the third of one's given names. Silly really, but there you are.'

'There *you* are,' corrected Pinball.

'Around here one gets one name to one's name.'

'Not even a middle name do we exalt to.'

'Stop!' cried the Chick. 'He's not crowing about it, it's just what he was born with.'

Can the cock stop himself cockadoodledooing?

'I'm making soup.' This Pinball announced, it sounded more like a threat than a foodstuff. She excused herself her soup was calling, what it said to her God only knows for even when she made Campbell's it came out in lumps.

But the Chick was right about the Prince, he did not crow neither did he crawk however the Chick herself was not averse to a little peep-peeping on his behalf. Although he had enjoyed certain shall she say privileges of upbringing he did not believe they made him a better person; indeed he felt rather disadvantaged not to mention embarrassed by them; they tended to mark him as a class specimen; people became overly impressed with his parentage and schooling while as an individual he became invisible.

This I could see.

'Where was it he went to school?' I asked the Chick for His Highborn had become horizontal in his chair.

'Eton followed by Cambridge.'

'Hoo ha,' I said for the reputation of these places had trickled down even to us. 'I'm impressed.'

The Chick did a little drum roll with her feet. 'Don't be. I mean what's so great about sending a little boy of seven off to boarding school by himself? It was cruel, right?' She looked to the lamb who looked cockeyed to the ground saying, 'Quite so.'

'Besides he believes in equality. Don't you?'

He did he did.

'An education for the privileged few is against his principles.'

His smile I could have tucked away in my cheek and gained slow nourishment for a week.

'A socialist?' I ventured in the direction of the Incredible Shrinking Eldest-Son-of-a-Lord.

'Labour.' He spoke with his lips he sank with his hips.

'God,' I said, 'created man that no one should say my ancestor was greater than yours.'

He offered his palms.

'He should have been born an American,' I said.

'That,' she explained, 'is precisely why he did his graduate work in this country.'

The Prince's eyelids descended behind the spectacle of their spectacles like Pinball's window shades against the great white throne of daylight. Meanwhile the Chick grabbed the porch railing behind her back and made as if to boost herself up. 'Watch . . .' The hand of protection flew out to her. The Prince's window shades flew up the little woven rings went round and round.

'Watch what?' asked the precariously perched Chick. A dangling thing, God preserve her.

Let me tell you something about the Chick, she was not a safe proposition more an experiment in advanced human life than a finite being. Take for example the work of Dr Frankenstein. He began with the body of a hanged man he sewed on the hands of a Rembrandt spliced the head of a nobleman the heart we don't know about the brain of a homicidal maniac was the crowning glory. In the Chick's case it was a matter of Pinball's perfection of feet lips chin nose eyes and hips cut with my legs teeth bust and ears. The hair was mine the colour (revenge blood let down with orange juice) was Pinball's. Poor chick, unfortunately we did not have Dr Frankenstein's freedom to shuffle the deck.

So there she was hanging on by a coil of blood from Pinball's blood when somebody threw the switch and snipped the cord and behold she screamed like one already in pain. You felt afraid for her as if a hand would fall off an eyeball drop out.

Fine-tuned in the head may be but on a flat sidewalk she could easily trip and break her neck. Balanced on that railing she was not.

The Prince's thumbs chased each other in a clockwise direction then changed their minds and went the other way.

'Let me tell you something,' I informed his thumbs. 'When this girl was five and a half years old she managed to flip herself up and over the railing performing a mid-air somersault came down on the point of a sharp rock and nearly lost an eye. Show him the damage.' She declined to show. 'It was nothing. My first day of school. I was excited.'

'Too excited, God punished you.' I pointed to the punctuated spot. 'Maybe you can lose the other eye this time.'

She threw up her hands. 'I didn't *lose* an eye!'

The Prince pincered up his newspaper.

'Excuse me,' I corrected myself, 'you *nearly* lost an eye, does that meet with your approval.'

It met. She slid off her perch thanks be kneeled between the Prince's knees and showed him her scar. Herr Doktor kissed it with his lips.

Feh.

Pinball screamed from her kitchen. My chubsticks moved yea and fast like a herd of elephants to a watering hole. Pinball had dropped the pot of boiling chicken soup on her foot.

Nine

A burnt foot. 'Annie,' I'd warned, 'put shoes on your feet even open-toed slippers.' I conjured splinters glass boiling liquids frozen toes fallen arches but she lived in faith the immortality of her own feet was the one thing she believed in. Filthy she trusted in those feet, so did I.

Pinball's feet glowed with soup-burn in the setting sun. I knelt down with my First Aid kit in other words a nice lump of chicken fat. The Prince said he didn't wish to interfere but. 'Then don't,' told Pinball. Still he spoke his wisdom. 'Cold water is recommended. Fat makes it worse, actually.' Actually our looks would have shrivelled David. 'Listen! He knows!' A cry from the fatherless one. And I knew in my heart he *was* right and yet he was not right. So I rubbed the foot with chicken fat nice and yellow round and round saying, 'Our ways are our ways.'

'Amein,' said the anointed one of the shining tootsies.

I awoke to the singing of birds to the hopping up and down with dry feet. They sang 'Tonight the Chick will fly away.' Friday the Sabbath the night the bride gets eaten and drunk.

We sat on our porch we rocked the sun also grew fat over our railing.

While the Chick and the Prince snoozed we celebrated with the drinking of salty water which represents tears and with the sucking on lemons which made our lips to tremble. The sourness of slavery, God deliver her.

When Solly left Pinball was free, nothing to stop her leaving. I said, Now you can go anywhere do anything. She sat and rocked and considered the nature of this freedom but by this time it was no longer so good. And so far away. I could have reminded her how close it really was (at the bottom of our stoop) but I did not. Two years in a camp, eight years in a marriage, pih. Too late my sister (Go where? Do what?). She hung on to the bony arms of her chair she hung on to the fatling arms of me, oh tell me what to do. And I thought, my sister shall curse and prophesy and I shall dream dreams and together we shall be free. And still she needed orders to live. Hoo, and I liked to give them. So we were in business.

'Consider yourself lucky,' she now pronounced through her lemon, meaning that I'd escaped marriage. I said I considered I wasn't given the chance. She said, 'Who would want to be married to a female Adolf Hitler?' Why is it the beauties of this world think they can get away with murder? Answer, because they can.

'You think it would have made a difference to Arthur,' I posed, 'if I'd had an upper lip like Marilyn Monroe's that you could see the little beads of perspiration trembling?' She said, God forbid.

Another reason I gave up on God. Him. Who needs Him to wag fingers? Who needs a Him to deliver our sons and our sons' sons? What about daughters! Who needs a Him with hairy arms like Solly the dumb bruiser I have my own hairy arms! Who needs a punishing prophet I have Pinball!

We became our own prophets.

So we rocked we rested our tea glasses on the arms of our rockers and we waited. And when I lifted up mine eyes behold! two feet shod in California sandals, what be these ugly things? Our porch boards trembled at each step of them. *Blessed the man she chooses*, we muttered our meditations on goodness while the lions inside us roared after prey.

Meditate terror!

What blessed is the kidnapper? Let there be no rejoicing in the taker-away of our child.

'Sit,' we offered, offering no chair. He leaned against the railing with his back which was as long as the sufferings of our people. Split crack we willed it to part and may he fall like Eli of the ninety-eight years and may his neck break and may the earth below receive his bones. But he stood and we rocked and he smiled with a terrifying sweetness.

And we did not.

Ten

It was morning a time of feeding. And so Pinball and I and our fatling Keziah sat down together on one side of our table, nicely polished and even with a cloth for protection, and we put the man on the other. 'You like bagels?' I offered and the man said, 'I do', for he knew better than to refuse. Pinball nearly gagged on the 'I do.'

'Does it surprise you?' he asked the Pin who did not take kindly to interrogation.

'My sister means only that there are certain gentiles in this world nothing personal who have never heard of the bagel much less developed a taste for it.' Mine eyes were on his eyes.

'I am especially fond –' he held it up to an eye and peered through – 'of the hole.'

'Ho ho,' I appreciated, 'a man with a dry sense of humour.'

'A man interested in holes,' observed my sister of the accurate eye. A man who has defiled our daughter. Who spreads his cream cheese who lays down his lox.

'So where did you learn about bagels?' I ventured.

'He made friends,' the Chick hopped in, 'with a Jewish family in California, Sephardic Jews.'

'Religious,' I conversed.

'Orthodox,' improved the Lover of Holes.

42

'Not like us,' said the Pin.

'No,' he agreed.

Before we were only a little displeased but now we were a lot displeased.

'What do you mean "No"?' This was Pinball.

The Prince tucked away his chin. 'Well, if you were religious you would hardly be eating bagels today,' said the friend of Jews orthodox or otherwise.

'Do we hear criticism?' inquired my sister.

'Of course not, I was simply giving an example, an illustration of your own point.'

'An illustrator of religious practices.'

'I'm not,' he protested, 'an expert on anything. One doesn't have to be Jewish to know that the eating of leavened bread during Passover is . . .'

'Is what?' inquired the Pin.

'. . . forbidden.'

'Knowledgeable,' I said.

'A reader of the Bible.'

'A rabbi.'

'A judge.'

'Oh dear,' he plopped about in his hole. 'This is quite absurd. It's not for me to judge.'

'You bet your sweet life.' Pinball flashed the sharp little scallops of her gums.

'Leave him alone!' wailed the Chick.

The mother ignored the daughter.

'So you don't think we should be eating bagels?'

The Prince leaned forward in his chair. 'I daresay it's none of my business what you eat. I was merely making an observation.'

'An observant observer.'

'Not at all. All I said was that one particular Jewish family, with whom I happen to be friends, are religious and therefore eat only matzos during Passover. A statement. No moral or religious value judgement whatsoever.'

'ENOUGH!' roared the Pin and the eldest son of a lord leapeth.

'The Jews you have known –' I tried to soften the noise of my sister – 'are not like us. We eat what we eat.' To which Pinball added, 'God passed over our heads a long time ago.'

After breakfast she invited him to a game of cards. 'Gin rummy. You play?'

'Very badly, I'm afraid.'

'Good we'll play', and she led him to the back of the house, a wolf's den smells sweet by comparison.

He caught his breath he opened his eyes. Prepare the table eat drink sit, ye princes. He sat down at a three-legged card table covered in peeling sticky green baize. The Pin sat opposite him. She shuffled and cut and made a moving rainbow and the Prince watched with the watching of a violet.

'Cut.' She offered him the deck. He cut and she cut and at last the treacherous dealer dealt treacherously and after that she smacked down with smacking the remains of the deck dead centre of the table. 'Look at your hand,' she ordered. He picked up his cards he made a fan of great evenness meanwhile considering their import through his red glasses. She saw he was in trouble, peradventure the Philistine would seek her help.

'Sorry, could you perhaps remind me of the rules?'

'Perhaps not.' My sister was not interested in rules. Her heart was wild her mind was wild yea even her twos were wild. 'Deuces,' she banged.

Hoo ha an high horse became a low. He lost his shirt also his undershirt. And in that day a prince became bare-chested before her, tee hee. And Pinball smiled through her slits. 'I like a good loser.'

And now she raised herself up and walked with her feet over to the thing in the corner of the room which was substantial and covered by a sheet the colour of old memories. 'Do you know what this is?' she asked him. He said, 'No.'

'God gave you a head.' The Prince worried with his

guesswork. If he got it wrong a terrible thing would come to pass: this he believed. He imagined my sister pointing to the front door saying, 'Out!' while she held Keziah locked in her lair, her prisoner her servant and her instrument. At last he ventured forth with his mouth saying, 'A trunk.' He saw the opening of a lid he saw secrets he saw things which would cause the eyes of their witness to tingle and shed tears. He girdled himself.

Pinball stood with the straight back of a magician about to reveal mysteries. And then with her arm she flung off the sheet the colour of memories Hosannah! and the Prince came to gaze with all his eyes on a great old-timey pinball machine.

For the second time that day my sister asked him, 'You play?' No he had never played he didn't know how. 'Then you'll learn,' she said, 'it takes quarters.' She reached into his pocket. She put money into the slot the machine juddered and winked and delivered a row of silver balls to the head of the spring. Pinball put away those balls one after the other like an animal tucking nuts. 'Your game,' she said holding on like a lover.

The Prince played but his spring had no spring to it.

At last Pinball the Pitiless led him back out on to the porch, she put him to recover in my rocker.

'You want a beer, I have cold Schlitz?'

He asked if he could possibly have it room temperature.

'Here we drink it cold.'

Cold beer trickled down the Prince's gullet.

They rocked and drank, drank and rocked but you could see by the way he leaned away from her he could not be sure if she would reach out and swipe him one for my sister had cultivated a set of claws scalloped like the Moosabeck sardine tin lids and the colour of their oil. Her ears had grown as mandrakes her hair was like the beard of a he-goat her nose like the tower which looketh towards Babel.

My beautiful sister Annie.

The Prince said, 'I'm not, you know.'

'Not what?'

'Not a prince. Or anything for that matter.'

Pinball rocked. 'A lord, no?'

'I'm afraid not. It's my father who sits in the House.'

'To sit in a house, this is a profession?'

He explained about the House of Lords. 'He was a Law Lord.'

Pinball saw lawyers wigs judges. She saw Judgement she felt sick.

'A life peerage. I don't inherit,' he heaped.

'Nothing?'

'Nothing.'

Pinball rocked she rubbed her feet together sole to sole the dirt gathered beneath them. 'Soon you will have another title.'

'I beg your pardon?'

'A doctor, I believe.'

'A Ph.D. actually. An academic doctorate is quite different from a medical degree.' An apology or a boast it was hard to tell.

'You will become a professor?'

He smiled with his dove's eyes bespectacled with red. 'With any luck.'

'What has luck got to do with it?'

After an interval not exactly decent she said, 'Let me tell you a few things about our Keziah.' She wiped her mouth with the back of her hand. 'You want to know what you're getting.'

The Prince was not so sure about this.

'In Hebrew,' she began, 'the word for new can also mean old. Did you know?'

This thing the Prince did not know.

'As a child,' she continued, 'Keziah was already old. Bald until the age of three. She would sit on the floor bent over her books like a rabbi. Once I had to search the house to make sure she was still breathing.'

The Prince let out his own breath.

'And she was very very constipated.'

The Prince did his cold beer less than justice.

'I spread her cheeks I pushed for her.' She demonstrated the procedure her face grew almost as red as the Prince's pomegranate seed spectacles. 'How many mothers would do that for a child?'

The Prince thought about his own mother. 'I wouldn't know. It wasn't exactly the sort of thing we talked about at home.' Poor Prince he said this almost sadly.

'I once dug them out of her with my bare hands, pebbles like rocks. What do you think of that?'

The Prince opened his mouth, no words volunteered themselves.

Eleven

While Pinball was shallumping the Prince at games and a few other things downstairs, upstairs I sat sidesaddle on a kitchen chair the chair sat on a white linoleum with red green and yellow stars. The Chick stood behind me braiding my hair. Have you ever tried braiding a Brillo pad? Not easy. She worked with diligence with a pulling apart of wires and with twisting. A slow and careful child. Woman. One two three. Braids are supposed to hang down smooth and obedient, these did not. 'They call them plaits in England,' said the Chick already well briefed. Do telephone wires stretch under the sea?

'I'll telephone,' she promised, 'faithfully.'

I liked 'faithfully'. Will we hear waves pounding back and forth between us?

'It's not all that far, Aunt Adolf, in miles no further than California.'

Far.

She braided she smoothed but smoothness was not to be. The way is twisted, so be it. What will become of her over there, O my niece my peach my bruised sweetness?

'What are you thinking, Aunt Adolf?'

It's the end, the end.

'I'll visit, I promise.'

Promises, pih. 'So long as you're happy.'

48

'I'm happy.' She yanked.

'One thing I don't understand.'

'What's that?'

'Your Prince studies American history in America, how come he doesn't teach it in America?'

She had trouble with my logic. 'England is his home.'

'This is yours.'

'His family are there.'

'Yours are here.'

'He has a job at the university.'

'What about your studies? You had ambitions.'

'I still do. Marriage won't change all that. It's not like it used to be in the old days you know.' She yanked again, this time I hollered. What do I know?'

'Aunt Adolf,' she scolded, 'stop worrying. I'm looking forward to it. An adventure. A beautiful quiet place near the sea.'

A drowning among infidels.

'Scenery very nice but what about people? You'll be a stranger.'

'That won't bother me. I'm quite independent you know.'

What do I know?

'C'mon, cheer up. Tell me about you. Tell me about Arthur, does he still come to see you?'

'Every Tuesday.'

'And he still brings Othellos?'

'Naturally.'

'And you're happy.'

'I'm happy.' Like this she was free to go.

Twelve

The Prince is on his way out, bye-bye. A pleasure he tells us and so forth. He calls us impressive he calls us formidable. I like formidable. He hopes to see us again, rinse his mouth with Clorox. He is relieved we are not as fearsome as he'd expected. Pinball's right foot is going *slap slap*, the porch boards receiving repeated shocks to their system plus her left eye is closed which is a bad sign. He pecks me on the cheek he does not peck Pinball. The Chick laughs with blubbering I hand her a hankie. 'Don't cry,' her mother tells, 'until you have something to cry about.' Her foot is a stumbling block in the Prince's path, hoo, how the mighty are tripped up.

And so we rock and watch as the taxi pulls up and she gets into the back seat with the Prince and her other baggage. She throws kisses out the back window her face is small. With us there is forsaking.

'She's going,' I observe.

'Removed.'

'Into exile. Far away.'

'Gone,' says Pinball.

'A disturbance of normality.'

'A cosmic upset in the universe.'

'God was also exiled, may she go with Him.'

Pinball corrects, 'She's going with *him*. Please distinguish.'

'Are not their princes altogether kings – Isaiah?'

'Not,' answers my sister.

'A gentleman and a scholar,' I try.

'A defiler.'

'A charmer.'

'Like the serpent.'

'A good head on his shoulders.'

'A receding hairline.'

For once will she not see good? 'Annie,' let me try again, 'never mind hair look what he *does*, he shops he cleans he cooks he sews, he even asked me for my Mandelbrot recipe, he talked to my birds he asked intelligent questions he told me not to use Harz Mountain foot powder it has a dangerous chemical and that gorgeous accent, what more could she want?'

'How can he know?'

'He loves her.'

'Love, pih.'

'Listen,' I tell her, 'intermarriage is common these days. He likes mingling you can see it. A cold man he needs her warmth.'

You could not melt Pinball's heart if you took it in your mouth. Just looking at her makes me shiver I feel like I'm marching. A march in the snow, you know where you're going but you pretend you don't, it will be all right after all just keeping going hope for the best. 'Tell me,' I say, 'when did he put a foot wrong?'

'It's not the foot I'm worried about.'

'Big nose big thing,' I try to laugh. 'But a gentle man, he won't hurt her.'

'Underneath the modesty, lordliness.'

This I cannot deny. 'She gives him the right.'

'He was born into it.'

'He was raised to believe.'

'In himself.'

'Please,' I try once more, 'consider. We could be wrong, Annie. He could be as David.'

A snorting of she-hogs, 'Ishbi-benob with hips more like.' Ishbi-benob was Goliath's brother, even bigger and uglier.

The hips you have to give her.

'Narrow shoulders,' she adds.

'Like a pear,' I giggle. Pinball and her nasty games, who can resist?

'A bad sign in a man.'

'And the nose. Like one of those elephant seals I saw on TV, they make love they crush their wives to death.'

'*Mates*, Adolf.'

'Droopy sweaters with holes in the elbows.'

'Knock-kneed.'

'Flat-footed.'

'Like a toad.'

'The Toad Prince,' we tee-hee like girls.

'Not a real prince either,' she informs. I stop giggling. 'Nor a real doctor.'

'Is that so?' I ask.

'That is so,' she tells.

'So what is left?'

'A sweet tongue in his head?' Please, Annie.

'May it consume away in his mouth.'

'Shy?'

'Like a fox.'

'Self-effacing?'

'To a degree not normal in a man.'

'When did she ever like what was normal?'

'Point,' Pinball gives.

'And yet . . .' I begin but my words are drowned out by the roar of an airplane as it flashes and flies over our land and we are left a couple of doleful creatures rocking and waving, waving and rocking.

'May they pass over the sea without turbulence or God forbid terrorists and come down bumpless and blessed in their new land and may the heavens give their dew on their heads.'

'Rain –' Pinball sees – 'rain without end.'

PART TWO

He raiseth up the poor out of the dust . . .
to set them among princes.
I Samuel 2:8

Thirteen

Who put out the lights?

In the morning she woke up an Englishwoman and it was not jolly. The Prince explained about the different qualities of light. 'California light is brilliant, golden. Quite seductive, of course. But looked at another way it's a light of high contrasts, so rather harsh.'

'God let me be seduced by harshness,' prayed the Chick. He put his fingertip on the tip of her nose she stopped speaking. 'Whereas this light,' he continued, 'this pearly sky, is quite different. It creates softer outlines, less defined edges. It has a subdued but silvery quality.' Superior he did not need to say. 'A gentle indirect light.'

A sneaky light that flattens out the world a light that makes you trip over things a greyness of ashes. 'You'll need a bit of time to adjust,' he tells her. 'But don't worry,' he slurps up one of her nipples, 'you'll get used to it; perhaps even learn to love it as I do. A relief after all that sun, which you have to admit is rather remorseless.'

Admit nothing, my Chick. What does he know about remorse?

The Chick and the Prince are in bed, raindrops fall on the roof of their cottage. The Chick listens and then she whispers into the grey dawn, 'The stars are crying.' The Prince who nestles betwixt her breasts lifts his head its silky broom hairs hang down as he blinks up at her with his dove's eyes. 'What did you say, my sweet?' 'Did I say something?' 'You did. Tell me,' he encourages. So she does. She performs an encore for his ears in a voice so small it gets him like a raindrop straight between his legs.

The stars are crying.

He is moved by the poetry of her words. His left hand is also moved. It moves under her head his right hand moves to her right breast and his tongue stops her vulnerable mouth like a plug.

Poo! Bite it off! Stop whispering! Blast those crazy words into his ears as through a ram's horn called a shofar until his drums split open like walnuts then fling him off you and run screaming into the night –

THE STARS ARE CRYING!

Run where? To who? Or even whom? For not a soul lived within blasting distance unless you counted cows sheep owls etc.

The Chick looks with her eyes up to the oak beams which are holding up their roof and which are full of character and also many holes of the woodworm. 'Dormant,' says the Prince who has rolled off from betwixt her breasts. 'How do you know?' She sees whole families of serpents growing fruitful in their beams.

He knows. 'When the woodworm is active you get signs of fresh borings around the mouth of the hole.'

'You mean when we get a trickle of sawdust in the eye we'll know they're up there?' Lying in wait?

He kisses her lids, left right. 'I'll deal with it.'

'What?'

'The woodworm.'

'I thought you said they were dormant?'

'Just in case.'

'How?' She sees him ordering them all down on their bellies saying, 'Eat dust.'

'Never mind. Forget the woodworm,' he says, by which he means I'd rather you concentrated on this other worm he's hungry again he wants you and he covered her in his great shadow like a crab apple and his fruit is sweet to her taste.

A premarital honeymoon, you get a lot of sex.

This too will pass.

Later he took her by the hand they walked out into their garden, she saw that it was infested with a rampaging green creeper.

'What's all that stuff?'

The Prince bent down like a doctor to examine his patient earth. 'Ground elder. It obviously likes it here. We'd better deal with it soon before it takes over.' The Chick saw an army of avenging elders coming for them in the night. 'How?'

'Pull it up by its roots, it's the only way. Unless you use weedkiller but we don't want to use poisons around here.'

We don't? She saw them pulling for days weeks years. A lifting of stones a crushing of toes. Quick, where's that serpent? Give me a bite of apple! Give me knowledge! Get me out of here!

The Prince explained what was wrong with weedkillers pesticides all things chemically invasive and the Chick listened and was duly respectful but when he was finished she was so hungry she could have stuffed her mouth with ground elder. 'Actually the young leaves are quite tasty in salads,' he said, leading her back to their new kitchen which was an old kitchen with holes for mice to come in and out and slugs too and other creepy-crawlies of the field. And here he filled their bowls with scrambled eggs decorated with the leaves of the herb tarragon which acted upon her like an aphrodisiac for no man had ever cooked for her before, may he choke on it.

There was no milk in the refrigerator. 'I'll arrange for it to be delivered every morning,' said the Arranger, lifting up his briefcase. 'Would you like the car? I don't mind taking the train. I'm sure you have things to do, places you'd like to explore.' 'No, you take it.' she said.

What things. What do?

They say Jews are good at going to new places setting up shop. Making Do. Making what do what? Bread from dying yeast? The last flinging out of blossoms by an uprooted apple tree? Behold a comely mummy goose-bumping in the English sun. Oh my Keziah, how I shiver for you! How I feel for you wandering half-naked in your California sunsuit in your soggy snake- and elder-infested Eden. What you do will be wrong, hisses the snake, so why bother? So you don't. So you wander so you think, why have I come to this place of my enemy?

Their new house was of a two-hundred-and-fifty-year-old oldness. The walls were a museum of secrets. The Chick discovered if she put her hands up against one of them and listened – shush – she heard voices. On this day she hears, *I am a wall my breasts are towers*.

The Prince finds her with her forehead pressed up against the wall of the larder, a thick-walled burial vault for ghosts and foods. 'What are you doing?' he asks, which translates, Why are you hugging the wall instead of me? He holds her close he smooches her forehead like the Pope giving absolution. Such a high forehead! So much wisdom inside! Why waste it on walls? 'I'll just get you an aspirin,' he says, assuming headache. Assume nothing! Listen to what she listens to! Hear what she hears!

'No, wait,' she says – a newly-minted act of rebellion – 'there's life inside those walls.' She means past life past memories. History. 'Listen, somebody weeping.' He puts his ear next to hers. 'Mice,' he concludes. She flies back. A wailing wall she can handle a rodent wall not. She prefers her own experiment in impossibility. 'Look –' she swipes it with a finger – 'their tears are sweating through.'

Whose tears, my Chick?

'Gloss paint,' explains the Prince, 'combined with dampness creates sweating. It needs sanding down, then a couple of coats of damp-proof paint. I'll do something about it.'

A man of Doing.

'I know,' says the Chick, 'what you think.' She sees or thinks she sees behind the concern in his dove's eyes disappointment. 'You think I should be out exploring my new environment, painting the house, going for bike rides, digging the garden. Instead of *this* –' she touches the wall with the tips of her fingers, taking leave of the ancestors which are not even her ancestors but speak to her of things in common.

The Prince takes her squarely by the shoulders which are not square. 'Listen to me,' he says.

She listens.

'My love, I don't care what you do so long as you're happy.'

Happiness, pih.

She throws him a look passed down from her mother's mother's mother to her mother's mother to her mother which begins with caution at the outer edge of the sender's eye and ends with an ice-pick to the left ventricle of the receiver's heart.

To survive in this place she needs to grow pale hair and pale skin and skinny ankles that cross themselves neatly among the folds of a soft flowery skirt. She needs to grow period. To learn ways which are not her ways. She needs Girl Guide lessons in hiking and chopping wood. In baking bread and bottling gooseberries and growing old roses. She needs elocution lessons so her own voice doesn't sound as harsh to her own ears as the California light to his eyes.

How can she believe him when she doesn't believe in believing?

'How are you?' I asked her long-distance.

'He doesn't love me I'm useless here.'

'He wouldn't have taken you all the way over there if he didn't. You're an original, what's wrong with you?' What's wrong with any of us?

'What if he's sorry he brought me? What if I was second best in the first place?'

What if what if? What if the sky falls? What if the words

SECOND BEST are branded into her heart like numbers on an arm?

I said, 'You will always be first best to me, now go let him love you', and I hung up and she went to him and smiled her cockamamy smile and flattened herself against the larder wall with her arms outstretched and she said, 'I am a wall and my breasts are towers', and as she was then in his eyes as one that found favour and as he was hungry he gobbled them up.

Fourteen

A derma, let me explain, is a sausage made from the see-through outer casing of a cow's intestine stuffed to bursting with onions and carrots and meat. A whole derma is maybe a foot and a half long, stab it with a sharp knife and fat dribbles out. The Prince's love grew and grew, a love that was not only long but wide. But you have to hand it to him before hurting her he would have chopped it off first. Of course that was then and now is now and now I may have to do it for him. Don't think I'm not thinking about it.

He pumped it in it dribbled out. I refer here to the thing he called love which he poured into her but which did not get absorbed for she was a thing riddled with holes.

He read her body like a map. The coastline the whole complicated exterior he crisscrossed he traced he charted from hole to mole, follow the dots. Love, pih. She lay there like a plate of fried liver and onions which looks and smells delicious but lies heavy on the heart. 'I wish you could believe how beautiful you are.' She crossed her arms over her body. Gently he removed them. 'Look here. And here.' A still-life framed by thumbs and fingers. Apples peaches varnished cherries. 'Lumps and bumps,' she corrected, pulling blankets over her head. He removed them with his hands. 'Why do you hide from me? Why won't you let me love you? Why do you dislike yourself so much?'

She knew not.

Hoo, but I do. It had to do with Pinball. A child doesn't know her mother she doesn't know herself. As the Chick said to the Prince, 'I don't know I don't know.' What didn't she know? Pinball for one thing, who knew Pinball? She learned to live like a fox she could not unlearn to live like a fox.

She had reasons for laying low. Lift up your head a little too high and it got smacked with a rifle butt. Or shot off. Or some part of the male anatomy shoved into it. So you lay on your belly you kept your mouth closed. The trouble with that was it left your tail open to attack. So you curled up pretending to be invisible which was impossible in Pinball's case, try hiding a burning bush.

For some reason they let her off having her head shaved like the rest of us. Lucky Pinball. Unlucky Pinball. You could say that for Pinball liberation never came.

Pinball as a mother. What kind of a mother does a fox make? Very protective, they say a vixen will chew off the arm of anyone trying to get at her cub. On the other hand if it's a choice between them she'll dump the cub at the hunter's feet, so long enjoy.

The Chick never knew what would hit her when she walked through the screen door, Pinball waving her fists or her feet or cookies in the air as if to say, My daughter where have you been all my life? Usually it was darkness, thick darkness. Pinball wrapped up in it, pacing.

A surgeon of nightgowns. I bought her pretty flowered nightgowns she operated on the sleeves the necks. Still she tore at her throat the necklines were too tight, God in heaven get me out of this thing.

Get us both out. Get us all out.

There was no way out so we waited.

Waiting, pih.

We arrived in this country famous for its freedom Pinball put bars on the windows and rocking chairs on the porch which was ribbed with railings and she rocked and rocked and a lot of the time we rocked together and I could see from her knuckles that she needed to rock just to stay attached. So no wonder the Chick never knew if the bars were to keep her mother in or the robbers and rapists and murderers out.

Pinball the escape artist. In the camp she was famous for trying to get out. Then one day she was *let out*. OK you can go. Go where? Do what? Why? So when Solly came along she looked at his dumb face and his muscles and said OK let's go.

A tragedy. She needed to get *herself* out. She never got the chance so she spent the rest of her life as a frustrated escape artist. Her greatest passion in my opinion was a commitment to imprisonment. Her greatest disappointment was Solly, as a substitute torturer he was too gentle.

My boyfriend Arthur (married), Pinball's boyfriend Moosa.

Moosa once shot a moose up in the mountains, drove with it slung across the hood of his car and flopped it down at Pinball's feet. Not kosher she told him. He liked to stand in her kitchen jiggling open a Moosabeck tin with his Swiss Army knife then eat the sardines straight from the can. He stank from fish from dead animals.

Moosa the hunter and trapper. The poacher. Poo.

Pinball in her slimy pink toga. Somewhere along the line she lost her foxy nerve she also lost her teeth and her nose lost its torque. Her spaces were great: between her lips between her ribs between her legs.

Men stupid men. 'You have to live for yourself and Keziah,' I told her, 'not him.' Feh, disgustwork, you could smell him coming: oil of moose oil of sardines.

'How do you think it is for a young girl to see a mother always waiting for a man like that!'

She threatened to leave with him.

I said goodbye don't forget to write.

She glared at me.

I said why don't you wash your floor for a change?

She said what for.

My sister the stink.

I made it worse. I worked I saved I washed my floors I fed my birds I said, 'To hell with Arthur', 'Come in come in' to Keziah. The more I did these things the worse she got. Spat and snarled, forgot to wash, forgot she had a daughter, lived from moose visit to moose visit.

Once she escaped. Moosa threatened to leave her so she went after him. I came home I found her gone. I called the police. They brought her home naked wrapped in a blanket. Bruises, a child should not see bruises on a mother.

The good sister the bad sister. Pih, it's not so simple really.

Go ahead blame me. The hard mean selfish sister, ha ha call me Adolf.

'Adolf,' she called up to me. 'Come down I need you.' I was on my way to work I saw her standing there with her housedress open her grey slip exposed no advertisement for bleach commercials. 'Do yourself up,' I ordered, orders she understood. She stared down at the row of buttons marching up from her hem an invading army of locusts. On my lunch hour I bought her three nice housedresses zippers up the front.

Carrots. She didn't bother to scrape her carrots before throwing them into her soup pot.

This kind of behaviour does not give a child faith.

Anyway there she sat in her rocker wrapped in a towel dripping out the bottom. Her legs were sticking straight out in front of her she was looking from one to the other as if to say, What matter of thing are these? What do I do with these? Doing, pih. They were fine legs as far as outline went complete with knee bones and ankle bones but coloured in with blue and red blotches. She waved them at me.

Pinball's ritual immersion, hoo ha. It happened from time to time.

Her hair was also wrapped in a towel underneath it her face

was a proudness of bones, Queen Vashti refusing to be summoned by King Ahasuwhatsis. Her knuckles were white on the arms of her rocker. But look closer and what you saw was a child saying, 'Aren't I good?' I wanted to stroke her face tell her how beautiful she was tell her no stupid man would banish her replace her with an Esther, I'd kill him first.

Good little Annie. I went for my bucket and scissors, the only way to get the felting of dirt off was to operate. She gave her feet up to me. 'Keep still! You want them cut off?' She opened her eyes a slit, 'Heil Adolf,' she hissed, and our laughing was one.

Once upon a time two sisters got sent to camp their parents went to a different one. The older sister was called Annie the younger sister was called Letisha. Annie was seventeen years old a beauty Letisha was five a chubfoot among skeletons who marched around the camp with a horizontal finger under her nose. *Shande shande* hissed the people. Shame shame, you couldn't blame them.

She was president of the Adolf Club. Admission to her Club was a vial of urine. The little children brought them to her she made them line up she questioned them, 'If this is really yours tell me how you did it.' *I squatted down and made a pee-pee, my hand got wet.* 'OK, you can belong.' They were sworn to secrecy otherwise she would have their blood in a jar she would drink it, more blood more fat. She buried the jars of urine with a shovel which was a dangerous weapon only nobody seemed to notice. 'Heil H—r Heil H—r.' She goose-stepped around the camp with her shovel and her finger under her nose. Her cheeks and her knees had dimples she could get away with murder, she was learning murder instead of her seven times table. She watched she sniffed she observed murder. Shame shame. She had a space between her front teeth. One of the old ladies put a curse on her face, 'May she grow a moustache where her finger is.' Which she did. Which is why you must believe in curses as I told the Chick.

One day little Letisha was sitting on the lap of her friend the guard saying, 'Take us on a picnic.' The guard roared, 'What do you think this is, summer camp?' What did she know to the contrary? 'You me and my sister Annie and don't forget the gooseberry jam. And wine bring wine.' This made him laugh a five-year-old brat telling him what to do. But her sister what a dish so he did.

He packed gooseberry jam made by his wife, a bottle of wine a cloth to lay on the ground. Letisha took Annie by the hand. 'We're going on a picnic.' 'No,' said Annie. 'Yes!' Letisha raised her shovel, she came up to her sister's bellybutton. 'OK, OK.' She allowed herself to be persuaded. They went in his jeep to a beech wood a dark place a place of darkness a perfect place for a picnic.

The fat guard lay on the ground, Letisha poured wine with her little hands she rested the cups on the mound of his belly the wine trickled into his navel and he roared and she stuck her fingers into his mouth smeared with wine and gooseberry jam and swilled him with more wine and their own wine they did not drink.

She whispered something in Annie's ear. Annie said No! Letisha pointed to the wine bottle the shovel. When he pulled Annie on to him Letisha crawled over his face and before horsy could get his tail up she swung round and broke his head a giant red gooseberry split open except it was only a crack it wasn't enough to kill him only enough to make him see red, yea the punishment of his humping was great.

A quarter to seven in the morning. 'Enough foot-washing,' I tell her, 'I have to go to work.' I did an early shift on the sewing machines. 'The worst is over,' I reassure. Pinball peruses her feet, naked and shorn cracked and black. 'Give them a good soak,' I prescribe. I fill two buckets squirt in Pine Sol, she likes the smell it reminds her of forest. She puts one foot in each bucket.

When I get home she's still sitting there. 'Your feet will fall off,' I prophesy. She laughs, the time of the singing of birds has come.

Pih.

Keziah comes home from school she drops her books she bends down she takes her mother's feet out of the bucket she scrapes with her nails she does a scrub job with a stiff brush. Finally she pats them dry with the towel from Pinball's head.

Behold! a pair of clean feet.

Correction: Behold! a pair of *relatively* clean feet, for no matter how much you scrubbed Pinball's feet would never be really clean.

And now for her head, a tangled mess. All that beautiful red hair. Strand by strand the Chick untangles it while Pinball dances with her relatively new clean feet at the same time singing, *Horsy, keep your tail up keep your tail up keep your tail up.* . . . The Chick makes a ponytail pointing towards heaven.

So there she sits smelling of rainbows waiting for Moosa to come back. 'Disgustwork,' I tell, 'you should be ashamed of yourself.' It was the wrong reason to get cleaned up. The Chick saw this too.

Moosa had been sneaking around for years. One day I said to the Chick she was drinking milk at my kitchen table after school, 'He's not bothering you is he?' While all the other girls were busy stuffing socks into their bras she was busy flattening herself with elbows. She said, 'Could I have some toast, Aunt Adolf?'

Toast. I put two pieces of Wonderbread in the toaster. The toaster was a rarity it was made of glass I have never seen another one like it you could watch the bread waddling through on its journey of electrocution. It fell out toast the Chick grabbed and buttered and ate.

Now she tells me in England they wait for the toast to get cold first, a precautionary measure, hot bread sits heavy on the heart. For a week I ate English toast in sympathy. Cardboard, feh.

Fifteen

She waits for him. She hooks him through the door like a hooker and moves him around their new-old English oak floor. He lets himself be moved. He does not ask, What's all this, then? for the look on her face says shut up and dance so he does and well well ho ho it's rather nice to let his bones and sinews be jiggled up and down.

This is no ordinary hip-hop. A gypsy conga, an Apache war dance, a flamenco fling (fling the Prince!), a Chick-dance which allows no part of the body to escape: arms legs hips heart, beat thump jump.

For the Prince dancing is an unnatural act, try to make a cow give a lecture. On the other hand he is a man crazy about being led around the dance floor of life, hoo ha to put it poetically.

Imagine a bed of earth, it comes in layers. On top you have a sand and pebble mixture. This is the Prince's topsoil, well drained and gracious yet humble. Next comes a layer rich in fish blood and bone prepared and laid down for a potential holiness with a good salary. Beneath these is a neglected tangle a wilderness of roots out of which comes a lost little boy, oh tell me where to put my feet. Not that the Prince was having doubts, a man with academic tenure is a man with a job for life. The last layer is bedrock stone.

He allowed himself to be pushed around the room yea and

it was good for it reversed certain imbalances in their stations also he was able to express certain hidden layers in the constitution of his soil.

As for the Chick she was celebrating. She had been for a walk. At the end of a lane she came to a field. She hung herself over a farm gate thus to consider the large black and white beasts grazing therein. Are you lonely? she wondered and decided no probably not since they had each other for company plus their minds were taken up with serious munching. On the other hand she thought there is something not quite right about these cows, like a bunch of ladies dressed in black and white polyester from the outsize department at Macy's attending a symposium on the practice of drinking tea.

Yes God help me I will walk across the field to the shore, this she decided. But first she had to get past the gate. She tried to undo it but it was tied in a mangle of pink string so she thought I must climb. Now let me tell you the Chick's legs were not made for climbing, putting a sock on one of those legs was like dressing a fencepost. We have the same legs the Chick and I, God has a lot to answer for. We'd walk down the avenue with our four sturdy stumps, mostly we kept them covered so as not to scare people.

I tried to protect Arthur from them as much as I could but one day I didn't slip fast enough under the covers and he saw, for shame. Is that why he did what he did? Afterwards when I looked at my legs combined with certain other unfortunate physical characteristics I thought, You can't blame him. But then I thought, Men stupid men.

The Prince was an altogether different item. Where Arthur the lawyer would see a pair of inadmissible female limbs the Prince of scholarly law saw the bottom half of his beloved, it could have been a fish tail still he would have worshipped it. But even so the Chick's doubts crept in like voles from the garden, she said to him, 'I think I have the wrong legs for this part of the world.' Those chubsticks were not made for hopping over fences.

Nonsense! he dismissed the leg problem. He dropped to his knees he ringed one off her ankles (two hands) saying, 'I love your legs.' They had something he called *gravitas*, hoo ha.

He worked his way up those gravesticks like a meat inspector at a health restaurant. He stroked the dimpled roundness of her knees. She pulled down her skirt he folded it back, let me. Stop let stop let, he won. He kissed one he kissed the other. 'How can you like such fat knees?' she inquired. The Prince said, 'I find them rather . . . poignant.'

Pooi.

But to continue with her cow adventure. The Chick managed to hoist herself over the fence and down the other side. She brushed off her hands she looked pleased with herself. She set off walking even striding across the field where there were rocks something called limestone outcrops placed here and there to trip up persons of foreign origin. By the time she rolled herself to a sitting position the cows were making their way towards her, what are you doing down on our grazing-room floor?

What did she know about those beasts? That they have four cloven hoofs for leaping upon the earth. They chew the cud. It is not an abomination to eat them indeed it is good to make a burnt offering of their flesh as a sacrifice to God.

They got closer and closer they formed a circle they kept coming with their bony poignancies and their divided hoofs and they looked mild and curious but soon they were so close she could hear their breathing and their faces grew great and so did their eyes and they drooled from their mouths and their tongues were charcoal greyish which was the last thing she noticed before she fell back on to a reasonably comfortable outcrop and got her face licked to death.

So now back to the part where she and the Prince are flopped down on their scrap of oriental rug, After the Dance is Over, huff puff. 'What was all that?' he inquires. The Chick answers, 'It's called the shag, Pinball and my father once did it together. The only thing they ever did together except for conceiving me. It was a New Year's Eve, I remember, I must have been eight or nine. Pinball rose up and crossed the room to where he was standing, I thought she was going to belt him. But instead she put her hands on his shoulders (she was bigger than him) and he put his around her waist. I'd never seen such a thing in my life: they were actually touching, moving together. They began to jiggle up and down hopping from foot to foot, it was the funniest thing I'd ever seen, I couldn't stop laughing.'

Or were you crying, my Chick? It was hard to tell. To us it was just a dance though I'll admit Solly looked like he was rope-skipping while Annie looked like she was doing an Irish jig, one hand on her hip the other in the air. Together they bounced, apart they twirled. The change in Solly's pants pocket jingled, Annie's busts celebrated their individual freedoms. Oh yes I was there too. What was Arthur doing? Dancing with his wife to Guy Lombardo. The Chick was clapping, please God or Someone let them never stop. But the Pin had to stop she had to run to the toilet. By the time she came back her enthusiasm for dancing had dried up also the floor had a sticky look about it. Solly who was no quick-change artist held out his arms to her but now her look said, 'What is there to dance about?'

The Chick finished up telling the Prince, 'Pinball ran to the bathroom, she had a weak bladder, and that was that. Next day she threw my father's bed out the window. He went out to rescue it, she wouldn't let him back in. We never saw him again.'

Amein.

The Prince helps her up off the floor he deposits her in a wing chair inherited from his grandmother the one who ran over chickens and he asks her in the manner of an Englishman educated in the USA, 'How was your day?' She tells him about her encounter with the cows, ha ha a funny story. But the Prince seeing cow-fear in her eyes does not laugh. He takes her by the hand. He leads her back to the same field which is just across the lane, he sits beside her on one of the outcrops.

'They're only bullocks,' he explains. At this the cows which were only bullocks but of a substantial size start moving towards them while the Chick tries to hide in the Prince's armpit only he won't allow it, cruel to be kind.

'What you must do if you want to discourage them,' he instructs, 'is breathe down your nose at them.'

Closer and closer. *And thou shalt cause a bullock to be brought before the tabernacle of the congregation of the Lord; and shall lay his hand upon the bullock's head* ... She sees their bowed heads she hears breathings through noses wide wet sad hopeful. She sees Solly coming towards Pinball, may I have this dance? She sees flies in their eyes and friskiness in their knees. Sweet revenge in the bends of their ears. *And thou shalt take of the blood of the bullock, and put it upon the horns of the altar with thy finger* ...

Suddenly the Chick yanks back a section of hair from the side of her head behold! 'My right earlobe,' she announces. The Prince can see that. 'Is it red?' she questions. 'No. Why?'

Why?

'Well, whenever my mother or my Aunt Adolf used to get a delivery of meat from the butcher they'd dunk two fingers in the blood and come after me to pull my right earlobe. Adolf told me it would wash off but I didn't believe her. I used to think I was permanently marked by a bloody ear. It was a reminder,' she explains. 'It might have been me being thrown into a pot with carrots.'

'How extraordinary,' says the Prince. He is in awe he is in pity. He is very fond of the word extraordinary.

'What you do to your animals you don't do to your children. I was being protected.'

We anointed her with the blood of our chickens as with lilies of the valley.

The bullocks were all around them.

'But ...'

But what, my Chick?

'But somehow it didn't feel like protection. More like a stay of execution, God intervening at the last minute. The great forgiver of human failure. But then you walk around with this funny feeling at the back of your head waiting for the blow to fall. You won't get away with it, says the feeling.'

Won't get away with what, my Chick?

This. That. It. Anything.

'Trust me,' says the Prince. 'I promise you, they're the gentlest creatures in the world. Watch this.' She watches she sees sweetness in their lashes, helplessness against flies in their eyes. The Prince puts his hands on his hips he blows out through his overendowed apparatus until they reverse direction they gallop backwards bumping into one another. 'There, d'you see?'

She sees.

She sees the Prince her friend her lover her teacher the genuine article smiling at her with his dove's eyes exhibiting true selfless pleasure at her progress in the Trusting of Cows.

We see otherwise.

'A teacher of lies,' says Pinball.

And I say put dock leaves and knuckles over your eyes! Wrap up your head in Afghans!

She does not. She looks she listens she lets him speak his smooth things and they are in her ears nectar as from God yea even without bitterness. 'Now we'll just stand up and wait for a bit,' says the Prince of Patience, 'and see if they come back again.' Lo and they do and he takes her hand in his and shows her how to stroke them between the eyes which they aren't so keen on but they forgive and they lick the back of her hand with their tongues which are not only blackish but of an astonishing roughness. 'Nice, isn't it? Like sandpaper. It tickles. Enjoy it. You see? They're quite harmless.'

And she says, 'Yes I think so.'

You think so?

Meanwhile Pinball is twitching in her rocker. 'What the hell is she doing over there?'

Lynne Alexander

'Cows,' I inform, for I am the one to receive letters and phone calls. 'Having lessons in bovine tolerance.'

She bangs the screen door shut. I hear the Disaster Drawer creak open and heavy it is too. 'One day,' I yell after her, 'the bottom will fall out and break your feet.' She comes back with an article about a farmer's wife who was crushed to death by a cow and not just the feet. She sticks it in an envelope hands it to me to address. So I write: To Keziah Prince, Jenny Brown's Cottage, England, Europe.

And now I must raise my hand to ask a question. Is it possible for an outrage to be committed without the committer knowing about it? A question perhaps for the rabbis for the Talmudic scholars for the Oxford philosophers for the Prince himself. What would he say? 'An extraordinary question, ahum.'

And I say may he be trapped in a field with cows whose calves have been taken from them and may they slowly converge on him – not a hoof shall be left behind – and lay on him one after the other and may the warm milk from their unemployed udders flow over him and cause him to be drowned.

What you do to your animals you do an hundredfold to your enemies.

Sixteen

Rabbi in case you didn't know it means teacher.

Teach me. Teach me to walk among cows and not be afraid. Teach me to identify cowslips and orchids even numerous varieties. Teach me to ride a bicycle and not wobble. Teach me to walk on rocks across a stream and not slip and break my neck. Teach me to swim in a rock pool beneath a waterfall. Teach me to believe in a Maker who will not send boulders to fall on my head for fun. Teach me to be made love to because I am lovable not because I am pitiful. Teach me to make a soufflé and know it will rise.

The next thing you know she'll be holding out her hand saying, Rabbi, teach me to walk.

'Teach me to walk,' she said, her toes were pointing to God. They were at the base of a mountain called Harrison. Harrison looked down on her his white beard flowing in frozen ripples down his front. The Chick said to the Prince, 'I'm not going to make it.'

'There's no hurry, take your time.' He showed her how to put her hands on her hips to fling open her lungs like closets. 'But it hurts it hurts,' she wailed, 'how come?'

How come? Ye shall not walk vertically into heathen lands – that's how come! Leave it to mountain goats not people! Go down, O daughter of the horizontal, on New Year's Day! Curl

up with a good book in front of the hotel fire. Sip cocoa.
Snooze.

'Keziah,' said the Prince pawing the ground at Harrison's
lower slope, 'if you'd rather go back to the hotel and curl up
by the fire with a book I don't mind. But . . .' He paused. But
what, my son? 'It's so wonderful when you get up there, I
know you won't be sorry.'

He knew, she knew not.

She turned up her face to the summit which was not the
summit for that thing was lurking among clouds even beyond
what he could see. The Prince moved his tail like a cedar. 'I
want to be up there with you.' A need greater than mountains.
'I'll help you. We can go as slowly as you like. Come. See for
yourself. It's another world up there, very still, you're surrounded by peaks, gullies, sky.' The path up the mountain
shone before him.

'What's it called?' she inquired.

'*Harrison Stickle*,' he replied.

'Harrison's Tickle, I like that.'

'Harrison *Stickle*, you noodle.'

Tickle, Princeling. I also like it.

A clean white snow-capped world. The smell of clouds. If
she stays below in snuggledom with the smell of wood smoke
between her toes, reeking of hot chocolate she will not know
and he will and the knowingness will divide them as surely as
it did Our First Mama and Papa and she will have to go on her
belly into the hotel dining room undeserving of her five-course
dinner not to mention the gift of the Prince's embrace and
from there on in she will be marked with blemish.

'Right. Let's go,' she said, and he was happy in her decision.
He flipped the end of her scarf which was his Old Etonian
scarf, wrapping her three times around with public school
blessings.

'Are your boots OK?' He'd taken her to a special shop where
they measured her feet like a child's. The boots he bought for
her were of sturdy leather and with the tread of truck tyres and

with many hooks and eyes for lacing up and the socks inside them were also high and of pure New British Wool and the colour of sacrifice blood. When she looked down the eyes of her boots seemed to look back at her. Must we? they said, but she denied them.

'They're great. I feel like a real mountaineer in them. I could climb anything. Let's get going.' And she huffed and puffed with her chest and the Prince called her a pouter pigeon and snapped her picture and although her toes were already screaming *Betrayer!* he smiled on her with his dove's eyes and helped her on with her new rucksack and its many zippers and pockets which he had also bought for her along with water-proofs and a hat and even a sweater made of the wool of a sheep called Herdwick.

In the store she'd objected. 'I have Adolf's sweater,' but he said, 'This is oiled wool it will be warmer.' So the betrayer of aunts let him buy it for her and she was warm unto perspiring though the earth was covered in snow.

'Ready?'

'Ready.'

New Year's Day. A good way to begin going up. On the other hand snow and sunshine are a lethal combination.

'Black ice,' says Pinball, her box of evidence on her lap. She sifts through clippings her fingers grip like ice tongs. Her Disaster Box overflows with avalanches snow drifts bodies buried above, a newsprint gallery of blue-white mountain graves.

The Chick begins the long heave-ho, her poignancies full of the Prince's 'you-can-do-its'. Soon her feet begin to flap her stomach to flip.

'Can we eat now, I'm starved?'

'It's actually better to wait until you get to the top, food tends to weigh you down.'

Weigh her down! Fill up her feet with chopped liver!

He unscrews his water bottle he holds it to her lips, the dribbles freeze on her face. 'We're almost there,' he promises.

Lunch on the skyline. Ah, the Chick closes her eyes, foresees a picnic with God. The Prince puts his arms around her and with words softer than olive oil informs her how brave she is and how proud of her he is.

Cut off the lips of the flatterer!

Up up into the sky. 'It won't be long now, just over that rise.' Hoo, a lie of love as big and white as an iceberg. They have come to a gully a frozen waterfall the only way up.

'Do watch your step, my love.'

My love. An ice floe of words. Even as they are climbing Pinball shows me pictures, a waterfall stopped in its falling, transparent with surprise at its own treachery.

'A little effort . . .' I try. 'Once she gets up there . . .'

'*If* she gets up there,' says her mother the optimist.

The Chick's feet slide out from under her, she flops on to her belly her arms are the arms of a supplicant loosed from their sockets. She claws at ice, smooth smooth, smooth and black, her toes tread air her tongue licks ice, her grip is no grip. A child on a sliding pond which is Harrison's fearsome belly.

'Grab on to my leg,' orders the Prince, his Goliath boot planted between two uniced slabs. No-ooo! She is afraid of unbalancing him of pulling him down, better that she alone be sacrificed to Harrison and his lethal Tickling. But her arms know about survival they do not think they grab on and he hauls with his tree-trunk leg until she is upright and then he scoops her up and with a sideways shufflestep they are out of the gully.

The Prince's relief is great but his guilt is even greater. 'I shouldn't have taken you out on such a day, I should have known. I did know, there's no excuse. I just wanted us to be up there together.' He hangs his head the tassel from his ski hat dribbles down the crack between nose and cheek like a woolly teardrop. 'It was selfish of me,' he confesses. No, no, disabuses the Chick, in the absence of chicken sandwiches she can make do with self-punishment.

'Shall we push on then?'

The path became steeper and rockier, a drip dripped from the end of the Chick's nose and froze. The Prince was already up there his shadow was long. 'I'm sorry,' she yelled up to him, 'I can't do it I can't get up there. I'll never know what you know. I'll always walk a million steps behind, I'll never catch up.' She was maybe twelve feet short of the summit.

He looked down on her and even as he did his head grew dark against the snow and a halo of light burned behind it which was the sun setting behind the mountain but the Chick's eyes construed the Messiah himself holding out his arms to her saying with a voice that boomed boomily, '*Yes you can.*'

'I can't.'

'You can.' He had Spoken.

'Come.' Let her obey.

She clawed her way up for it was steep and the way was made of loose rubble called scree and she kept slipping, two steps forward three steps back and it was a thing terrible and wondrous to behold.

'You can do it, try to stay upright.' His arms were held out to her, the moons of his fingernails about a foot from hers.

'Nearly there.'

An inch a half-inch at a time, wet with snow and sweat. When she was just below him he stretched forth and caught her hands with his hands and pulled her up and her toes dragged and she was as a sack of Jerusalem artichokes and he held her in his arms while he rejoiced and she rejoiced too only with trembling and whimpering.

'Here.' He sat her down on a pile of rocks called a cairn which proved they were on the summit and the wind blew fierce and the view was of clouds and anyway she couldn't see for the wetness over her eyes. He wrapped his scarf on top of her scarf which was his and he removed her wet gloves and put her poor frozen hands into his armpits and when they were thawed out put his black suede ski mitts upon them.

He fed her with pigs of orange, he slid the sections through her lips one at a time. 'No more.' She closed them. 'One more pig,' he insisted, but she was too tired to eat so he popped it into his own mouth, along with a sandwich or two, may he live on cheese sandwiches for the rest of his life.

The Chick went down from the top of Harrison on her bottom while a troop of Boy Scouts leaped over her head. The Prince became a briber. A hot bath, he whispered in her sacrifice ear, and other things, and so they got down.

It was dark. She wanted to kiss flat mother earth but he held her upright and when they got to their room he undressed her and put her into a bath that was hot and steamy and had clawed feet and when he saw that she was all right suffering only from temporary exhaustion he went and abluted himself in an adjoining bath also with claws.

And God came down off the mountain and made him to fall asleep and his head to bob in the water and then He pressed His hand over the Prince's nose until he went down and stayed down and from his mouth bubbles rose up with a sound as pretty as music.

The Chick should be so lucky.

Instead they sang and splashed in tandem.

In reality it was the Chick who rose pink and slippery from her bath like Venus on the half-shell and let me tell you when somebody like the Chick who is dark with no-can-do-ness raises her arms and yells Wahoo! I did it! it is a wondrous thing. The Prince had her before dinner on the bathroom floor. He had her after dinner under the feather quilt and her cries were damped by goose down.

Seventeen

She was drinking English breakfast tea. The Prince offered coffee but no no his poison was her poison. A letter arrived an official red stamp. She stuck a nibbled nail under the flap, rip rip. It was from Her Majesty's servants and it was not gracious. 'If we do not receive word of intention to depart within twenty-eight days we shall be forced to take immediate action. Please report to your local Immigration Office at once.'

'They're threatening you? Come home,' I advise, 'it's flat here. Never stay where you're not welcome.'

'I don't want to go home, this is home now.'

'Then marry him, what's the big deal?'

'I don't want to.'

'You don't want.'

'No.'

'Then don't.'

'They'll throw me out.'

'Then marry him. You're living with him anyway this way you'll inherit.'

'I can't.' Around and around we go like a wedding ring.

The thought of being married makes me want to puke. Pinball's refrain, once you have it in your head it's hard to get it out.

To the Prince she says, 'Let's just forget about it.'

'I'm afraid we can't.'

'What are you afraid of?'

'Them slinging you out.'

'No way', and she tears the Queen's letter into little pieces and throws them up in the air where they twirl and whirl and come down as confetti on his head. The Prince who is nervous about eating an ice-cream cone in public already has the look of a hunted man. He shimmies with his shoulders but the incriminating evidence sticks to him, a Prince with platelets of dandruff for shame.

'The Queen will not be amused.' A sardonic remark.

'Fuck the Queen.' A non-sardonic remark. 'I mean, what's she going to do? Come fluttering up from Windsor swinging a flamingo, Off with her head!' Hah. To the Chick the Queen is a joke a paper doll a character out of one of her Little Golden Books a dumpy modeller of crowns the perfector of the corkscrew wave. 'Let her threaten.' Bones and bloodstains can bring her pains but the Queen's threats, nah.

The Prince smiles the Prince admires but the Prince is his father's son so he bangs his gavel of judgement saying, 'It won't wash, I'm afraid.'

'It doesn't need washing,' she told him.

The next thing she knew a FINAL WARNING dropped through their letter box, a summons to appear before one of Her Majesty's civil servants at the Office of Immigration and it was printed in a flaming flow of letters. FAILURE TO APPEAR meant BIG TROUBLE.

'What do they mean? What can they do to me? I mean really.'

'Really deport you.'

'How?'

'Extradition.'

'They can't do that I'm an American citizen.'

'Precisely so.'

She looked at this man, what was going on here? Was it the

law he loved, thou shalt not disobey thy Queen, or her? Did he really want to be married to her? Or did cohabitation make him as nervous as the thought of marriage made her? Not possible, she concluded.

'Possible,' I correct. 'You're dealing here with a man who believes one thing with his head another with his um-pah-pah. A sentimentalist.'

The next thing she knew banns were being published. Hear ye! Hear ye! Miss Keziah Little, a.k.a. Chicken Little, Spinster, is being sold into lawful wedded slavery to the Honourable Geoffrey Anthony Osborne Prince. It was posted in the post office window in the centre of town next to a Missing Person poster of a young girl with black circles around her eyes and a black dog under her arm, it did not say if the dog was also missing.

They rang the bell of a so-called man of God with false teeth and a stained moustache, feh, at least mine is black and shiny with cleanliness which makes me closer to God than the so called. He rubbed his hands together, 'And what can I do for you, hm? Is it married you'd like to be, hm? And when is it you'd like to be married, hm?'

The marriage room was a cell with four walls each one covered in a different flowery wallpaper, stained by smoke of chip fat to match so-called's moustache, double feh. The fire was fake the flowers were fake the man shuffled in his backless English house slippers.

The Chick fled. 'I need to get some air,' she cried, and left the Prince to back out, as was his wont, more gracefully.

The second Register Office was no better. Instead of chip fat, bacon. 'Uch, bacon.' The Chick held her stomach. 'I'm sorry,' said the Prince of Sorriness. 'We'll try one more place, perhaps it will be more salubrious.'

'Salubrious, I like salubrious,' I said to Pinball. 'Like what the Italians say when they drink a toast. *Salut*. Good health.'

'Since when is marriage good for the health?' She went to her Disaster Drawer she brought back an article saying it was good for men bad for women. I couldn't argue and even if I could where would it get the Chick? Marriage according to Pinball was an open prison sentence, once you got in you never got out the divorce laws couldn't help you. A fancy cage without keys. Go ahead leave who's stopping you. You retreat to the back of your lair you turn off the lights you bury yourself in burying, deeper and deeper.

The Prince and the Chick worked their way down the list and each place was worse than the last until they got to the main Register Office, Charles Dickens would have loved it. Keziah loved, the Prince loved. Dark polished mahogany gleaming brass. Bars on the windows where you went to register and behind the bars a young woman filing her nails. 'Perfect,' said the Chick, 'let's get it over with.'

The Prince went to the window to make his petition.

'Yes?'

'We'd like to get married.' He looked to the Chick for corroboration she was busy studying mahogany grain, an intricate subject. The clerk handed him a form. 'If you'll just fill this in and post it, we'll send you an appointment by return post.'

'How long will it take?'

'The wait list is at least three months, sir.'

'I'm afraid it will have to be sooner.'

'I'm afraid that's impossible, sir.'

The Prince explained the urgency of the situation but alas the clerk was not impressed. 'I'm sorry, sir, but you can't jump the queue. If we made an exception for you we'd have to do it for everyone and we couldn't do that now could we?' The Prince of Parity had to agree. 'Perhaps if you write to the Home Office they'll grant you an extension. Or you could opt for a religious service, they're much quicker. Next, please.'

So they opted.

Eighteen

'I take it you have both read the marriage service?' Yes we can read they nodded with their heads. 'Is there anything you would like to discuss? Changes you might like to suggest? I'm afraid it's rather an antiquated document.' 'Never mind,' said the Prince. 'It certainly is,' said the Chick.

The vicar stretched forth his lips. He put his spectacles down on his desk he clasped his hands before him saying, 'Well, now' and 'Ahem.' And then he invited discussion towards possible emendation of the service. So the Chick discussed. 'Would you mind taking out the references to Jesus Christ?'

Now the Prince had chosen this particular Church of England partly for the aesthetics of its architecture but also for the liberality of its vicar. Rumour had it he was ecumenical. He had met Jews before and not come away pierced like a strainer from their horns his skin welted and bloody from whiplashings of their tails.

So when the Chick asked him to remove all references to his Lord Father Master Messiah Jesus Christ he did not spit and order her out of his temple but sat there in what the Prince would have called a thoughtful silence while the tips of his fingers rose up and consulted each other. He prayed for patience but in his heart he longed for a trickle of wood dust from the borings of the deathwatch beetle to fall into the eyes of this outrageous young woman's sockets.

The Chick meanwhile hung her head saying, 'My poor Jewish mother.' Tee he, she should have gone on the stage.

'Jesus Jehovah Yahweh Shmegegy,' fired Pinball, 'call Him by any name if He condones marriage He's a Jailer.'

'Quite, quite,' said the liberal man of God picking up his pen and drawing a neat line through each and every reference to the name of his Lord Jesus Christ and there were many. But what to put instead? 'We'll say God simply, shall we?' God Simply, a nice name for a Creator. Pinball went to play her machine. The Chick agreed.

And God Simply's representative on earth sat back while haloes of rainbows appeared round his head. 'Of course, we in this congregation,' he smooched, 'are firmly committed to openness. We always take the requirements of the particular couple into consideration. In your case, such a service as this, which happens to be according to the Church of South India, is dreadfully anachronistic. Rather embarrassing actually.'

'And how,' said the Chick, and the Prince put the edge of the sole of his shoe on the edge of the sole of her shoe and pressed.

'Yes, well,' said the vicar, 'is there anything else you would like us to look at?' He shut his eyes in order to encourage what he called their Creative Dialogue.

'Um, I don't care too much for this bit here: "Love, honour, cherish and *obey*". I don't call that very liberal, do you?'

'Oh dear oh dear,' he oh-deared, 'I thought we'd already taken that one out', and away went wifely obedience to God's representative on earth, her husband. 'Jackpot!' yelled Pinball from the back of the house. 'Amein,' I rocked.

'As a matter of fact, we haven't included that one for years.' He mopped his forehead with a handkerchief of terrible whiteness. 'Would there be anything else now?'

The Chick scanned her copy. 'Let's see. "Be fruitful and multiply." I'm not so sure about that. I'd rather not promise.'

He looked at the Prince who shrugged so he took that away too.

Soon there would not be many words left.

'You know,' he said, and a knuckle or two could be heard cracking in the wilderness, 'it always amazes me how people will go along with ceremonies which are quite meaningless or even antithetical to their beliefs. Most people, that is. I suppose they think of these services as coming from some God-given source; they wouldn't *dare* suggest any changes. So this is all quite ... refreshing to me. Ye-e-es, give and take, that's the name of the game, hmm?'

'In that case,' said the Chick, 'would you mind taking out the references to God?'

It was like when He heard about how Eve had wangled knowledge out of the serpent.

'I beg your pardon?' He was about to become an anti-Semite.

'Keziah ...' warned the Prince.

Pinball perused the sky. 'Looks like rain.'

'I mean, I don't really believe in God.'

The vicar advised them to go home and think about it. In other words, take it or leave it.

So they took.

Nineteen

The night before the wedding and all through the house not a creature was stirring not even a mouse.

Especially not a mouse.

The Chick could not sleep she rose from her apprentice marriage bed she went down to the kitchen to sniff out what was what. It was four in the morning she smelled an abomination. She put her nose to counters to drains to the floor to the garbage she even stuck it praise be between her own legs where she discovered the odour of morning-before bridehood, pih.

What must the Jewish bride do? You want to know, my Chick? I'll tell you. First she is made to wash away the ooze and slime of her womanhood in the baths called a mikvah. Then she is made to hide her shame under a veil called modesty, then she is gagged by a mouthful of pretty gauze. Then she prays she repents she confesses her sins. Of course she fasts. Under the wedding canopy her belly growls she waits for her beloved who has eaten a bellyful of bagels and lox to lift the veil and feed her with his lips. Meanwhile the shadows pass over. The rabbi and her betrothed pray over her head, mumbling bees in cahoots. Pray hard and the Lord may take pity on you and make you like Sarah Rebecca Leah and Rachel. Comely respectable maidens, hoo ha.

Still she smelled the smell. She began to clean. She swept the floor she scrubbed the insides also the outsides of cupboards with disinfectant she rubbed the taps with lemon juice she emptied the refrigerator of sticky jars and mouldy lemons and filled it up again. She washed the floor not even a cushion under her knees.

Do not go down on your knees on your wedding day!

She went out into the garden. She drank tea the sun was rising the floor was drying. She went back inside the smell was still smelling. Aha! it was coming from the stove otherwise known as a *cooker*. She opened it up she took out the racks and trays she scrubbed inside. She did the broiler tray with steel wool and there followed all the rings and the rings' rings and the tray under the burners and when she was finished she was filthy and tired and still the smell smelled.

Aha! it was not coming from the cooker it was coming from *behind* the cooker! So she wriggled and pulled until it was far enough out for her to see behind it, behold! dust balls.

And now the smell was not coming from behind the cooker it was coming from *inside the back panel*. Something in there some rotting creature she had to get the metal plate off it was held on by screws. Did I mention it was an electric cooker? It was an electric cooker. Gas had not come to their village.

No more, my Chick, you have smelled enough you have seen enough. Go get dressed or you'll be late for your own wedding, let His Highness do it. But the Prince was still asleep in the cosiness of his tent so she did it herself.

She went to the tool drawer she found the Philips screwdriver. One by one she twirled and the screws which were in the shape of stars came out in her hand. She took the steel plate by its sides and lifted it away so she could see what was what and what she saw was a crucified mouse. Actually it had been electrocuted but it looked like a crucifixion because its little arms were stretched in the shape of a cross each tiny hand attached to a terminal, red for live black for earth.

The Chick put the star-shaped screws into her pocket so they would not get lost. After that she went upstairs, took the

Prince by the hand and led him downstairs as to Golgotha. She did not speak but the Prince did saying, 'Oh dear, it was only a field mouse.' And when he saw the Chick's face, 'My poor sweet, I'm so sorry. It can't have been much fun finding it', and he held her against his chest and tried to smooth down her hair which also looked electrocuted and which would not allow itself to be smoothed. And then he suggested she'd better go up and get ready.

'What will you do?' She was studying the mouse. 'Don't look –' he shielded her eyes. She threw his hands away, I'll look if I like. And then she went upstairs.

The Prince unwound the mouse's tiny hands he laid it down on newspaper as if he was about to diaper it he bundled it up and took it down to what he called a rubbish bin. *It was only a field mouse*. He scrubbed his hands like a doctor and after that he proceeded to his grapefruit.

The Chick was trying to weave a ribbon through the horsehair of her hair when the bell rang. Her hand jerked her hair came undone, what now? The Prince arose from his grapefruit. At the door Shiloh! there stood a man in a beret and beside him a bicycle draped with onions from small to fat. 'I wish an onion seller would come round to us,' wished the Chick only that week. And so it came to pass, a thread of luck a banishment of mousy omens.

She threw her arms around the Prince's neck they danced up and down, the Chick the Prince and the string of onions and he dangled them high over her head like mistletoe and kissed her on her lips and the crucified mouse kept its peace.

And the Prince put his white linen suit upon his flesh and a flower he stuck through his lapel. And the Chick guarded her gravesticks with a skirt that was long but not white because she was born after all contaminated and they drove to the Church in the sunshine where there was no canopy and she was not gagged by a veil and did not have to walk around the Prince three times in adoration nor cut her feet on glass lest she forget the sorrows of her people and her right hand lose its cunning.

She holds out her hand to receive the ring. Circular and without end. The two rings get stuck together and the best man who is a woman can't get them apart and the Chick begins to see the crucified mouse dangling from the vicar's neck and she steps on the hem of her long skirt getting up and she hears it go *rip rip* and she says 'ooh' instead of 'I do' but it doesn't matter because the vicar takes her moving lips as read and so she is sworn consecrated married bound into bondage before God Simply and the vicar and a handful of strangers and the twin presence of her Aunt Adolf and her mother Pinball, God help her.

The Prince her husband kisses her with his lips. 'Excuse me.' She unhooks her lips she runs out of the chapel and into the toilet. *The thought of marriage makes me want to puke.*

Meanwhile back in the chapel the mystery guests of the congregation (two interesting-looking dames, one fat one thin, one beautiful one hideous) come into their own. They reach into the laps of their housedresses and pelt the bridegroom with the nuts raisins and candies they have hidden there. A hailstorm of hard candies to his head. Candy stripes. Strong mints. Rootbeer rocks. For luck. And now the women reach under their pews for the bowls and jars and crocks the candies were stored in. And after that come the flowerpots and cooking pots and frying pans and griddles and girdles and anything else they can find to hurl. And now they stand and file out of their pews until they are all around him and they beat his head with ladles. And when they think he has had enough they stop and repent each one in her turn bending down to kiss him with her lips. For it is said in the Torah, 'Whoever weds a suitable woman Elijah kisses him.' Their kisses are charged with electricity, his lips are charcoal.

Dreams, pih.

Twenty

'**W**here is he taking you for your honeymoon?'
        She huffed she puffed she would have blown my house down. 'Aunt Adolf, he isn't *taking* me, we're going together.'

'So where are you going together?'

'He doesn't know yet.'

'Let him take you to Jerusalem.' The Red Sea. A cruise. Let her wrap her poignancies in blankets snooze with her nose in the sun, a nice package deal. Show him the Wailing Wall teach him to blub.

'Are you crazy? It's dangerous. I hate Israeli politics.'

I thought about Palestinian bombs. 'You could be right. Why not the Riviera?'

'Not his scene. Listen, I better go, this is expensive time. We'll go somewhere nice don't worry. Talk to you soon. Bye.'

I rocked I thought about honeymoons. How once upon a time Pinball spent hers watching Solly try to climb their new green walls like the trunks of trees, he tore her paint job to shreds. Together they searched the house for phantom burglars, Pinball in the lead. Pih, more of a lemonmoon.

Arthur and I were planning to go to the Alps he showed me pictures. We would bathe in a hot springs surrounded by mountains snow-capped peaks. We would go we would Do.

We would see the flowers in the meadows sink our toenails into buttercups attend a concert of cowbells spread out a picnic on a red and white cloth clink glasses, shalom. To you. To *you*, my dear Letisha, have this nice piece of goat's cheese. And he would put it between my lips.

They went to see a bed.

The John and Josephine Bed. Made of gilded wood with a canopy hanging down from the ceiling a circus tent with silk tassels a fat brocade sausage for a pillow, an invitation to neck trouble.

Do not be so quick to condemn, I told my sister, it was her choice not his. He would have taken her to Paris Rome Athens Casablanca. He would have strolled her along the banks of the Seine filled her belly with Viennese pastries her eyes with paintings from the Uffizi. He would have handed her into a gondola filled her shoes with holy water her cleavage with stinky gardenias. But the weight of his generosity sat on her chest the carcass of an unclean creeping thing. She fell on the grass. 'I don't know. Let's just explore the area up here. Why go to Europe I haven't even seen England yet.'

'Are you sure? Don't you want to do something special for our honeymoon, something you'll always remember?' The Prince of No-pressure Salesmanship. She said, 'Wherever we go I won't forget.'

Free choice, pih.

So there they were on their sweetmoon enjoying the Great Bed. It had only recently been restored. The Before Bed had been in a saggy and rumply ('sadly deteriorating') condition so four dedicated lady quilters took pity on it. Win Maddison, Maureen Avery, Elsa Charlton and Jean Turner, they worked on it for a year. Nice names nice ladies. Maybe not nice, who knows? Anyway a lot of work.

When the Chick called me up I said I didn't know they had beds in museums. I thought of Solly's bed a museum piece if ever there was one also very much in need of restoration it had been on display in our garden for years by then daisies grew out of its rusted skeleton. I said, 'Maybe they'd like to put Solly's bed in a museum.'

'Oh, Aunt Adolf.'

'Why, what's wrong?'

'John and Josephine slept in this one.'

'Who?'

As a matter of fact that was what she wanted to know but was too embarrassed to ask. Ask! Yell! Shout it to the chandeliers! WHO THE HELL ARE JOHN AND JOSEPHINE? You hear? Instead she asked a fishy question, 'Which king and queen were they again?' She was not big on English history.

The Prince called her my sweet he explained they weren't king and queen at all but the owners of the museum and its collectors. John Bowes a rich country squire and his wife Josephine.

She felt like diving under the newly restored silk brocade quilt. 'I feel so dumb.'

'Please don't.'

'I should know the kings and queens.'

'Why should you? I only know them because we got them drilled into us every day at school. You probably know all the early American presidents.'

'Well . . .' *Washington Adams Jefferson* . . . who came next?

'In any case, knowing names and dates and facts is not what matters. Let me tell you a story, it's about my mother's funny school.' He held her elbow.

'Tell me.'

So he told. 'For each subject they had an expert who taught them intensively for two weeks. When it came to French history it was a famous Oxford don, a woman. My mother and her schoolmates were sitting under an apple tree full of blossom while the old lady lectured them on French history. It was magical; they were transported. She felt she came away really knowing that period.'

What, wondered the Chick, does the Prince's English mother-to-be sitting on the grass with her legs folded away under her frock have to do with me and my appalling ignorance?

'On her next visit home my grandfather questioned her on French history. "And what have you learned about Napoleon?" he asked. "Who's Napoleon?" was her reply.'

Hah. You see how clever this Prince is, how little the ordinary things matter to him, how outside all the rules he is, how he sees the Chick's real worth even under all those rumpled crumpled layers? How he sees his mission not to mention the investment potential in a restoration job, how he is prepared to work on her even if takes the patience of four unpaid ladies of leisure?

They walked on. The windows in this Bowes Museum were wide and high and with many panes and lo! she beheld a great forecourt and beyond that rose gardens sculpted into giant leaves five leaves each side exactly symmetrical. Two heraldic beasts hung on by their claws to a pair of great stone balls. As she looked the beasts twisted their heads and snarled up at her. She shrank away from the window. No shrinking! Snarl back! Only stone!

She caught up with the Prince who was busy looking at a life-size Dresden porcelain baby wrapped up like a cabbage roll.

'Swaddling,' he explained. 'I believe you call it bunting.'

'I do?' *Bye baby bunting Daddy's gone a hunting*. 'Let's go,' she says.

'Soon. Let's just have a look at the toys. They're said to have a rather splendid collection. D'you mind?'

She hangs on his arm like an elderly relative.

'What is it, my sweet?'

'Nothing.'

He takes her to the toy section he points out all the teddies and trains and toys he had as a child. A wood and wicker doll's pram, a children's go-cart, a toy farm wagon, a big round revolving child's play table with a seat in the middle. The Chick imagines him sitting in the centre of that wooden spool with its play table and spindles spinning round and round and round.

Give me give me give. She wanted she did not want, she was fascinated she was repelled. Solidity security privilege destroy it all. No. Preserve it everyone should have such things the Prince had such things by being here she had them too. His past her past, his toys hers. Don't touch. Teddies, doll's houses, doll's clothes with white tucks at the throat, cot quilts railway models toy soldiers fire brigade, horses cows sheep . . .

The Prince held her elbow. 'All right?'

All right.

On their way out they stopped to view the tableware collection. Gold dessert spoons egg spoons candle snuffers. Fabulous terrible. Now as she sits at her play table with the world spinning round her she bangs with her cup and her Mummy comes running *Yes, darling* brings her an egg, taps at it with the golden spoon feeds it through her rosebud mouth.

'Dreadful ostentation,' says the Prince whose own egg spoon was of mere bone his candle snuffer of simple silver.

Simple silver, God simply. Amein.

On their way out he offers to buy her a catalogue. 'It will remind you.' She doesn't want to be reminded. 'Too expensive,' she says. Instead she picks out two postcards, one of John and Josephine's Bed and one of the revolving play table.

I have them in my box.

Twenty-one

The Chick wished for a castle she got a castle. Romantic ruins turrets hanging moons, slits for the escaping sighs of non-escaping damsels. But those slits according to the Prince were for arrows headed for the heart of the invading horde. Very poor toilet facilities too.

The Prince spread out his rug with a view of the sea on a grassy mound. He opened his picnic basket which he called a hamper an inheritance from his Gran. Wickerwork with two handles and many compartments for holding the cucumber sandwiches the scones the fruitcakes the butters the jams the flasks the mugs the wine bottles the silverware. There were even loops on the lid for the serviette rings and serviettes.

'Serviettes?'

'Napkins,' translated the Prince slipping her a grape. She closed her lips to the passing of further fruit. 'What's wrong, my love?' A darkness passed over her face not a cloud in the sky. She wiped her mouth with a remnant of toilet paper. This I taught her to do, always carry a few squares in your handbag, you never know. Your picnic hamper may have lost its serviettes.

Hoo ha.

After the picnic they went for a walk they came to a bridge over a stream. The Prince stopped, 'Shall we play Pooh sticks?'

'Poo sticks?'

He could not believe his ears neither could she. 'Who poo? what poo?'

'Do you not know Pooh?' Such a lack such a gap! Such literary underprivilege! pitied the Prince.

'Find a stick,' he instructs, and they lean over the bridge which is stone and curved and at the count of three they drop their sticks and run to the other side and behold! there is the Prince's stick.

'Where's mine?' wails the Chick. Lost drowned, even her Pooh stick is doomed.

'Never mind,' says her husband, and he takes her to a pub and buys her a glass of sweet cider and after that he buys her a skirt with flowers on it so she can swish it past her gravesticks like an English lady and at last he drives her up to the high moors where the heather is in flower for it is the end of August and he rootles as he once rootled as a boy in short trousers and he finds her a sprig of white heather, 'For you, my sweet; for luck.' He removes his red glasses he gazes on her with his dove's eyes he says a silent prayer that one day she may come to trust him but most of all trust in herself. And may her Pooh stick not get trapped by rocks and may she cry out I won! I won! And her winning would be his winning.

And may they bring me the dove and I will put him on my altar where I will wring off his head and burn it and wring out the blood and sprinkle it thereof and pluck away its crop with its feathers and then I'll burn it until it be ashes and all this will smell sweet to me.

Don't forget the salt.

Her first opera, he took her to Mozart. '*Cosi Fan Tutti*, All Women Do It,' he translated.

'Do what?'

'Are unfaithful.' The Prince's nose-channels ran down with rivers for the sweetness of the music for the sadness of it all.

'What sadness?' asked the Chick.

The Prince called it Profoundly Cynical and Disturbing.

'What is disturbed?' she wanted to know.

'Fidelity. Love. By the end the couples are switched around and yet it doesn't seem to matter.'

'Well does it?'

The Prince held her hand he squeezed and manipulated until it was as imprintable as butter. He could not speak. He took her to An Hotel where he fed her things that melted in her mouth and poured a wine offering down her throat. After that he took her back to their room where he held her until her flesh was itself butter and into that he imprinted the words. *I will never leave you.* '*You* may leave *me* of course,' he said taking his Mozart to heart. 'But I will teach you that it is possible that love can go on and on and on that promises can be kept that marriages can endure that we will care for each other in our old age in sickness in health in madness and badness in boredom and in wrinkles.'

In his passion he lost his punctuation.

Pooh sticks on him.

Twenty-two

'It won't last,' said Pinball. Sour moons curdled milk, Pinball's recipe for a long and miserable life together.

Maybe yes maybe no, already the Prince was busy breaking rules. I entered my plea saying, 'You never know.'

'I know.' Her threats were like a fishbone in the mouth, even after you fished it out you were still afraid to swallow.

'Give them time,' I gave. We rocked. We discussed wedding presents.

'Sent,' said the Pin.

'What sent?'

'A box.'

A moan a groan a denial from the heart. 'Don't tell me.'

She told.

'Keziah doesn't need such a thing.'

'She will.' She thumbed in the direction of England. She meant of course a Disaster Box, basic equipment for the newlywed no home should be without one.

'Annie, what does such a present say? Think about it. Put yourself in her shoes.' She looked at her feet, impossible.

I tried again. 'Keziah doesn't need a box she doesn't see marriage the way you do. For her it's an opportunity an opening up more than a shutting in. A box of opportunities. They have a lovely cottage right by the sea.'

She plucked at her nightgown she chewed on air like an old lady.

'She walks with boots on her feet.'

Pinball saw combat.

'He's teaching her to walk up mountains she'll be closer to God.'

She saw Him stretch forth a Finger zinging with electricity, the sound of screams filled our ears the smell of burning flesh.

Withdraw thine hand let not thy dread make me afraid.

'Listen, he's teaching her to distinguish grass from grass, tree from tree, to plant tomatoes to camp in the woods to be one with nature.'

'Poison ivy.'

'Ha! they don't have poison ivy over there!'

Still she saw poison ivy.

'He bought her a bike he's teaching her to ride he's even teaching her to drive a car.'

Metal smacking metal.

'He takes her to the opera to plays he reads her poetry stories even children's books, the whole world is opening up before her.'

A black hole.

'Picnics.'

She stopped rocking.

'Listen, Annie. It's not just doing. He's teaching her to think how to talk, you should hear her fancy accent on the telephone. *Aunt* Adolf, she says it rhymes with want. *Aunt!* Philosophy, sociology, history, the Latin names of plants, birds . . . He has put her in a house with roses round the door.'

'A prison, a high stone wall.'

'He has shown her –' I was getting mad – 'sea-birds with long curved noses.'

'To peck out her eyes.'

That did it. 'I'm going up to my birds.'

'He'll leave her, watch. Just like Moosa left me like Arthur left you.'

This last I took exception to. 'How can you say Arthur left me? He visits me every week religiously.'

'He left you.'

'What are you talking about? He walked out the door a few hours ago you saw for yourself. He took her wedding present to the post office for me.'

'What?' she rubbed the bottoms of her feet together like a fly.

'What do you care?'

She said nothing.

'For your information, pearls.'

'*Pearls?*'

'A single strand, best quality. From Hawaii.'

She banged the screen door. 'Where are you going?' I yelled after her. She returned waving a clipping she stuck it under my nose.

MAN STRANGLES WIFE WITH WEDDING PEARLS.

'Take it away.'

'A choker,' she said, her gums were terrible. I saw the Chick's neck dissected with pearls.

'Give me that stupid thing.' I grabbed the clipping, a photograph of the pearl strangler. 'You're comparing butcher's eyes with dove's eyes. What are you, crazy?'

'Wait,' she said, and my mouth was filled with fishbones.

PART THREE

Put not your trust in princes.
Psalm 146:3

Twenty-three

It was their tenth anniversary.

'May they live happily ever after,' I said not so originally.

'May she live,' Pinball spat pins. A tuck here a tuck there at each end of my sentence. My sister could have been a seamstress of conversation snipping out sentiment pinking pity and look out for your tongue.

May she live usually translates, May she live a hundred thousand years and be rich and fat also her children and her children's children. But lest God think His suppliants forward and smite us with fallen arches we say humbly, *May she live*.

They lie through their humbles.

Not Pinball. Pinball was not usual. Pinball was no creative translator. Pinball meant what she said. Breathing to Pinball was an accomplishment. *May she live*. A prayer for breathing.

So Keziah breathed and the Prince breathed, in fact ten years of mutual breathing passed between them.

And God who doeth marvellous things without number and also miserable and unsearchable had caused certain already existing tendencies in the Chick to be exaggerated which is to say her busts had become bustier her legs leggier (in width) her ears earier. 'Where is your hair?' I wrote her. 'All I see are ears. Listen to me do not pull you hair back like that it does nothing for you. Let it loose let it fly.' Only her hips her nose her lips and her chin (Pinball's elegancies) remained intact. In fact they'd contracted. The combination was terrible. Her front teeth were also Pinball's (as from when she had them), pearly white straight up and down. But the space between them was mine, hah!

Poor Chick.

There was only one curse from which she was free (so far) and that was facial hair. Thanks be.

She did not believe it. She had no faith in facial hairlessness. She had nightmares of sprouting she woke up furry and exhausted. The morning of their tenth anniversary was no different she stood at her mirror making use of a pair of tweezers.

Don't! You'll make them grow! Dope!

I also stood at my mirror plucking. Pinball snuck up behind me on her bare feet saying, 'Why bother? Why not join a circus instead?' My sister the still-pretty torturer even without a tooth in her head. I showed her the gobble hole between my teeth she showed her baby's gums. 'The fat bearded lady: two for the price of one they'd save money on you.' 'A plague of bunions in your slippers,' I gave her which was stupid since she never wore slippers and her feet were even more perfect than her gums. She sat on the edge of the bathtub she stuck one of her oars in my face saying, 'find me a blemish', knowing I could not. Pride of feet, another of her sins.

I miss those feet.

She padded off I looked at myself in the mirror I beseeched the Lord, Why send me such a hairiness in my housedress, why? And, Am I a balloon that you should have blown me up like this? No answer. Maybe I should have eaten handfuls of Harz Mountain instead of M&Ms. The Othellos were Arthur's fault. Once I went on a pickle diet I lost thirty pounds. I gained back sixty. 'Eat,' said my sweet sister. 'You won't live so long anyway.'

Pinball as a prophet was a flop. I lived. (I still live. She does not.) I'm fat and hairy. As for Keziah and the Prince, wrong

wrong one hundred per cent wrong it was not over. Ten years thanks be and the honey the sweetmoon was not over it went on shining into their bedroom window the booming of the bitterns accompanying. A bittern for your information is a depressed-looking bird with hunched shoulders that stood in the reedbeds near their house, it made a noise like when you blow across a milk bottle, *bhoo bhoo*.

They lived happily if not ever after at least for the years you could count on Pinball's filthy silky toes.

Praise for toes.

To prove it wasn't over the Prince put into her hands a square wooden contraption oozing with wax.

'What's that?'

'A honeycomb.'

She licks with her tongue.

'Don't eat the wax, silly.'

She eats the wax. She spits with her tongue but the wax is a stubborn wax. Prince Oral RotoRooter puts his mouth, on her mouth. Siamese twins joined at the tongue. All gone.

Feh.

Anyway here they are still very much together as I said to Pinball even after the passing of so many years.

'It's only the beginning,' says the Prince trying his mouth at prophesy. 'We have a whole life together.' The Chick looks forth from her panes. 'It seems like a long time already.' This he ignores.

'Think of how many times I have been inside you.' His hands are honeyed with love he says he hopes to visit often in the future.

No! Cut off his hope! Visiting hours are over!

Pinball points out the unusually high ovarian cancer rates among the wives of uncircumcised men.

She closes her ears to us she opens her legs to him, honey and sour milk are under his foreskin.

Poo.

Do not misunderstand. I do not say the Prince was bad. No,

he held no one prisoner. This was not his method, free to go free to stay. All he was doing was making it so nice so smooth so slippery, enclosing the Chick in his garden a fountain of gardens a perfume of roses a well of living waters a netting of raspberries – that she would be crazy to even think of leaving. Come. Come into my garden my beloved and taste of my fruits.

Feh! Spit! Yell Poison! Howl! Neighbours! Animals! Wake up make rackets! A banging of pot lids! Let my Chick go or I will smite thee with frogs and froglets! Into his underwear drawer let them come down!

Did I say Happily Ever After?

A no-such thing. The Chick and the Prince went up in their happiness they went down they wobbled around so-so. A little unhappy a lot unhappy. You could plot the days the weeks the years like the Prince's graphs, learned articles accompanied by diagrams, see Model 3 it says and you look you see dots plotted on a curve. Opportunity factors.

Or medical tables you see in magazines, life expectancy of people with cancer measured in hundreds of weeks. Plot the dots join the dots like the stars at the planetarium where I took the Chick when she was ten years old. Down and around up up up and away the Chick and the Prince after ten years they still twinkled together like those twins I forget their names.

Meanwhile Pinball staggers around like a drunken thing pouring contempt not just on sisters but upon princes too. 'Wait wait,' she says, coming to rock and her feet rock too.

Wait for what? How long?

Twenty-four

The Prince was by this time a Ph.D. not to mention an Honourable. He was at peace with his stones and in league with the beasts of his field. At peace with the ground elder in his garden in league with the badgers in his wood. The property of his body was fenced with bones and sinews, he knew where he was. He removed his glasses which were no longer red but rimmed with the shell of the tortoise, he held them in his teeth while he raised binoculars to his eyes. He saw a heron with a fish in its mouth, the heron was also at peace. The fish's peace was an altogether different thing.

The Chick was by this time a Peripatetic Driver of Library Books and a Knitter of Afghans not to mention a Childless Matron of 37. She was not at peace in her tent. Music by Mozart made her ears to water, a fire from a woodburning stove smarted her eyes, red wine rolled around her bloodstream. She wasn't so happy.

She had a problem with the cold. She suffered chilblains, her big toes which were little toes were like sandpaper also itchy and hairy. I said, 'So what, you take after me.' She said, 'It's not funny.'

She got too near the stove she burned, she got too far she froze. Her fencing was in need of repair, she did not know she had a tent. She sat in the warmth shivering. She made mistakes she cursed she dropped stitches she watched them unravel and then she mourned.

Mourn not! Dance a sword dance! Jig! Stab him with needles! I waved chubarms and chublegs, Pinball rocked.

'Why is she knitting?' asked Pinball for whom the making of garments knitted or otherwise was a thing of wonder. Also hanging in the air like a line of her grungy washing was the proposition of baby clothes.

'Nothing doing,' I said. 'She's knitting because she's cold.' How could that slow and careful child become a mother? A rhetorical question as the Prince would say. She could not find her own nightgown. Besides where they lived nothing grew except outcrops and ground elder and thorn trees. Not a place for multiplying.

So I thought.

Then she sent a picture. 'Me sitting under a gnarled crab apple.' Two crabs wasn't all I saw. I saw cherry blossoms I saw lilacs I saw roses from Sharon and from other places. I saw poppies and peonies the size of cabbages. I saw some garden, hoo ha.

But inside her nothing grew.

'She went to the frozen North with the enemy what does she expect?' This from Pinball. I had no answer, my feet filled my shoes.

'What is she knitting?' Again.

'Stop asking. An Afghan. I sent her the pattern, very complicated to follow.'

'She likes complicated.'

'She'll figure it out,' I said.

Pinball denied it. 'She can think but she can't figure.'

'She will.' I had faith in her. Maybe she could not find her nightgown but she could find answers.

'She won't. *He* will.'

This time the Pin scored. One hundred per cent.

The Chick sat with her lap full of tent. She gazed into the woodburning stove a thing more interesting than television.

As she stared frolicking Swedes made merry in the firelight. 'What are you staring at?' asks her Prince.

'You'll think I'm nuts.'

'No, tell me,' he insists.

'I can see people dancing in there. Witches and devils hopping about. Scandinavian Rumpelstiltskins. Putting curses.'

He laughs he takes her chubpaw, 'Of course you can see figures dancing – so can I. Those figures are sculpted into the cast iron – it's called relief-casting. You're not nuts at all.'

'I'm not?' She sounds disappointed. She groans.

'Now what's wrong?'

'I'm stuck. It's too complicated to explain.' Her lap is full of the rough wool of women's work. Local sheep, black grey brown.

'May I?' He takes up the pattern he reads with his scholar's eyes. 'Look,' he shows, 'you need to twist the wool around the needle several times, it makes a bump. Does that make sense?' He directs her with his hands like a conductor. It makes sense it makes music it makes a bump.

Mozart is happy in his slow movement.

The Chick was born into trouble. For her sparks shot forth also hexes. The dancing Swedes lifted their legs they sprayed like cats, the cosy woodburning stove was a fiery hell a metal dungeon carved by Hieronymus Bosch brought to brilliant flaming life, oh comfort me with demons.

She threw her knitting at them. The Prince saved her work from destruction but the needles fell out. 'It's ruined I'm lost,' came her cry in the wilderness of their tent.

She was ready to mourn even before she knew. All her stitches were falling down. 'I'll never be able to pick them up now.' Sheep's wool filled her mouth.

'Nonsense,' said The Prince. He picked up her stitches one by one he handed her women's work back to her. She glared at him. 'Why is it called an Afghan?' A reasonable question. But the Chick, deliverer of books to the unenlightened, knew not the derivation of her own stuff. 'I don't know, I don't know anything.' She dropped her head. He picked it up it weighed so much. Could such a thing be a mother?

'No matter. Perhaps,' he suggested, 'it's a kind of nomadic blanket such as the Afghans used on their camels in the desert.' The Chick whose lap was full of the rough wool of local sheep said, 'You're probably right.' Her eyes were full of worship her muscles were full of flop.

No! No! Remember your tutu! Remember your dance at the Casa del Rey! Prize pupil! Golem's dance! Do it again! Lift up your knees! Twirl! Whirl! Spit on him for knowing!

The Chick as a child had been a dimpled doughnut of a thing singing along with Dinah Shore, Little Golden Records, hoo ha. Then she grew up she slimmed down she did she went she read she drew. She descended into subways she arose still wearing the blouse on her back. She showed us up for what we were. Rockers. File clerk to a Disaster Drawer. Mother of birds, janitor of birdcages. Pinball was green before the sun. My birds sang but my own throat was closed up like a scar. Once upon a time I might have been an opera singer.

Yet next to the Prince she lost her volts, forty watts max. How did this happen? Who knows. Even the Prince scratched his head his dander fell like snow upon his shoulders. It was not what he'd bargained for. And yet he had chosen her for better for worse in sickness and in health and so he would not replace her even when she made high-pitched whining noises, even when she threatened to go pop in the night. Even if it meant groping in darkness.

We also sat in darkness, rocking and waiting for IT according to Pinball to happen. Who can help? Who can stop this thing? The Pin's grin had a horrible Swedish look.

Twenty-five

The Prince is showing slides. Recollecting in the tranquillity of his tent how with his big lens and his great knees creeping along the earth he tracks this creature and that. The Prince enjoys blow-up vision he zooms in upon God's small things he crawls upon his belly to Nature in Her tabernacle.

The Chick also enjoys the fruits of his crawling. She gets to sit in thick darkness without the comfort of movie candy watching a three-foot caterpillar of many legs and much hairiness, the colour of a Lime Rickey.

And I say unto her, 'Maybe he'd like to do a close-up of my upper lip I could dye it green wiggle it up and down, sideways unfortunately it will not go.' My ears fill with laughter.

Her eyes fill with his sharpness of focus. His compositions his sensitive eye they are indeed a wonder to behold. He touches a button and lo there comes into view a giant poppy with petals like orange wax paper the sun shining through. After that comes a blurring a whirring a brightness all round, a halo of burning crackling haywires. 'Hey, that's my hair!' And now comes her foot. Followed by a hawk's foot. Keziah's teeth. An ape's teeth.

'Stop. Let's see that one again. Now go back. Forward.' Her teeth, the ape's teeth, her fears are founded. 'What are you trying to show here?'

'Nothing.'

'Don't tell me that's a coincidence.'

'Of course it is.'

'So you admit there's a similarity?'

'No! Look . . .' The projector whirrs, the Prince behind his projector also whirrs. What can he do? How can he get out of this thing?

He sits beside her he lifts her lip like a fond veterinarian. 'My love, your teeth are no more like that ape's than your foot is like the hawk's foot. I put them together for *contrast*, d'you see?'

'Are you sure?'

'Of course I'm sure.'

Pinball says, 'Never mind those gorilla teeth of hers what about the feet?'

'What's wrong with them?' Sometimes Pinball's drift is a little hard to follow.

'Nothing. Him. No footwork there.' She means no one to work on Keziah's feet. 'Footwork' is what I do for Pinball. The foot plopped in the spoon of my lap. Between each toe I go furrowing with a finger coming out with black bitlets. A twiddle here a caress there a good scratch around the heels. Pinball's feet are so calloused I can run my nail across the instep and all she registers is the sweet flutter of a caress. Torture makes Pinball purr.

'Mmnn, don't stop,' she says.

'Mmnn, don't stop,' says the Chick for the Prince is at that moment doing exactly with his left hand what I am doing with my right.

'Wrong. He does,' I inform her.

'Does what?' She is far away her feet are wings.

'Footwork. *Fancy* footwork.'

'Is that so?'

'That is so.'

'He doesn't mind?'

No more than I do.

She goes to her Drawer she comes back waving Oscar Wilde at me. '"All women,"' she quotes, '"become like their mothers – that is their tragedy. And no men do – that is theirs."' She sticks her foot back on my lap I pinch up a piece of instep, she feels nothing. 'Wrong! wrong! He's just like his!' I tell her about his mother Lady Hoo Ha who was also at peace in her tent, her tent dating from the eighteenth century. 'A more maternal man she could not have found.'

'A tent-peg in both their heads!' Her eyes are nostrils they sniff me out. 'How do you know? Because he plays with her feet? A foot pervert!' She reads me about the one who tied up his victims and tickled their feet before he cut them off.

'Nothing to do with feet!'

A lie. The Prince's crime had everything to do with feet. He held them so tight two feet in one hand like a fowl's she couldn't walk. He stopped her mouth with kisses she couldn't answer her own questions. He held her hand she couldn't get lost.

'What should I do? Where should I go?' She stood with her arms at her sides, two empty bags. She went for a job interview she asked him, 'What should I say?' He took her on a walk she asked him, 'Is it cold out? What should I wear?' The prophet of weather looked to the sky saying, 'I should wear long johns if I were you.'

You're not! You never will be!

Each morning when she was a child the Chick would stand looking into her clothes closet past the ghosts of dresses into the dark hole of used Kotexes and water bugs. 'What should I wear for school?' she'd ask Pinball of the exquisite dress sense. And Pinball would say helpfully, 'A skirt, a blouse.' After that Keziah went to the toilet. 'Come see!' she'd yell. Pinball hung herself over the bowl. 'Praise be,' she'd say. Praise for taking in praise for letting out.

Beyond that only the sound of my canaries. Twoo-twee, the time of the singing of birds was entirely questionable.

The Chick is his fledgeling. She falls out of the nest he puts her back she falls out he puts her back she falls out ... His patience is legion, what mama bird could compete?

What mama bird would *want* to?

Stop being so *motherly*!

Pinball gave up trying a long time ago.

The Chick went into her bedroom she dug out her long johns which were made of Chinese silk which the Prince had bought for her, very light very warm. They got up on the hills the sweat ran down between her breasts. 'You said it was cold.' The Prince smiled his ointment smile. 'I do get it wrong occasionally, you know.'

No! In God the Father the Weatherman We Trust not to cock up on His predictions! She looked at him with such a rise and fall of her bosom it branded his heart. 'I'm sorry,' he said.

'For what? It's not your fault.'

It's true it wasn't but he felt it was.

What am I saying?

Never mind. It comes from too much whistling duets with my canaries too much missing too much slow steady banging. Othellos. Pinball's feet. The Disaster Box, Keziah. So many things gone missing. I'm so hungry I could eat the runners of Pinball's empty rocker.

No! Fee fie fo fum! Give me the Prince's elbows to crunch! Give me his feet to tickle!

The Chick lay on her back her arms crossed X over her chest like a reclining mausoleum nude. 'You always hide yourself, why? Tell me,' encouraged the Prince. 'I can't.' 'Why not.' 'I can't.' 'Please, my love. Did something happen?' 'Something happened.'

Moosa. The oily sneak I should have known. I should have grabbed him and strangled him with a cow's intestine then stuffed him into it. Moose derma. Every morning the Chick told the Prince he crept in while Pinball lay on her back snoring and stinking. He crept over to the Chick's bed where she slept in her innocence with her arms crisscrossed over the gap in her pyjamas but Moosa loosened them like laces he opened them up the arms the buttons all her openings his morning appetizer.

O my Chick, why didn't you tell me?

The Prince groaned and then in his kiss-the-boo-boo voice said, 'I want to make it better for you. I want to make it so it doesn't hurt any more.' He peeled away her hiding hands he kissed her right nipple and her left. He cupped her cups with the hot pads of his palms he thrust his face between them. He made collops of her fatness on the two sides of his face. He warmed his cheeks he plugged his ears with pink stethoscopes. What does he hear? A heart prepared for deceit, a belly ready to be run through.

Behold, his sword awaits.

Twenty-six

The Prince made it so good she forgot to be afraid. She sucked in breath she threw out her chest a mermaid on the prow of a proud ship. Pih, how was she to know he would smack her in the nipples with the oldest fish in the sea?

Pinball also got smacked. Smack smack take that. A fish in the face from Moosa, poo. She wasn't prepared.

'You'll leave me,' she told him before. He raised his lip he showed her his dead tooth he said never. To prove it he baked her rice pudding he fixed her radiators he changed her light bulbs he screwed her loose screwings. She beheld him on his ladder she beheld God in his overalls. She could not hold her water.

She set him a test, this was her reasoning. If he loves me he'll love me like this. She unmade herself with the dedication of a scientist conducting an experiment. She drank whisky from a bottle. She peed on her feet she peed on her rocker's feet she peed on his feet. She didn't get dressed she didn't get undressed. Her hair hung in an oily red tail following the sad bumps of her backbone. Her elbows went rough her nose went west her belly dropped. Her few remaining teeth rattled in her head. Her beauty was consumed away like a moth. She became like the blue striped cloth upon my sink, feh.

How long can a person love a cheesy cloth? Answer not

long. Moosa failed her test. Pinball won. She proved what she already knew.

Poor Pinball. She went down so far she met bottom, lo and she saw that it was a slimy place. A place where no life lived not a wavy leaf of vegetable matter not a simple speck of spawn. Help, get us out of here said her legs and kicked. Hard. Bones toes knees heels, whoosh she was launched begotten spared. Enough. Time to Do said something or other inside of her. So up up she comes a parting of waters a parting of air, Pinball the rising silver mermaid lands beside me in her rocking chair, plop.

Welcome back. She opened her mouth and lo what came out was fish-speak. Dumb bubbles. I turned my head. Come closer, I can't hear you. She tried to stand she wobbled she fell back again. Come, let me help you. I went to her she kicked me in the belly. I went back to my rocker I rocked I rubbed my belly I saw she had to do this by herself.

She did. She rose up she found her feet she tilted sideways, reached for the side of the house, pushed off again, left skid marks, a trail of tail moult. Our porch-boards were painted battleship grey from salvage paint. Yea and she walked a straight line towards me with her arms stretched forth: I am shut up no more.

I sat I rocked. Let me watch while you Do. Let me watch while you rise up and live and about time too. She smiled with her gums I cried with my eyes.

My sister my spouse my much defiled.

It was only afterwards I figured out that Pinball was a woman who had to be left alone by men before she could Do for herself. Free of Solly free of Moosa free of stupid men. Even with her lumpy veins and her crooked saggy nose Pinball was a special thing. Like treasure you find washed up on the beach. Cheekbones anklebones kneebones, selah.

I threw her into the bathtub. She slipped and slid, she was bigger than me but I was fatter. I made her laugh she hadn't laughed in ten years. She tore my dress she pulled me in on top of her we flopped around. Water flew out. I cushioned her head on my hairy arm she rested in relative peace. When I brought her out of that place I rubbed her down she came up like a diamond, I had to cover my eyes.

I pushed her on to the toilet seat I dried her feet. I turned her around I made her a baby's topknot, her hair was fine and streaked with grey. I wrapped her around with bathrobe I strolled her into the kitchen I spooned Cream of Wheat into her mouth. She ate the pap I ate the lumps. For dessert she had strained baby peaches. 'Look,' I showed her the picture on the jar I told her she looked like the Beech-nut baby, all shiny and clean. 'You look like Adolf Hitler,' she returned the compliment. I scraped the remains of the peach goo with the spoon and stuck it in her mouth.

I loaned her my Singer and a piece of practice material. This way she'd have something to Do, maybe even earn her keep. (Pinball money, hah!) She put her big toe on the pedal and off she went. She was smoke she was dust she was a squealing of tyres. She travelled near she travelled far she broke the speed limit. She broke my best needle. The piece of material came out crisscrossed and puckered with her terrible tracks. I took back the Singer. 'You'll have to go on welfare,' I told her. She said she'd rather eat my birds.

Twenty-seven

'It's the Good Humour man!' The Chick as a child ran with her chubsticks after the ice-cream man. She rang of his bell she bought of his refrigerated Humorous popsicles. Now women and children hear the Chick coming they yodel to one another, 'It's the Library lady!' She drives a beat-up van full of beat-up books with sticky covers. She takes orders from literature-starved ladies, some of them also battered and with sticky covers. She has no bell. She bumps along from village to village offering up her wares. Iris Murdoch, Doris Lessing, Muriel Spark. Thank you very much they say and slip another Catherine Cookson under the pile. She opens her mouth to cry Aha! Aha! I saw that! yet all she can do is smile with her teeth which are my teeth, the lion hath lost her roar.

'Smite them on their cheekbones!'

She calls me a virago.

'What's a virago?'

'A big strong quarrelsome woman.'

Hoo, honoured I'm sure. 'Let them read trash, what do you care?'

She cares. She cares what they read she cares what they eat or don't eat she cares about their children and their children's goldfish. She should have stayed in California and become a teacher, a civil rights lawyer, a social worker, a psychiatrist, a

121

doctor. She could have been anything if not for him.

Instead she's stuck in a truck. They hand her their dog-eared library cards they hand her their dogs they hand her their marital problems. A shrink-vet combo on wheels on the salary of a pin.

'But I like it,' she says. 'It's non-demanding.' Dulling lulling a pleasant job a pleasant husband.

'Is it not Written: *Is there taste in the white of an egg?*'

For shame she has forgotten her Bible.

Hard-boiled eggs. Bally eggs. Oh how I love the yolks, dry crumbly bright. But the whites, feh, try to grab an egg white see what happens. It slips out of your hand.

When I was three (before Pinball and I got sent away) our father who was no father dangled a valuable bill in front of my nose. Mine all mine if only I would eat *the whole egg*. White, poo! You want to know what I did? I yanked the money out of his hand. I tore it in half I kept tearing I tore until it was in little pieces which I threw over his head. Confetti: go get married. I took the egg from his other hand I stood there I peeled away the slivers of slime behold a yolk bare and bright as the sun. I popped it into my mouth I stood with my fatlings apart I chewed in his face. You want to know what he did? He hissed he called me cat but it was too late. He couldn't hide the twitch of lip with the shred of bribe money on it.

Whereas Pinball – nowhere is the difference more between two sisters – Pinball Annie would have killed for that smirky smile. Approval, pih. With all her looks and all her smartness that was the thing she wanted most and yet she couldn't get it try as she might and don't think she didn't. Men stupid men. Crooks wife beaters child molesters cauliflower-eared sleep-walkers. Her taste in men matched her taste in eggs. Slimy, feh.

Her daughter sends me a picture. There stands the Princely Egg, his hips and his lips are legion. His arm is around her waist. The Chick is wearing the floppy heather-coloured beret I made for her, it looks like a pancake on her head.

I dial her number. 'Listen to me. This is what you have to do. Take bobby pins draw it together play around with your fingers until the shape is right you can't just sit it on your head and expect it to look perfect, nothing is perfect.'

'Wrong,' she says.

'What? Who?'

'The Prince.'

Let me hold my water. 'What did he give you for Valentine's Day?'

'Aunt *Aaaa*dolf.' (Since when did I grow so many As in my name?) 'He doesn't need a special day, he's always bringing me presents: flowers books toys.'

Toys?

'Anyway Valentine's Day is no big deal over here. It's another one of those pernicious American commercial holidays engineered by card and flower companies.'

Pernicious, I like pernicious.

'Arthur sent me lilacs.'

She did not say, So what else is new? Arthur's lilacs are religious. Once upon a time he went out of my life but the lilacs kept coming. Winter flowers, hoo ha. He left me but he didn't leave me. Every week for thirty years he came back.

Arthur's Day.

Thirty years thirty dollars, it's about time I had a raise.

Lilacs, pih.

'Tell me,' I said, 'did you give *him* something?'

It turns out she wrote him a poem it came out surprisingly pernicious all about St Valentine the Christian martyr who got torn apart by lions.

Twenty-eight

'Tell me about Arthur.' She was eight years old. 'Why did he leave you?'

'Who says he left? Don't listen to everything you hear!'

Keziah listened she knew she was born knowing. Her ears were wide her mouth was a question mark. Her father had not long gone the way of his bed. 'What did you do wrong?'

What did Job do? I chewed a corner of fresh magazine I told.

'I fell in love with Arthur, Arthur fell in love with me. I put him through law school. Nine years I drilled holes in fabric I gave him every penny I earned.' It might have been my flesh that got drilled every drop of my blood that got poured out and given him to drink. Cold fruit soup. 'That,' I told her, 'is what I did wrong.'

'I went down and Arthur went up. Up and up and up he climbed his books got heavier so did his shoes. Florsheims, hoo ha, I paid.

'After nine years he graduated he got his first job he got his first secretary, black seams up her legs. Bye-bye, Adolf.'

'It doesn't make sense,' she pronounced, 'after what you did for him.'

'No.'

'It's not fair.'

'No.'

'What did he say?'

'He said, "I'm sorry." And I said, "You're sorry." I was a parakeet. Then he said, "I'm very sorry," and I said, "You're very sorry." I was a very parakeet. Now he said, "Look, Letisha, what can I say?" and he said, "Do you want me to tell you?" but he did not wait for telling, he pressed my hand he ran away. The pressing left thirty bucks cash.'

'What did you do?'

Doing stories are more exciting for a child than not-doing stories. But I wanted the Chick to know the truth, that doing sometimes takes time so I said, 'At first I did nothing.'

'It must have been a shock.'

'I sucked lemons I ate of bitter herbs. I was busy gathering my strength.'

'You had to recover your equilibrium, right?' Equilibrium, hoo ha. Eight years old.

I rocked. My bones rocked inside my flesh, my heart was wax. I listened to the hopping of birds the sound of gravel the tinkling of bells. I fed my birds I fed my face I washed my feet. I stared at my legs which were trees, I supported them with support hose. I thought of the floozie's spike heels the black seams up the backs of her stockings. I went to the toilet bowl and threw up my bile.

'He made you sick,' said the child.

'Sick? He made snakes slide from my guts!'

'So what did you do then?'

'I opened my throat which was like a sepulchre and I spoke to God.'

'What did you say?'

'I said, "Lord, you see a woman who is sick of being sick. You see my humiliation you see the mark of my disgrace." I held up my hand. "Give me light so that I can pray to you."'

'And did He?'

'He gave me a flicker of dying match, you could hardly honour it with the name Light.'

'Oh.'

'So then I said, "How shall I defile my enemies?" I considered the way of Jael.'

'Ooh.' Her Os were increasing.

'You remember what she did?'

'She gave Sisera milk to drink and covered him with a mantle and then she took a tent-peg and nailed it into his head with a workman's hammer.' She pointed to her temple. 'And then she smote off his head.'

She remembered.

'You did *that*?'

'I considered but I did not do it. I consulted God.'

'Phew. And what did He say?'

'He said nothing He showed nothing. But I saw something else.'

The Chick looked, 'What?'

'I saw a lady God, a Mrs God, a Lioness God, I don't know what to call her. She was Light. From her my heart caught fire my prayer was a flowing flame I said to myself, this is the One, to hell with Him.

'You mean God?'

'I mean God.'

She giggled. 'So what then?'

'I went home and slept. In the morning I went down to the garden of nuts in other words the A&P. I looked for Brazil nuts but there were none so I chose a large can of unshelled pecans I took them home I tore off the key and wound it round the outside of the can and dumped the nuts into my handbag.'

Comfort me with pecans for I am sick of love.

I looked at the Chick I posed her this question. 'Who is she that marcheth forth hot as an eclipsed sun and terrible as an army armed with the wrath of nuts?'

'You?'

'Correct! No more lemon-sucking! The time had come to Do! I polished up my pocketbook until I could almost see myself in it, a sickening sight, and I hung it on my arm. Pinball said, "You look terrible." I said, "I am."'

The Chick put her hand over her mouth.

'I hid in an alleyway near their workplace. I waited until they came past and then I made my move. Arthur landed on the sidewalk, his floozie landed in Emergency.'

'What did you do?'

'I Did. I beat them up.'

'Both of them?'

I nodded.

'With your bare hands?'

'Hah! What do you think the handbag was for? A handbag with nuts is a fine weapon. I pointed to the specimen hanging from the doorknob. 'Just like that only bigger. Black patent leather. With a big gold-plated clasp.' My grin was also gold. Thus armed I demonstrated the arm action of an avenging prophetess. Instead of a tent-nail, nuts.

'Oooh,' went the Chick.

'It clipped her in her nose. A big nose.'

'Was there a lot of blood?'

'A lot of broken nose. I crippled them up good.'

She took a deep breath. Watch out, my Chick, I spit on the faint-hearted.

'Did you get into trouble?'

'No charges.' I bit into an Othello.

'How come?'

'Call it Arthur's conscience. To him a bump on the head equalled nine years of law school. So now we were even.'

We chewed together we sucked up sweetness we filled our bellies with the chocolate butter cream of an Othello. The Chick licked her plate.

'Revenge also doesn't last long,' I confided, 'but it's delicious while it does.'

'What happened to the floozie?'

Oh to hear her call the floozie a floozie! 'She got her nose fixed he married her. A year later he landed on my landing.'

'What for?'

'For bringing lilacs for bringing a cheque. Guilt money. The bump still didn't add up to the years I spent sewing in the sweatshop putting him through law school.'

'Did you take them, the flowers and the money?'

'I took I forgave.'

Her face said, How could you?

My face said, 'It was better than nothing. As a matter of fact it was better than something. Once a week romance, highly recommended. Stays fresh, like flowers.'

The Chick sniffed at my wet lilacs saying, 'I see.'

What did she see? What did she feel with her nose? Lilac tears, pih.

'Do men always leave women?'

'What kind of a question is that?' A good question. I had the answer on my tongue, my tongue clove to my palate. I had the evidence in my bloomers, it chafed between my legs. Pinball had the evidence in her Drawer. I said, 'Not always.'

'Do couples ever stay together?'

'Occasionally.'

'And are they happy?'

'Happiness, pih.'

'Do women ever leave men?'

'If they're lucky. If they aren't saddled with children. If they have the money and the wherewithal.'

'What's a wherewithal?'

'Hoo ha, a handbag with nuts in it.'

Twenty-nine

Let me rest let me swallow my spit.
Let me eat straw like an ox.

Let me sing (I, even I, will sing!) of the Chick and the Prince and of their Doings.

How they cooked together and ate together how they talked together and walked together. How they cleaned toilet bowls together. How they listened to unkosher Bessie Smith records while jiggling around with knives and wooden cookspoons raised above their heads. *His frankfurters are oh so sweet ... How I like his sausage meat*, feh with poo. How they made love in beds in tubs in woods in sheds on beaches on moors on floors. *Any time he wants to he can use my sugar bowl ...*

How he chopped with his axe and scythed with his scythe, how he built bookcases he rewired the house he crawled through a crawl space on his belly like a serpent, how he ate crawl-space dust in order to install spotlights, yea how he made light to shine down on the Chick's head.

She presented him with a twisted baby challah (the way is not straight!), a wreath for electrical accomplishment. He came down dirty filthy. She stuck her nose in his armpits mmm-ah the perfume of Doing. Peradventure she could not Do herself but what's to stop her absorbing his Doing through the lining of her nose?

129

Stop snuffling at his sweat glands! Do for yourself!

She was not ready to Do she was not ready to Know. She was happy to be unhappy, comfort me with pits.

He would do anything for her. 'Let me draw you a bath,' offers the artist. Pih, he means *run* her a bath. 'You can soak while I cook.' That too he does. 'I'll make a cheese soufflé and the artichokes from the garden, shall I?'

'Whatever,' she says, and she goes to her bath which is his bath and she soaks. And he brings her a glass of sherry and then he goes downstairs to grate his cheese and divide his eggs which he does as effortlessly as drawing a bath. And when her bath runs cold and she begins to wail he bears her pots yea even several (up and down he goes) of boiling water. And when her bath dribbles over on to the floorboards he gets down on his poignancies and wipes it up.

Which is my case against him: is there anything he *doesn't* do?

Tailbone! Menace! Noble abomination! A vomiting of gratitude on his tootsies!

What, he doesn't mean it that way? He means to be generous? Give give and more give? Aaah, I see. He had too much the Chick had too little so this way he makes it up to her. Give give grate pour mop feed anoint. An heap of towels at her feet a bombardment of cookies on her head.

Feh.

Listen to me, O Princeling. Too much sweetness can be a terrible thing. She has trouble taking? This I don't deny. A failure to give? Denied not. For I remember what it was like when the Solly Boys came to liberate us with their Hershey Bars and we took and we ate but their sweetness made us sick.

She took from him she spat him out, poo. She adored him she cursed him for making himself adorable. She walked ten paces behind him up mountains, she gave his back the finger. By his side, not by his side. A chained-up married lady, a Harry Houdini. A heart full of singing canaries, the heart of an artichoke. An high horse, an abject. A tosser of flame-coloured ringlets, a bower of heads. A piss off I'm busyer, a creeper up of behinds. A leave me aloner, a where are you I need youer.

With him and yet not with him.

'Ready!' he calls, and she comes she comes, newly washed and the colour of cheap rosé wine. 'Ah, there you are.' He sticks a corkscrew into the top of a bottle of Crusty Old Claret given him by his papa (pronounced pa-*pah*) Lord Hoo Ha. He screws and lo the arms of the contraption raise themselves up like angel's wings. He lowers them with his two hands picture the patriarch patronizing his offspring: sit, my children.

The Chick sits. She grabs a topknot of bread she screws it off with the technique of a torturer. (Spare the bread! Screw him!) They raise glasses, *Cheers*, they sip wine of a goodly heritage.

L'chaim.

He has taught her how to eat of the vegetable artichoke. How to pull off the leaves one by one dunk them in melted lemon butter scrape the flesh with the top teeth. Instead she turns each leaf upside down scraping with her *bottom* teeth.

'You lose the butter that way.'

'I know that.'

'I'm sorry.' He waves a dug-out artichoke leaf. Butter dribbles down the Chick's chin.

Now comes the hairy heart. The Prince would warn her but his tongue hides in his mouth. *Stop telling me what to do what not to do!* His tongue curls further into his cheek. 'Feeyuch,' she spits and picks. 'Why didn't you tell me it was all stickery?'

'I'm sorry.'

Sorriness upon sorriness. Beware says Adolf-Solomon of love as strong as death. As Eden full of palms with hearts raised up in longing. Artichokes into giant thistles.

She slings on her coat.

'Where are you going?'

'Out.'

'May I go with you?'

'No.' Denial, this she can Do.

She shuts the door on her only friend. (She has made no league with the inhabitants of his land.)

She walks in moonlight she sings of her well-beloved touching his accomplishments.

More a croaking than a singing, so what? Let the frogs and froglets appreciate.

So she croaks of her well-beloved. Of his reading of Greek and Latin poetry of his reading of philosophy of his reading of Pooh. Of the playing with toes. Of the planting of plants even wildflowers if not wild grapes. Of their garden which he fenced with fenceposts which she helped to bang in, and which he scythed and gathered out the stones therefrom.

My beloved hath a greenness in his thumbs yea also a dexterity in the rest of his digits.

My well-beloved walks long-legged among other leggy sea-birds. My well-beloved rescues hedgehogs even to the stopping of traffic. My well-beloved has a sweet singing voice he also bakes sweetness into his Reine de Saba otherwise known as chocolate cake. My well-beloved is skilled in the reading of maps in the taking of photographs in the giving of flowers. In the anointing of sore bellies. In the sewing the sawing the seeing the listening.

Amein.

She stands in the lane looking up at their cottage. The Prince sits illuminated at his study window. She squats in a puddle of moonlight. He scratches his hairs he jiggles his finger in his ear. She puts her hand to her mouth, her heart is double. My prince my prophet my teacher, pih.

She takes aim at the humpbacked one in his wing chair. She prays for no witnesses. She puffs up her cheeks and her tongue goes out before her: *A raspberry on your perfection!*

Children desecrate houses of worship because they believe there's a God in there who is all-powerful, a bogey a Wizard of Oz who makes them feel small and inadequate. So they try to destroy Him to show Him up, to part His curtains to reveal

Him in His dirty drawers, behold a *shlump*!

But the Prince was no *shlump*.

So the Chick took to a secret seething to a rebellion to a wriggling inside the straitjacket of her perfect tepee. Only the more she fought the tighter the smelly skins of animals wrapped themselves around her. She dreamed of tent-nails and hammers and woke up screaming. The Prince wrapped his arms around her. 'Such an extraordinary little person. It's what I love about you, you know.'

'What is?'

'Your vulnerability.'

They were walking along the cliffs near their house. 'You're sweet,' she said collecting rocks. 'Also,' he added, 'your fierceness.' 'Me?' Her fingers were itchy on her rocks.

Fling! Smite! Push! Break his spell! Break his head! Do it on a cliff! Now!

She dropped her rocks. She poked at his chest but her finger wore a lily pad of devotion.

They sat on a grassy ledge overlooking marshland and estuary. Sheep had cropped the turf to a bowling green. The mud was arranged in parallel wavy lines. The tide seemed to be moving in several directions at once around the sand banks. Waves in slow wrinkled motion. So quiet!

The Chick lay down she wrapped her head in the Prince's lap. She fussed she fidgeted at last she found peace on her pallet, shalom.

ZOOM! An Air Force fighter bomber passed low over their heads it ripped open her belly. She lay there waiting for the ravens to come and nibble up her organs, come partake of me. She was ready she was open to the sky she was dead before she was dead. O Keziah, why so willing?

Only with stroking and a kissing of the nose-tip did the Prince convince her she was still alive. Comfort me with the shield of your hand. He stroked her brow he cupped her chin. The ridge of his nose got closer and closer, his lips landed giant butterfly wings on the landing strip of her forehead.

Hoo.

Hoo hoo. The warning hooter went off. The Chick raised herself from the Prince's lap. She observed the incoming tide she saw flotsam and jetsam and the fish-eyes of the drowned. She saw motorbikes, horses, stagecoaches going back hundreds of years. 'You needn't worry,' soothed the Prince, 'it doesn't happen very often. Just be careful when you walk down there not to get yourself trapped by the tide.' She said, 'I know.' He said 'Promise me.' She tickled his nose with grass.

The wind was an even more gentle lover than the Prince, it caused her T-shirt to puff out with pleasure. A gull cruised over their heads. 'Wouldn't it be nice to coast like that?' The Prince had a talent for flopping, his meat was fillet. He explained about warm thermals. 'What if you let yourself go and suddenly the wind drops and you end up smashed among the rocks?' The Prince said birds were aerodynamically equipped to deal with such eventualities. 'People aren't,' said the Chick. 'One day,' he said, and he took her in his arms, her breathing passages were filled with chest-wool.

One day what?

A bee sat on a daisy. A big bee a small daisy. The bee strolled on the flower in its furry yellow-and-brown striped jacket. Around and around suck suck it went from the flower's private parts. The flower collapsed, the bee waddled away. The Prince lifted the flower's head with his finger but the stalk was broken beyond even his powers of healing. He looked sad.

'This is a surprisingly hostile area. It's surprising how much damage wind alone can do.' Ordinarily it was a wind-whipped place but today it was mild. He embellished. 'Hardy tenacious plants come in and take advantage of conditions. You have to be salt-tolerant if you're a plant.'

And if you're a person? Tell me, Dr Tenacious Plant, what is my Keziah's threshold to damage, her chances of survival in this place you took her to live where the sands shift under her feet where the stars wander in the sky where rocks are cracked with depressions?

'What are those?' She was pointing to some hardy tenacious yellow wildflowers.

'You know what those are.'

'I do?'

He held one to her chin, her chin glowed yellow.

'Oh yeah, buttercup.'

He licked her chin.

She grabbed his face he yelped.

Good! Do it! Crush his bones and his sinews!

Pinball joined in.

Bang bang the banging of sisters. 'Let her eat butter!'

The Prince said, 'I love you.'

She said, 'You'll leave me.'

He looked pained, 'My sweet, I wish you wouldn't say such things.'

I also wished.

He said, 'Believe me. I swear it. I never will.'

'Oh but you will,' she said, and she laughed.

So did Pinball, a terrible sound.

They walked on. He took her hand she let him. Another couple passed them by two scrawny old things in floppy hats, eyes fishy with cataracts. Holding hands. The sight of them brought tears to his dove's eyes. 'You see.' He rested his chin upon the parting of her fiery fuzz. 'It is possible for couples to go on loving and taking care of one another for quite a long time.' An affirmation a confirmation. Hoo ha. For the Chick it was rubbing her nose in the impossible.

The sun is going down. A worried bleeding tomato she cannot take her eyes away. 'Don't stare,' warns the Prince, shielding her eyes with his hand. She removes it. She sees a burning bush a bush which if any bird flies into it will shred its wings. And out of the heat-rush of that ignited bush (which is only the setting sun behind a coastal blackthorn) she sees not a bird or a plane but her Aunt Adolf crying, 'Feh!' and beside her her mother Pinball crouched over vomiting on to the sheep-grazed turf.

For ever and ever. 'I do love you, you know,' says the Prince. The Chick smiles like a sunset, 'Yes, I know.' Her nails are fierce in his palm.

Thirty

Pinball picked up her telephone she did not put it down. She covered her wall with numbers. She invited men in yet she did not lie down in beds with them. Face to face she made deals. She was no more on bottom. 'What's going on?' She blew smoke in my face she paced up and down. Her jaw was square her feet were wide she shimmied in her new skin. 'Praise be,' I told her daughter.

'What is she doing?'

'Doing.'

Keziah was also Doing. Her chest rose up full moons with the help of a couple of stiff supports. Her nose grew straight upon her face her hair was an heap of reddled sheep. Her neckskin smelled of crab apples. She wore heels yea even pumps very slenderizing to the leg. She said to the Prince, 'I'll see you later.' He looked with his dove's eyes. 'Where are you going?' 'Out.' 'Out where, my love?'

He liked them to stroll together through their garden, to entertain the death of a weed here the curve of a new flowerbed there. He liked them to sit together under their ancient crab apple tree. He liked them to pick of their vegetables and thereafter to chop of their vegetables meanwhile discussing their days in companionate tandemness.

Dead men's fingers, her favourite vegetable.

Where is hope?

'Shall I prepare something for dinner? When will you be home?' The Prince followed her to the garden gate. She said, 'I'll see you when I see you', and she banged the gate in his belly.

She had a job. A secret job. Volunteer work. She phoned me collect. I said, 'What exactly are you doing?'

'Doing.' Hoo ha, a familiar word.

I felt my counters. Sticky with something perverse. I took my nose on a hunt I found a pile of old dishcloths curled up together under the sink. My birds thought the time of singing had come. Dopes! I threw sour J-cloths all over their yellow heads.

She was collecting evidence. Instead of a Disaster Drawer she had a file drawer marked 'Cases'. The Herberts, the Wrights, the Porters, the Blumers.

The Chick had become a marriage counsellor.

(Her mother had become a bookie.)

'How interesting,' I said.

'Oh it is,' she replied. 'And quite challenging.'

'What about the Prince?'

'What about him?'

'How does he like you doing this thing?'

'It's none of his business.'

Pinball bet, 'She'll use it against him.'

And so it came to pass. She brought out her evidence she presented her case(s) to the Prince. The Blumers: agreed to separate. The Porters: agreed to separate. And so on and so forth, her accordion file accordioned but the tune that escaped was always the same. Her couples fell out of love they fell out of marriage they fell into her case drawer, *thyunk*.

The Prince begged to differ. 'It doesn't signify. You can't extrapolate from a few cases.' His knowledge in this area was of significant significance.

He was a tree. His feet were root-feet they went deep. The whole world of couples could get rent apart but he and Keziah would cling unto one another every night for the rest of their lives, amein.

The Chick heard thunder she saw a cracking of branches.

'People fall out of love.' She held on to the side of their bed.

'Feckless,' he pronounced. 'Love requires commitment, trust.'

Already she slept.

'Don't give in.' He reminded her of the raspberries in their nets.

The Chick lay in the circle of his arms repeating the words she heard in her head: *I just don't love her any more . . . I just don't love him any more.'*

'But what does that mean?'

'It means they don't love each other any more.'

The Prince argued against what he called instant gratification. He poured cold water. 'A long marriage isn't like that.' He had learned at the feet of his ancestors he absorbed through his soles. Marriage is like a garden: it requires water sun faith patience determination, also a little manure from time to time does not go amiss. Its roots go deep its scent is sometimes stinky. Lust after your neighbour's garden and you are deluding yourself. Bury your nose in new blossom your weeds will grow again.

'Ha,' said the Chick.

The Prince held her in his arms he held not a treemate but a board. 'Leave me in peace,' she said.

'He'll leave her in peace for ever,' bet the Maker of Books. I passed this piece of information on to the Chick, she said, 'Don't be ridiculous.'

'It happened to us.'

'That was different. The Prince is no Moosa, no Arthur.'

I could not disagree with this and yet, 'He's a man.'

'Not like other men.'

'You're very sure of him.'

'Absolutely.'

'God is allergic to absolutes.'

Pinball blew her nose into the hem of her slimy pink toga saying, 'Wait, you'll see.'

Her daughter sees desolation she sees weeds. Crack-ups and break-ups. She wants to prove she is proving.

'I don't understand.' This I say to her mother.

'What's to understand?'

'She pushes him away from her saying "Go!" and yet she believes in her heart he will not go. She tells him, "You will leave me." He says, "I won't." She says, "You will." And yet to me she says "He won't" and "Never." Explain to me what is this game.'

'A game.'

Still I do not understand.

'His words have begun to take,' she explains. This sounds to me like gardening.

'Just so. She pokes him in his sides with thorns but her roots drink up his sap.'

'Feh.'

'Worse than feh.'

'Don't tell me.'

'Look,' she tells. (No more!) 'A belly preparing for deceit.'

The Prince leads the Chick down to the bottom end of their garden near where the rows of raspberries and gooseberries and rhubarb grow and it is sheltered by pine trees and she lays under him upon the earth and the tits twitter and the sky is sky-coloured and it's a jolly nice scene.

My sister perceives otherwise. 'Wrinkles,' she points out.

'*Wrinkles*?' I could dump her over the porch, 'Go sleep in Solly's bed! On your face! Eat dirt!'

If she laughs again I'll strangle her.

'She has filled him with wrinkles and for this she will be cast out.'

'What do you know?'

'I know what I know.'

'His ripe green olive. Never!'

'Consumed to the size of a pit!'

I cover my ears. No more. Rock rock make her stop.
'Thrown to the ground, trampled underfoot.'
I run away her voice runs after me. Why won't she stop?

Thirty-one

The Chick delivered her books by day she listened to stories of deceit defection despair at night. *Please make him hear ... Please sort her out ... Maybe the problem is I'm too weak ... Maybe I'd like him to be strong ... I just don't love her any more.*

Children called clients. Children with wrinkles and pot bellies and a heap of unpaid bills on their tables. *Help me please help me.*

A not-so-young woman, call her Lisa. She is thinking of getting married she is thinking of not getting married. What's the problem? asks Counsellor Keziah. Well, says this Lisa, am I in the right place? Am I wasting your time? A melon of a woman half ripe and half unripe she could split open and go either way or close up and keep rolling around in circles.

Keziah listens. Lisa says she's scared. Her parents are morally strict she is their good little girl. But she has another self: secret sexy bad mistress. If she gets married all that would end. All what? The excitement the secrets the sex. What about him? 'Oh, he's so dependable, he's always there ... He does my laundry ... He fixes my car ... He adores me. Isn't that good?'

The Chick says he sounds like a prince (hah!).

'Yes, aren't I lucky?' She bursts into tears.

Keziah says, 'I know, it's all right.'

'Do you? Is it?'

Keziah wants to say don't marry him but she lets the woman's questions dance around the room in a professional manner. After a decent interval she says, 'I'm sorry we have to stop now.' With such timing she could have been a musician.

Next. This time it's a couple, young. The woman wears big black motorcycle boots she lurches from side to side. The man has wild eyes. They both wear leather jackets. She has an eye-twitch and a vacant smile. She does not speak. Keziah wonders if she's deaf.

'How can I help you?'

The husband points at his wife. 'She is a worry to me.'

Keziah nods.

'She doesn't like sex.'

Nod nod.

'She doesn't feel anything.'

This time Keziah looks directly at the wife.

'She thinks it's dirty.'

The wife nods her head.

'You see? She's like a rubber doll.'

'Tell me,' asks Counsellor Chick, 'have you ever had an orgasm?'

She looks at him. 'Have I?'

He looks at the ceiling and blows. 'You see?'

Keziah sees what she sees. 'Could you say how it feels?'

'What?'

'Intercourse.'

The wife says, 'Dry.'

'You mean it hurts?'

'Hah! I can hardly walk the next day. He goes on for an hour. He rubs and rubs me in the front . . .'

'Wait a minute,' says the husband.

Chick Keziah says it's all right many men do not realize the clitoris is a very sensitive organ which responds best to an indirect touch. The wife puts her crash helmet on. She says,

'He rides the bike too fast I'm always coming away – that's another thing.'

'Coming away?'

'She means falling off.'

'Oh dear. Well, we can talk about that next time, OK?' The husband puts one arm around his helmet the other around his wife. 'C'mon, let's go', and they stump away to practise the joys of subtle sex, good luck.

That night in bed the Prince licks his finger and with it traces a message up down and around the most sensitive parts of her body. This man needs no instruction in the art of direct or indirect stimulation.

'Where did you learn to do that?' she asks him.

'From you.'

'From me?' She doesn't remember ever telling him what to do.

Not necessary. 'Your body speaks for you.'

It does?

Panic. She sees herself a peeled split-open squashy Sharon fruit. Shame! Quick! Close up! Watch out or he'll turn you inside out! She crosses her legs she wraps herself up in nightgowns.

'Don't worry, I love you.' He reassures he pets he backs off like a brother.

'Liar, you're just saying it.'

'My sweet, you know better than that.'

True. She knows even better than he knows but something makes her contradict, a curse a need to unravel to destroy.

A heap of denials on his head.

'You're so lovely.'

'Fat and ugly.' She traps a bunch of thigh skin between two fingers. 'Look at that disgusting cellulite, you call that lovely?'

'My love ... Women have a layer of fat, it's natural. But if it bothers you, go on a diet.'

'So you *do* think I'm fat!'

'No I don't. I mean do whatever pleases you. If you feel

better thinner then go on a diet. But please try to understand it doesn't matter to me; I love *you*, all of you.'

'I'm getting to look like my Aunt Adolf.'

Hoo ha hoo!

'No you don't. You look like you. There's no one else like you in the world. I wish you could see yourself as I do.' He lays his hand on her belly, an heap of wheat. She pushes it away. 'I'm tired. Leave me alone.' She turns her back on him a besieged city in a garden of cucumbers. He presses his vegetable matter against her, feh. 'Tell me something, do *you* love *me*?' An interesting reversal. 'I don't know,' she says. She can't bring herself to say it. *I don't know I don't know I don't know*. A tragedy a stupidity a miscalculation, even a Prince needs a return on his investment.

He strokes her back. He loves how she goes in at the waist out at the hip, his flesh bloometh between her legs. She butts him with her behind. 'No! Cut it out!'

Good idea! Chop it up, rub with garlic, roast!

What am I saying? Cut out my tongue. Cut out hers. Crazy Chickadee. Why does she have to say these things? What possesses her? Why torture a man who loves her?

Why. Because she's Pinball Annie's daughter. Because she likes testing. Push push prod prod, she should have been an animal experimenter. Does there exist anywhere in the world an animal that will withstand more pain than any of its predecessors in order to stay with its mate?

The Prince loved her his faith was greater than ever. He would never leave her (an original, irreplaceable!). But what if she got fat and ugly? What if a demon took up residence in her mouth and made her to spit dirt on his head? What if she was no longer an extension of his pinkie? What if she stopped walking ten paces behind him up mountains like a geisha? What if she stopped thinking he was perfect and she stopped saying yes and yes and I'm sorry and instead said, You did this and this and this. And if she could find no thing he did that was wrong – for his iniquities were indeed scarce – yet she would say, 'The reason you love me and stay with me is because you lack the imagination to do anything else.' In other words, if the devil climbed into her heart and made her to stab at him with pitchforks until he was bruised all over his tender fruit – what then? Answer: Then she would be able to prove to him what she already knew.

'You'll leave me,' says the only one of her mother.

'I won't, you know.'

'You will.'

'You're quite wrong. I love you.'

'Go away!'

He went to his garden he pruned his undoomed roses. His arms were tracked with blood. He presented her with an armload of not-yet-open blooms she spat between her teeth which were my teeth. 'Roses! Who needs them!' She scattered them to the four corners of the room. The Prince picked them up he put them one by one into a vase with water.

Why a rose? Why anything? He thinks of his mother Lady Hoo Ha with her stiff joints bending over her rosebed with her basket and trowel. The roses suffer black spot their heads drop off. 'Oh dear,' she says, yet she laughs saying, 'Never mind, next year they'll come back better', and lo they do, they do. The Prince her son-without-spot also goes away yet he always comes back. She puts roses in his guest room. She expects nothing her blooms bloom.

'Smell that.' The Prince offers an old-fashioned rose to her nostrils, she grabs its stem she sprouts blood.

'You'll find a nice young Englishwoman,' she bleeds. 'An empty-headed skinny blonde.'

'She would bore me.'

'*You* bore me.'

'I'm sorry. What can I do for you?'

'Leave.'

'I don't want to leave.'

'Why do you want to stay?'

'Because I love you.'

'Creep.'

What more can a creep say? He understands her pain her need to deny, his patience grows even greater. Clobber me with roseheads I shall not stop creeping around you.

He bears her wrath he holds her feet he comforts her with the stroking of them. 'There there.'

Where where?

'I'd rather you went,' she told him.

He went for a walk she wept, 'You left me alone.'

He stayed home from work he tended his garden. She complained of being a weed widow. 'The weather is foul here. I may go back to the States. Don't think I'm not thinking about it.'

'I'll come with you.'

'No you won't.'

'Then I won't.' He reached out for her in the night she was not there.

'Wrong,' says Pinball, reaching for her pay-off money. Her clients were multiplying her business was paying off, praise be.

'What wrong?' I bang.

'She is there –' the emphasis is on the is. She means underneath the flannelette nightgown the Chick is as naked and defenceless as an hoopoe. I rock I knit, my lips swivel to one side. My sister's words are toothpicks in my side – quick! get them out.

The Prince scoops up his Keziah he strokes he massages he snuffles up her doubts. His loving is endless, yea his promising thrusts bespeak for ever. 'I will never leave you, I will never stop loving you.'

And so on and so forth.

The Chick lets go. The Prince's faith fills her with the scent of earth and grass and manure. The besieged city flings open its gates, Hosanna!

Is this a cause for mourning?

Pinball hangs her head and mourns. My mouth calls her a perverse thing. 'Go swing a chicken,' her mouth calls back.

'Go take a bath! You stink!' I want to hurt her I want her to stop planting her unpleasant plants. 'Look at you! Stupid stupid! Passing money around in broad daylight. They'll see they'll know they'll covet.'

She was hiding her 'take' in her Disaster Drawer. 'A drawer is no hiding place. They'll break in they'll bump you off.'

She wriggled her toenails bruise-coloured nail polish.

My sister had a spin on her tail like one of her silver balls. Bells went off as she passed by. She was hot she was in orbit she was charged. She lit up lights as she went.

'Setting the world on fire is fine if you have fire insurance.'

She had nothing.

To hell with Pinball. Two sisters two noses two pairs of eyes. A parting of the ways. My eyes see a white horse called Keziah and he that sits upon her (trot trot he rides and his riding is gentle and long) is called Faithful and True. The miracle had come to pass.

The heart of his wife trusts in him.

Pinball sniffs her pay-off envelopes, mmn mmn who needs stuffed cabbage? 'They trusted in the Pharaoh too,' she delivers. 'They leaned on the staff of that broken reed it went into their hands it pierced them.'

No! Stop up our ears with cotton balls! Don't listen! I say ho ho come forth! Trust! Swing high, sweet Chicklet! A blasting of trumpets! Blat blat!

To my sister I give the curse of Adolf. 'May you disappear! May they gobble you up!'

'Let them, try,' was her reply.

PART FOUR

You have spoiled the daughters of my people!
Adolf-Isaiah 22:2

Thirty-Two

Pinball was talented she rose out of nothing. She had what it took, quick mind dirty feet, dirty mind quick feet. Every man in the neighbourhood had placed a bet with Pinball, numbers ballgames horses. Men coming on to the porch with fat wallets men going off with skinny wallets, men handing their pay-offs over the railing. Other men coming to collect.

Between the two Pinball made out. As I said she hid her cut at the bottom of her Disaster Drawer. It wasn't much but even so I warned her, *Hold on to your bloomers.* But Pinball who had spent her life imagining a KEEP IN: DANGER sign on her screen door didn't seem to notice it snuffling around under her porch.

Pinball had what it took to rise out of nothing, she also had what it took to get herself bumped off. She progressed to a dead sister in less time than it takes for a silver ball to fall back into its starting trough.

May they gobble you up. Please God I hadn't meant it to come true. May the stars fall from the sky in mourning. And then gobble *me* up.

Why don't those stupid stars listen?

I was asleep in my bed my birds were asleep in their cages, cover us with flowery linen. It was four in the morning Pinball left her side window open. The crumbums had no trouble leaping up Pinball was awake before she was awake, her mind was quick her reflexes quicker. 'Adolf, get the gun!' she yelled. My ears heard pih. She saw the eyes peering up over the twenty fingers. Next came noses chins feet legs whole bodies pipsqueaks with guns. The heathen had entered her sanctuary, Good Try Lady Hand It Over.

What lady! Do as they say!

Not on your life – not on *her* life. I know my sister, a woman who once flung a bed out the window. This time she went for her Drawer she handed it over, You Want It You Have It! She slid it off its tracks she pushed into their bellies. It caused surprise it caused a crushing of guts and giblets. The other one of his tribe took his revenge he cracked her on her skull with his gun, she was no more.

He spread out his hands upon all the contents of her Drawer saying, 'What is all this crap?' and he buried her under it: newspaper clippings letters postcards photographs Keziah's school albums. The money came last like an afterthought in its black leather purse. Not a lot.

But for her feet she was covered in Selected Items of Disaster.

'All her pleasant things,' says her sister Adolf newly arrived on the scene but old and worn as linoleum.

'You call these things "pleasant"?' A little skinny cop had squatted down to read off the desk that was Pinball's stomach. '*Her* pleasure, Sonny,' I informed him. I thought I saw a smirk. 'Laugh,' I told him, 'and I will sit on you.'

The ambulance men arrived. They sat on her body with its leaf-mould of clippings and bashed her in the chest, her heart had cause to reconsider. Stupid heart. For now she would remember her end. How I slept and my birds slept and she had no comforter in me, her sister her snoring spouse.

Annie forgive.

They put us both in the back of the ambulance. The sirens screamed I held her hand – still warm! I heard a mumbling of prophets upfront saying, 'Too late.' I told her, 'You went out wonderfully.'

Far away the telephone rang in the hallway of Jenny Brown's Cottage the Prince picked it up put it to an ear still attached to its pillow. 'Hallo? Hallo? Is anyone there? If this is a prank . . . Look who is this?'

'Put Keziah on.' I could not remember my name.

'Letisha?' he says. 'Is that you?' Like Arthur, he could not bring himself to call me Adolf.

'The one.'

'Do you realize it's the middle of the night?' He's holding on to the stripes of his pyjama bottoms better than his patience.

'I realize. Put Keziah on.'

'I'm sorry but this is a dreadfully uncivilized time to ring.' He was about to hang up, I was not civil.

'Is something wrong?'

'Something is wrong.' Is it fit to speak to a prince about bones? I spoke.

'Oh dear, how dreadful. I'm so sorry. Where is she?'

'Hospital.'

'What are her chances.'

'Not good.'

Keziah grabbed the phone.

'Aunt Adolf?'

'Kezie.'

'Aunt Adolf.'

'Kezie.'

'Aunt Adolf . . .'

Comfort me with the naming of names, our back-and-forth song could have gone on for ever. The Prince touched her with the wand of his hand, the spell was broken. Time for doing. 'I'll be on the first plane out in the morning,' she says. She revolved she hit the Prince's chest a wailing wall with stripes. She bounced and rattled he held on tight. 'Would you like me to come with you?' 'I don't care what you do,' she said.

My sister Pinball had many disgusting habits. I will tell you her most disgusting going back to the time Keziah was a girl at home. She would pee she would not wipe herself. Instead she would stuff a bunch of toilet paper between her legs, insurance against leakage. She wore no bloomers for holding. You see the problem. I saw, the Chick saw. She became a prophet she warned of droppage she knew whereof she spoke, Sir Isaac Newton, hoo ha. The problem landed on the floor.

Pih, what will come down will come down. Once it left the premises of her swampy place she knew it not. 'Annie –' I'd point to the crumpled uriny wad – 'you lost your toilet paper.' She knew me not. I said as to an untrained dog, 'I'll rub your nose in it.' She howled her nose was also wet, my sister was not housetrained.

Now though I walk through the rooms and hallways of her shadowy valley I find no evidence of her disgust work. Lord, drop me a sign – a remnant a scrap a square. A crushed flower palest pale yellow . . .

Let me not bang the screen door behind me.

I am become as a widow empty as a rocker. I do not weep. A city without its people. A monster brown paper bag without its delicatessen. The one comforter who should relieve me has been squashed down, she was my sister. The other her daughter is far from me. Who is left? Arthur and his Othellos, pih.

My feet are wrapped in nets they sit like wigs upon the floorboards they do not carry me. My hair is a flock of goats my beard grows barbs my rocker groweth elbows. Don't anyone come near me. I spit through my teeth at the worm in the garden, 'Where is my sister? Who did this thing?' 'There is no revenge against murderers,' sneers the worm. 'Who says so!? I'll fix their wagons!' The worm does a shimmy which also reminds me of Pinball. 'Shut up! Rat dust!' The worm obeys. Twoo twee, the time of the singing of birds with a rotten sense of timing is come. 'Shut it off or I'll feed you to the worms!' They also mock me. Who will listen? I bend my knees to the ground my nose to Pinball's rocker saying unto its lingering stink, 'You were my sister.'

Thirty-three

'I don't believe it I don't believe it I don't believe it.' The Chick stood on one side of Pinball's hospital bed I stood on the other. 'Believe it,' I advised. The Prince stood at the foot. She went to him she leaned against him, oh comfort me with sweetpeas and roses. She opened them to the remnant of Pinball, her chest going up and down her sackcloth falling open. Breasts, pih, dried cowpats. The Chick went to cover her up, I said, 'Leave her.' Cowpats sweeter than roses.

'I mean,' her Chick beseeched us both, 'she spent her whole life not going out because it was so dangerous *out there* and what happens? The danger comes *in* to get her.'

The Prince cleared his throat saying, 'There is a Greek myth. About a man who believed he would be crushed by a house. To avoid this he spent his life out of doors. Then one day he was crushed by a falling tortoise.'

I did not clear my throat. 'It did not rain turtles on my sister.'

'Aunt Adolf, he's just trying to draw a comparison.' His all-of-a-sudden defender.

'Drawing is nice but how does he *explain*?'

He calls it Cosmic Jokery. Hoo ha, this I like. My sister believed if she went out something or someone would get her so she stayed inside. She put up bars, spears she would have put

156

shards of broken glass. Beware All Ye Who Enter Here! But the door-to-door cosmic jokery salesmen found a way in. Don't Come to Us We'll Come to You! It was not a Tupperware party they entertained my sister to.

'I'm sorry.'

'You're sorry?' I looked at what was once my sister. What was left? Life in her heart in her kidneys in her bowels her veins. Her eyebrows twitched upon her forehead. We took it as a Sign. The doctor shook his head saying, 'I'm afraid that's a purely physiological response. Aside from the basic biological functions she's virtually dead.' 'Virtually dead!' I hollered to his retreating back, oh restrain me from punching him in the kidneys! My fists became meat hooks for dragging him back by the neck, my knuckles dusters for beating his face to chopmeat. Sweetly I said, 'Maybe she'll virtually come back.' The saliva was gathering on my tongue. 'I wouldn't bet on it if I were you.' 'YOU'RE NOT ME! WHO'S ASKING YOU TO BET!' My voice registered on the ECG machine, I spat into a cardboard spitoon, one of Pinball's eyelids started winking.

Annie, are you enjoying this?

The doctor went forth on his belly at quite a speed. The Chick followed in his slimy trail; but the Prince brought her back. 'Sit.' He led her to her mother's bed, I sat on the other side.

We are a sandwich. Pinball is our filling she warmeth our hips with her hips.

'Look,' he explains, 'I know this isn't easy. The doctor is rather a clod, but he's trying. He doesn't want you to get your hopes up. He's being straight with you.'

'Straight, hah! Remember the challah, the braided twisted loaf!'

He shuffles with his feet the nurses shush with their fingers. Pinball in her own way joins in. Boo hoo for hope.

Yes, I know. The Prince was trying to help. He knew what the doctor knew which we also knew but did not wish to know. Knowing, poo! Doctors, also poo! Physicians of no value!

Raise my mother my sister from the dead, this was our bargaining position. Not easy even for a prince.

'I'll be out in the waiting room if you need me,' he told.

We need you like we need lice.

Our tongues went forth after him.

We dropped to our knees on the two sides of Pinball. We prayed with remembering. How her feet never left her porch but her spirit went wandering. How she was there and yet not there. It didn't seem right she should be trapped in a house. She paced on the brown linoleum flecked with gold stars. The heavens turned upside down, be our guest.

This I could understand. Were I heaven I too would have laid down my life for her. Yes, walk on me.

Her flesh was bruised where the drips and needles went in. 'I used to think,' said her daughter, 'that one day when I came home from school she wouldn't be there. That she'd do a disappearing act. Shoot out the roof, go into orbit. Like a rocket.'

'A shooting star,' I improved.

'Or one of those circus tigers bursting through a fiery hoop.'

'A flaming doughnut.' Hoo ha, I also believed one day she would make an exodus.

We saw fire we saw wild animals we saw rockets and stars. We put our dreams into Pinball.

'We failed to see the real person.'

Annie, forgive.

'When circus tigers are finished with their act,' so she once read, 'they go moping back to the safety of their cages.'

Dragging their tails through doody, feh.

Pinball rocked. Pinball brooded in darkness, paced in darkness. Occasionally she rose up early she played *Eili Eili* on the piano. Her hand was a paw her claws were long. Click click, *Lord, Lord, Why hast thou forsaken me?* Gold stars on a floor, pih, they do not illuminate a life.

For most of the Chick's childhood Pinball hibernated. Why get up to button buttons? She went forth as far as the toilet she lost her way she lost her toilet paper on the stars.

I banged down the lid of the piano I nearly crushed her fingers. 'HIM!' I yelled. 'So He forsook you. So how come you sit around waiting for another Him to save you? Wake up! There is no Him!'

She said, 'Two words', they were not Happy Birthday. Her lids were long she doodled beside her telephone table. She drew the profile of a girl with a top lip like the curl of a can opener. A lot of wavy hair hid the side of the face. A squarish jaw like Pinball's. To finish off she took the point of her pencil and ground it with unusual conviction into the space between the upturned nose and the snarling lip. 'What's that?' I asked. 'A beauty mark,' she said. 'Mole,' I begged to differ. She insisted beauty mark. To me that black mark said it all.

'Doomed,' I said over the remnant of her body.

'Trapped,' added her daughter.

'Imprisoned.'

'Who locked her up?' was the next question.

'No one,' I concluded. 'She did it herself.' One attempted escape in a lifetime may have been one too many. She travelled a long way, my sister, mostly back and forth, back and forth. Clunk, she threw away her own key.

Rock no more, my Annie. Be our specimen. Be still.

Bodies were not meant to be looked at in such a way. Yet we looked we studied we found fault we praised. Praise be we called her SisterStinkyDybbukWitchMother. We touched we kneaded we pinched up skin we watched it ooze back into the landscape of her flesh. We traced bone with our fingertips, cheeks jaw knees elbows. A body.

'Such rough skin,' said the Chick.

'Washerwoman's elbow,' I explained, 'common to women all over the world.' I held up mine as a for-example, the folds of laundry hung down. The Chick laughed, 'Except she never washed.'

This was true.

We massaged her elbows. I hoped she was enjoying herself. After a while the Chick went round to the foot of the bed she found a foot, Shiloh! It was cold and blue so she rubbed. 'She made me afraid, why?'

'She was afraid herself.'

Look, Chicklet, at what her heart is telling you. The ECG machine was doing a fandango. We did some more urgent footsy-work.

'But that doesn't fit. You told me yourself how she wasn't afraid of anything when she was young. A daredevil you called her.'

'This is true.'

'It doesn't make sense.'

'No. Yes. Once she was safe she got afraid. It happens.'

'She made herself a prisoner, why?'

'She saw there were things to be afraid of.'

'What things?'

'Disasters.'

'She exaggerated.'

'She was trying to protect you.'

'She was protecting herself.'

This was not so crazy. 'You may be right.' Her daughter cried into the crook of her mother's elbow saying, 'She did a lousy job.'

Pinball's eyebrows jumped.

'Yes,' I agreed, 'but she didn't realize.' Pinball had spent all her time snipping and warning and rocking. She saw shadows she saw evil eyes she saw faces in stockings fingers ready to grab. Everywhere but under her own roof. She invited Moosa in, she suspected nothing she did not allow herself to suspect.

She delivered her daughter up to a molesting moose. Go with him, she said. Her daughter said, Let me obey. She followed him to his basement his hideout his hole in the ground. A thing that liveth lower than an animal, feh. Keziah was ten years old.

Meanwhile Pinball lay on her bed which was no bed but a rancid old sofa, it stank of old memories, old feet, new blue cheese which Pinball was partial to. Her blanket was a thing never washed, fake fur with spots, feh. Once I pulled it off her I took it upstairs I threw it in my washing machine. 'Give it back,' she cried, you'd think she'd lost her best friend. Her howling was hard to bear but the stench of that blanket was harder. Let her howl.

Two hours later Keziah crept through the screen door, Pinball yelled 'Come.' The Chick came. 'I'm home,' she said. This her mother saw. 'Your eyes are red,' said Pinball the observant. 'It's very windy out,' her daughter replied. This Pinball accepted.

Fake fur fake wind, whose fakery was greater?

'Why didn't you tell her?' I sunk my thumb into the soft part of my sister's arm, it left a black and blue mark.

'I didn't want to upset her.'

Pinball dribbled blood.

The Prince of Good Timing strolled in I gestured for him to take the Chick away. 'Go for a walk.'

'Will you be OK?'

'I'll be OK.'

'Are you sure?'

'I'm sure.'

'We'll come back for you in an hour or so.'

They left I sat. I called my sister terrible names I spat at her through my teeth. I accused her of never having loved anything or anyone in her life. Only men stupid men and that wasn't love that was sex. What and who did she ever care about? Not her husband not her daughter. Me, pih. I was just there to clean her floors to wash her feet to pick up her slimy nightgowns her matted old fur her greasy wigs. To raise her daughter for her because she was too busy playing *Eili Eili* on the piano. Not to mention tragedy queen to a moose. She suffered me to love her. Her horrible big ugly fat freak of a sister with a moustache who no man with the exception of

Arthur thanks be would ever look at once.

The time of the singing of sisters was come. So I sang. *Eili Eili*. Pinball rumbled along. Then her eyes flew open I heard, 'Don't let them.'

Don't let them what, Annie?

Nothing.

'I'm sorry but your sister is dead.' The nurse shut her eyes I would not let them pull a sheet over her face.

Don't let.

Don't let them pull a sheet over your nose don't let them forsake you don't let them betray you don't let them get away with it. Make a noise! Make a stink! Make a racket!

So I opened my lungs and sang like a Steinway. *Lord, Lord, Why hast thou forsaken me?* A few other patients sang among their tubes. Some wept. One raised an arm it dropped back on her sheet. My stroke is heavier than my groaning. She might have thrown a grape, I deserved it. Soon Keziah and the Prince came to take me home. I was so happy.

My sister was away.

Thirty-four

'I presume you would like,' says the director of funerals, 'a double plot.' He has three lips, his tongue sticks out betwixt its puffy portals.

'No, we would not like!' we say unto the fool. '*She* would not like.'

The top half of him oozes across his desk. 'As you wish, of course, but it is my duty to remind you that according to custom most married couples wish to go to their rest together. In death as in life.' An heap of fingers performs an unholy act of group sex, feh. 'Furthermore,' he flops back against his chair, 'you get an overall reduction of thirty per cent.'

Will you pollute me for a handful of shekels?

Our breasts gang up on him. 'She would have gone to bed sooner with the garbage man.' 'She probably did,' giggles the Chick. His tongue wags without speech in its hole.

Pinball and Solly in 'His and Hers' coffins, Double Deluxe plot, Double Deluxe, feh. Side by side, not a lot to do, nails and hair growing away. Solly's brain even less agile than in life. Pretty soon their flesh falls or gets nibbled away by worms and so on and so forth until they are bones. Next the earth beneath them which is wet begins to sag, yea like a soggy mattress in the middle causing their skeletons to roll towards one another. Closer and closer, Pinball and Solly, Solly and Pinball headed for a collision clatter clatter. I now pronounce you hipbone and hipbone.

No! Dig up her bones! Get her out of there!

It made me sick to think about even as a just-suppose.

'Look,' explained the patient one of us, 'her so-called husband disappeared over thirty years ago.'

'He may reappear. He is still legally . . .'

'Nothing. Look, Sonny, this makes it official.' A time for the banging of pot lids. Pinball's final escape. Bury her with Solly and the tearing out of hair would be upon us.

Hold on to your waveset, pimplet!

'Do you suppose,' Keziah posed, 'I would sell my mother into eternal bondage for a few dollars?'

He did not reply.

Don't worry, Annie. You'll get your single bed, no thirty per cent betrayals.

'No deal no bargains –' I slammed my wherewithal on his desk – 'we'll take one single plot.'

'Wait a minute, what about you?' asks the Chick. A good question.

'Make it a double after all.'

He picks up his pen.

'Wait.'

More pornographic diddling.

'What about *you*?' Will she lie down for ever with princes? A tough question for a tenderized child. Slow and careful. Take your time, my Chick.

'Make it a triple,' she says.

Amein.

'As you wish.' In other words, On your heads. If he'd been a Catholic he would have crossed himself. Instead he sticks a Clorets in his mouth.

Our heads feel fine, Death Breath, just get on with the paperwork.

Meanwhile we put our temples together we study a plan of the cemetery. Our fingers come down on a scenic spot for Solly about three miles away from our sacred place. 'We'll have that one for my brother-in-law. Wherever he may be.'

The funeral director says, 'I'm sorry but that land isn't developed yet.'

'Neither is my brother-in-law dead yet. So far as we know. But just in case we'll take a reserve option.'

Is that you, Annie, cackling among the trumpets?

Thirty-five

Yea, though I walk through the valley of the shadow of death, I will fear no evil.

I'm glad to hear it. Pinball walks with her feet her feet are paddles they are not clean. It doesn't matter. Water slides down their smooth tops and gushes forth between her toes. She walks on grass. No more rocking, she goes forth to Do. She is girdled with no girdle. Her shoulders shimmy her wings are spangled. Liberty never looked so good.

Keziah reaches out for me. I take her right hand in my right hand. There is no more any Pinball. Praise her.

A man steps forth with no shine on his shoe tips, who is this man? He stands over the hole that is my sister's grave, he unfolds a piece of paper from his breast pocket he clears his throat. Glasses he puts on his nose. Not red thanks be. Elbows poke through holes in his tweed. He opens his mouth to speak we bow our heads. A few Irishmen and Italians in yarmulkas who were my sister's clients also bow their heads.

'My mother-in-law was not an easy woman to get close to,' says the Prince, for it is he. I pass tissues. Hoo ha, listen to this.

'People do not go through what Annie went through without paying a price. She paid and arguably her daughter Keziah and her sister Letisha also paid, but I believe they would have paid twice over for the return. She was not your

166

conventionally nice person; she was much much more.

'This family that I had the privilege to observe played an odd sort of game. Two sisters who appeared to deny their love for one another. They talked nasty, mumbled mockeries, chided one another under their breath. Their cutting remarks left me feeling skinned.

'At first I was shocked, this was not part of my culture. But soon I saw that it was part of a ritualized defensive battle, and God help anyone who got in their way. I realized, too, that this state of play – if you can call it play – came out of their need to demolish the very things they most longed for; things which I, as it happens, hold quite dear. Love, faithfulness, goodness and, above all, trust. A need to deny which arose of course from their terrible experiences during the war.

'Where, then, did I fit into this, a foreigner, a gentile? I did not. I can just imagine the curses they heaped on my head; actually, I'd rather not. I'd grown up on the other side of the world and enjoyed a relatively privileged upbringing. And now I'd swanned in and taken their Keziah away – what could be worse? Nothing, apparently.

'Each time I visited Annie tested me; she certainly made me sweat. She beat me at pinball and gin rummy and even chess, which I'd prided myself on. She was one of the most brilliant women I have ever met. I truly believe had she been born in different times and circumstances she could have picked any profession she chose and gone straight to the top of it – and that was both hers and everyone else's loss. But instead she did nothing; and yet I don't believe it was nothing. For something was brewing, as we know. In the last year of her life she took up a most extraordinary profession for anyone, let alone a woman of her religion and generation.

'In England we talk of "wicked old ladies" – not wicked as in sinful, but tough, sharp and ornery. Annie was all of these things. Pinball Annie. I saw for myself from the photographs how beautiful she'd been in her youth; how proud and even a little wild. I am told she once bit an SS guard in the leg. Her repeated attempts at escape were legion. Who could blame her for becoming, well, a bit odd when she finally got away? But for the dreaded blue numbers she bore no scars, yet she was wounded in spirit, as was her sister Letisha, and to some extent –' this he whispered – 'her daughter Keziah.

'I know that this loss will be most difficult for Letisha because they were constant and faithful, if sour, companions. Even as they bickered they spoke as one.

'It will be hard for Keziah, too. Apparently Annie had trouble expressing love directly. She could be cruel, and withholding. Her worries about the outside world became neurotically exaggerated, but it was through these fears that she expressed her love and concern for her daughter.

'Annie led an apparently confined life; for most of us it would have seemed like a self-imposed prison sentence. Yet in another way she rose above her surroundings. Arguably she found a kind of freedom. And if not then, with any luck she has found it now.'

There is no more any Pinball.

The Prince steps closer to the hole in the ground. He throws on to the lid of Annie's coffin a yellow flower which he has brought with him, an act of calculated disobedience.

There shall be no flowers at a Jewish funeral.

The rabbi gives him a dirty look but is not prepared to get down on his fat knees to fish it out.

Amein.

We went to a diner my feet were lumpy in my shoes. We filled our faces with bagels and cream cheese. The Prince tried to take Keziah's hand under the table, she shooed him away. Let him! Even I was ready to kiss his ring.

She went to the Ladies Room I turned to him. 'I suppose you don't know flowers are forbidden at Jewish funerals, why should you?' Comfort me with fibs for I am in a mood to overlook transgressions.

He said, 'I know.'

I bit into my bagel my bagel bit back. I thought to myself, Who is this man who will not cover himself with lies and yet denies the truth?

I thought of the snowball bush in our garden, how the flowers held on and held on. The wind battered their stems the rain whipped their heads – yet they hung on even into winter. Then one day the sun came and smiled on them and they let go, *phloomp*.

Thirty-six

I looked across my kitchen table at Arthur. 'You,' I said. He didn't contradict me.

'So,' he said.

'So,' I said.

'So,' he said.

We might have gone on like this for ever or until I had to go to work the next day. I couldn't afford any more leave. 'So what are you going to do?' I challenged.

'Do?' All of a sudden he was interested in a calendar on my wall, it had been there since 1952, pictures of exotic birds.

'Since when is "do" a foreign word?'

'Letisha, what do you expect me to do?' He offered me his hands, I gave him my mouth.

'I expect you to use your wherewithal, Arthur. A big lawyer like you. Pick up your telephone, ask questions, bother a few people, find out who did this thing and tear their fingernails out.' I bit into one of his precious half-melted Othellos. I meant of course Pinball's murderers. I wasn't asking much.

'Letisha, be reasonable.'

'Reasonable!' I banged. 'Why? Were *they*?'

'What is this, an eye for an eye?'

My moustache was bitter chocolate. I said, 'I said fingernails not eyes, they can keep their eyes.'

Arthur groaned. 'Letisha, please.'

'Please what?'

'Please you're asking the wrong person. I specialize in law not retribution. Get the Mafia to do something – she was working for them, wasn't she?'

'She wasn't big enough for them to bother about. They sent flowers, I threw them out the window.' A backyard strewn with lilies. 'They could at least have investigated.'

'They get a million break-ins a night, they can't be bothered.'

'Makes you wonder what we pay taxes for. Makes me wonder why I have you, Arthur.'

He looked hurt, he looked into his Othello box. 'That's not fair. Letisha. You know very well I can't afford to get involved in something like this.'

'That's what they said.' That's what they all say.

'What am I supposed to do?'

Men, stupid men.

At least when he was eating I didn't have to listen to his stupid talk. Even so he said, 'Did you hear Ebinger's is going out of business?'

'You don't say.'

'A terrible thing after all these years.'

All of a sudden I was sick of chocolate, comfort me with no more Othellos.

Arthur tried. 'I see an Othello I think of you.' An Othello is shaped like a burial mound. 'I mean they symbolize our friendship after all. Without them things just won't be the same.'

'Arthur, things aren't the same.' All my birds were singing at once. 'Shut up!' I flung bird food at them.

'Of course not.' He hung his head. 'Forgive me.'

While his head was dipping up and down pretending to pray I picked out of the box a prize specimen, a brown rock a shiny rock. I thought of Pinball's brown linoleum with the stars, I flung the Othello at his bald patch. 'Of course I forgive you, Arthur.'

He lifted his decorated head.

'Letisha . . .' He was as one having trouble with his bowels. 'I guess I better go now.'

I did not disagree yet my heart was not completely turned within me. I handed him a washcloth for his head. He did not move. 'You have something on your mind, Arthur?'

'Letisha . . .' He had a lot of stickiness in his hairs. 'Letisha, I know it's very late in the day to say this, and maybe you know it anyway, but I just wanted to say I made a mistake.' He was thinking of his floozie who was no longer his floozie but his wife.

His eyes were mournful in their sockets. 'Please, Letisha. So I made a big mistake all those years ago, but I've been paying for it. Believe you me.'

'I believe.'

'Let me tell you.'

'Don't,' I stopped him. 'It was a long time ago. You have three nice girls, your wife still grows black seams up her legs.'

'She has a black seam on her brain like tape.'

I thought of Pinball's brain which was dead, I said, 'I don't want to hear it. Everybody makes mistakes, Arthur.'

'That's very generous of you, Letisha.'

Generosity, pih. 'Think of it as an opportunity.'

He sucked his cigar, his tip lit up. 'What kind of opportunity, Letisha?'

'Well, a day off every week for thirty years, don't knock it.'

He tried to take my hand, my hand was not willing. 'I wouldn't have made it without you. He looked into the Othello box he looked into a grave, his hand was on his heart. 'The last Othello,' he said.

Dear God, is this a man?

Thirty-seven

Once the Prince had spoken at Pinball's funeral it was as if He had Spoken. He owned their tent he owned their garden he owned the sky over their heads. Now he owned her mother too.

God rumbled so did I.

Get your mitts off my sister! Nobody owns Pinball!

As for Keziah I saw she had given herself up into the hands of the enemy.

OK, so Pinball was right. Hoo ha for Pinball.

The Chick knitted with wool the colour of daffodils, *clickety clank*, her hank was tangled. 'Who said anything about enemy? He's my best friend. He's knows everything about me. He takes care of me.' Yea, the Prince washed her with water he anointed her with smelly oils, he put her to sleep on sheets specially ordered under a duvet of great puffiness and the highest of tog ratings. He washed her hair he clipped her toenails, he might as well have swallowed air for her.

She gasps like an asthmatic into her mouthpiece. 'Look how he spoke at my mother's funeral.' I'm looking.

'The eloquence of birds,' I give her.

'So how could you say such a thing?'

'OK, he's your best friend.'

She slides down her wall, her mother is a vine in her

wallpaper. 'What am I supposed to do now?'

The Prince was in his garden counting out his seeds. He dropped to his knees he embraced dunghills. He pressed an ear to the ground and behold he heard a voice saying, *Plant!* so he called to the Chick to come forth and be his helpmeet. 'What do you want me to do?' The helpmeet's pockets were filled with fists. He held out his string to her.

The Chick held one end of his string he tied the other. He drew a straight furrow with his stick and into the ground he plunked his seeds: Parsnip (Tender & True), Radish (Red Prince), and Summer Spinach. The Chick watched. It wasn't in her thumbs to make things grow. Pinball had also had a talent for making her plants to shrivel. The Chick was happiest pouring weedkiller on the heads of the ground elder.

She poked a hole with her finger but her plopping carried no conviction. 'It's still winter – will they really grow?' she asked. He showed her the packets, February–April sowing. 'Of course they will, assuming the slugs don't get them.' He put a watering can into her hands he closed her fingers round its handle saying, 'It's rather a simple equation.'

And after they'd finished their planting the Prince led her up to their bedroom for a rest. Rest, pih. The Prince was no calculator but when one plant died he naturally replaced it with another. Winter made him think of spring. According to his uncalculations it was time for *that* planting, hoo ha.

So he put his fruit into her hands he closed her fingers around it he instructed her on the principles of propagation. And then he opened the furrow of her plantation he stroked its wetness he took aim, his fruit was ready to fructify. Shloop, he squirted his seeds in a straight line and deep.

And so it came to pass that a representative of his seed said 'How do you do?' to a representative of her seed.

And I said, 'When are you expecting?'

'Aunt Adolf, I only just got the results of the test.'

'How does the Prince feel about it?'

'He feels.'

'And how do you feel about it?'

'Sick. Fat. I can't button my trousers.' Her hand is on her belly. He has filled her with gravelstones and bitterness. He has broken her teeth with pregnancy and covered her with ashes.

'Don't button your trousers! Be fat! Eat sweet butter!'

The Prince tells her it's normal to feel sick at first, the body is adjusting to its new hormones, soon it will get better. Oh jolly good. How does he know? He knows. He reads books, he consults his local representative of the National Childbirth Trust. He instructs the Chick in the workings of her own body. So exciting! She does not find it so. 'Don't touch me, I feel repulsive.' 'My love, you are the furthest thing in the world from repulsive.'

'Is that so?' Her belief is no belief. 'Go plant your garden.'

He sticks to her like greenfly. 'I wish you'd let me do something. Please. What can I do for you? Shall I draw you a bath? Fill you a hot water bottle? Play with your feet?'

'Go play footsy with your flowers!'

'Keziah, please . . .'

'LEAVE ME ALONE!'

Oiy.

Thirty-eight

Spring. A season of new lambs trying out new legs. A day of sunshine laced with breezy breezes. The Chick wears her padded jacket yet she shivers. 'Why am I cold?' she beseeches, her legs are as newborn lambs.

Why? Because you have strayed! Because the foreigner's dampness has entered your bones and sinews! Because your thermostat is cockeyed!

The Prince and the Chick lean upon a farmer's fence, four elbows in a row.

New lambs! New beginnings!

The ewe chews the lambs butt. They stick out their woolly white behinds and suck. They leap for fun upon their mother's back. She is busy with her chewing work, she knows them not. Side to side on its hinges slides her jaw. Don't bother me I'm having lunch!

'Implacable,' says the Prince.

The Chick thinks of Pinball. One butt of a sturdy lamb to the nipples and she'd be down on her side waving her legs in the air.

Yea, she waveth no more.

A zipper of sadness slides down the Chick's cheek. The Prince wipes it away with his finger, 'My sweet, what is it?'

'Not sweet.' Who can fill such a breach?

He strokes he mops he croons into the circularities of her ear. 'You musn't be afraid. I'll be with you. I'll help you. It will be all right. You'll see.'

She saw but she was not comforted for she did not see with his seeing. He saw a mother wide in her lap and her orifices, a mother who squats down her babies plop out. The Chick saw a mother otherwise known as Pinball whose lap was narrow whose orifices opened in a rending and a tearing of flesh. She heard, *May you never hear the screams of a labour ward.*

She held on to her belly.

She saw four heads joined wings, terrible things. No feet no face no ears. A pretzeled heart. She saw 'what ifs'. What if it's mad like Pinball? Has a brain like Solly's? Looks like Adolf . . .

Stop right there.

'I have to pee,' she announced. He was on his knees consorting with primroses. 'So pee,' said the Prince of received rabbinical inflexion. 'Where?' asks the lost one, oh lead me to my toilet. 'Over there –' he points – 'in the wood.' 'What if someone sees?' 'There's no one around. And if they do, so what?' 'Will you wait?' 'Of course I'll wait.' The Prince is her horse, he will wait for ever. She strokes his nose. 'I'll be right back.' 'Take your time.' 'What if I have to *make*?' 'Then make. *Really*, my love.'

Make on HIM! *Really*!

She went into the wood she found a flooring of many leaves and damp. She thought of burying herself under them but the movement in her bowels forced her to attend to the business of squatting. She held on to the stump of a dead tree. She pushed she sweated she saw stars, she felt the movings of a movement. But even her waste products were stillborn. She whimpered for help in her woodsy loo.

Hoo ha, half in half out.

The Prince came to her rescue. He pulled the reluctant matter from her body she leaned against him like the grateful dead. My wife my sister my defiled one. She is smeary she is stinky yet her shame is to him no shame. 'Well done,' he celebrates, handing her new leaves for toilet paper. He camouflages with an heap of leaves, on top of that he plops a rock. 'There you are,' he says, scrubbing his hands in moss matter like a surgeon.

Where?

'Don't you ever have to go,' she inquires, 'I mean when you're outside?' In other words, give me a sign you're human. 'Of course,' says the human, 'I just don't make such heavy weather of it.'

The Chick looks up to the firmament. Black clouds picking up their skirts heading in her direction.

Thirty-nine

If having a garden assumes faith in a future what does having a baby? Answer: Too much.

She was no more marriage counsellor. Up and down and up and down the estuary she went like some burden cast out of the sea. A wandering bird rejected by the tribe of Sticklegs. She slipped on rocks she slopped in mud. Fresh sea breezes slapped her across the face like a wad of horsehair from an old mattress ('so exhilarating!'). Healthy mind healthy feet, pih, she came home weighed down on two sides like justice. What's for dinner? Rocks and shells. A woman's work is never done.

Never mind, the Prince is an excellent cook. Sit down put your feet up I'll make you a fire I'll make you some soup.

I'll make YOU soup! Puree of Prince!

Listen to me, my Keziah. Do a little less staring out to sea like that French Lieutenant's Floozie and a little more gazing into your Farberware. Eat and drink for tomorrow, pih. Make a feast of fat things. Make matzo balls make pom-poms (make *his* balls into pom-poms!). Make Aunt Adolf the Merry-hearted's Dynamite Cheesecake.

She read the recipe she mourned.

OK make Mandelbrot, simple and wonderful.

So she did.

The Prince put one hand on the hill of rejoicing that was her

179

belly the other in the valley of her back. 'Stop bothering me –'
she shimmied like her mother – 'I'm trying to make cookies!'
I sent her the recipe. Beat together eggs honey and butter until
light and fluffy. Add orange rind and vanilla. In another bowl
sift together flour baking powder and salt. Make a well in the
centre and stir in first mixture. Now add nuts and fruit. She
made a well in the centre the earth opened up under her feet.

'What is it, my love?'

'Nothing.'

The Prince stood behind her as she stirred and sifted, his
arms a loose noose around her neck. 'Are you sure you're
doing the right thing?' He referred (lucky for him!) not to her
cookie-making but to the quitting of her job, for he saw that
baking and walking on the earth alone could be hazardous
occupations for a Chick.

Her earth and the Prince's earth were two different geo-
logical stories.

'Keziah –' he led her into the restful captivity of a kitchen
chair – 'please stop worrying.' He took her two buttery hands
in his. 'We will be fine and so will the baby. We're quite solid,
don't you see?' She saw loose rubble held together by old sand
blown in from the Ice Age, poised to crumble should God
decide to put in his finger and stir. He rested his chin on the
parting of her ways. 'Ow, your chin is digging in. Get off!'

She butted like a lamb the Prince was thrown against the hot
oven he did not know what hit him. 'Stop being so self-
congratulatory. Stop gloating,' she ordered this man with
hardly a speck of a gloat in his body. He opened his mouth he
closed it again, all this will pass.

Oh yes.

Their marriage would go on because a prince marries for life.
A prince does not go back on his word. The heart of a prince
trusts in his wife.

Smash his trust! Dash his expectations in pieces like a
potter's vessel!

He rolled out of her way she opened the oven door. 'Have

a hot Mandelbrot.' 'Half,' he allowed, for his Mum had warned, Do not partake of hot baked goods. The Chick dug with her spatula. She served him a whole slab, his hands dropped down with its weight.

'Thank you.'

'Don't mention it.'

He raised his fork his mouth was filled with falling rocks.

I knitted her a yellow angora sweater she wore it she bumbled around looking for her stripes. She still worked in her yellow library van checking books in checking books out. 'Early spring,' conversed a borrower. 'Isn't it nice the crocuses are out already?' 'Terrific.' She opened the front cover of *Someday My Prince Will Come* she stamped the date of return the whole van shook. The borrower presumed low-flying aircraft.

The Prince requested permission to visit a mountain called Helvellyn, he was interested in taking photographs of early spring flowers. 'Go,' she told him. It was the weekend. He took her hands in his. 'My love, are you sure you'll be all right on your own? What will you do?'

'I'll do.'

He did as he was told. He went forth with his big camera bag over his shoulder and his big boots on his big feet, he said, 'I won't be late.'

'Be late! Who cares?' She shoved a wooden spoon into her mouth like an epileptic, it nearly broke her front teeth. 'Please,' crooned the Prince drawing it out, 'I wish you wouldn't punish yourself like that.' He put his lips to her lips and hung on, feh.

He left, she waved a chicken over her head.

I also waved a chicken.

Pinball waved nothing.

The countryside is never a lonely place according to the Prince. Infinitely interesting to the observant observer, infinitely treacherous to the uncertain foot. When the Chick got home from her library round she made her way down to the shore. Tufted seacakes, runnels and channels. She watched while a gaggle of boys went leap leap with a ball. 'Face defeat!' one of them cried, and the Chick's foot slid sideways though she stopped herself from falling. 'Rather awkward,' she recalled the Prince's words, 'if you're a sheep.' Rather awkward if you're a human!

Only the sea-birds knew how to pick their way with elegance. Guillemots and razorbills and great crested grebes oh and don't forget the Prince in his britches and garters.

An elderly couple stopped to ask her the way. 'Oh just follow the path around the coast, it's well marked you can't miss it.' An authority! She turned to go she nearly disappeared into a stone cave. A lime kiln, a sort of oven. A ruin. She tried to grab on, a crumbly bit came off in her hand.

There were many species of plant life living in that strange land I gather which did not belong yet managed to take root, for example bluebells. Bluebells get covered by high tides yet they hang on. Tough tootsies.

She sent me literature. *A dynamic coastal area*, I read. In other words, Beware. Come in come in make yourself right at home, don't mind us battering you with eighty-mile-an-hour winds and high tides. If you're worth your salt you'll survive. Adapt! Exploit the niche! Stop complaining! Pull up your one hundred per cent British New Wool socks!

The tide was out the mud flats were showing like the backs of wallowing pigs, the Chick was no bluebell. Her socks were thin her floppy shoes were caked with mud. Wrong wrong all wrong, what kind of an outfit is this for basic survival? She doesn't care she doesn't hear the warning hooter. *Hoo hoo*. Up and up the water comes she observes the level on her legs, oh let me be a human tide marker.

Hoo hoo.

Tweedledee in espadrilles.

Sounds of splashing and of struggling. What's this? A sheep staggering as if with strong drink. Tilted at a crazy angle. Trapped in a tide pool. The Chick goes forth to help, O fat-hearted but ill-advised one. Mistake mistake! It sees her coming it struggles more it falls in with all its legs. It SOS-es with its eyeballs. Blue rectangles.

Hoo hoo.

Higher and higher the water swirls about her poignancies. One sheep one Chick, six gravesticks up to the knee in mud.

Baaaa! Maaaaaa!

Hoo hoo.

A toy train with a yellow face tootles across the railway bridge.

Toot toot.

She looks to the sky, a bunch of purple eggplants. From out of their midst comes a flash of sunlight and the tidal bore smacks her in the belly.

The earth reels the earth is broken down the earth is dissolved in swirling the earth wanders exceedingly.

Yet she does not fall.

Selah!

Another woosh, she drags one leg free. She grabs a hunk of turf she pulls the other one out of the pit. Unfortunately she cannot save the sheep. Choices, pih.

She flops down on rock she listens with the ears of the newly washed. She hears the Prince's car. Whoopee she begins to run. She runs and she runs a great running. And as she runs she hears the bubbling of the curlew with a nose like the Prince's and the tongues of sea-ducks sing songs upon her head and other wading birds whose names she does not know but with twinkling elegancies, all these and more join her in her running.

Down the inside of her legs blood also runs.

PART FIVE

Didn't I say it would be so?
Pinball Annie

Forty

Three months. This much time has passed since Pinball's burying.

I sit on my porch snipping pom-poms for the Chick's chick. Red wool, hoo ha. Give me a good strong red, she said. So I give.

Snip snip even all around, my pom-poms dangle down. Pinball is no more.

Balls says my sister.

Let me correct. The *old* Pinball is no more. There is no more any Disaster Drawer. The slime of her nightgowns is no more nor the loose fit of her flesh. No more sackcloth. Layers of veils shot with gold threads. Also earrings rings chains feathers. A headband embroidered with stars.

Unto me a new sister is born, her name is Wow.

'Who did you over?' I address this Thing. It laughs with teeth which are new pillowcases. Its eyes are searchlights it is all lit up. How can I look?

Snip snip, go my scissors.

Bang bang, go her feet. Stop snipping, she orders. No more stink but a smell as of wood musk rises from the floor-boards.

'Why should I?'

Why should my soul, she raises palms, be still among lions?
She calls me Dreadful (some things never change!). I call her
Dead. This she does not deny. I pick up my needles. *Put them
down.*

I put. *Look at me.* 'No.' *Yes.* I look. She tells, *The time for the
knitting of baby booties is past.* 'No,' I deny. Yes, she yesses. 'I
could mess up that fancy outfit but good.'

Underneath the fancy feathers she's afraid of me. She bumps
bones along the porch railing. 'Coward,' I accuse. I go after
her with my almost-finished red pom-poms like a bullfighter
without the figure. She could rip them out of my hand with her
claws. Instead she brushes my shoulders with her wings, their
wind is a soft wind. Soft skin soft feet. Pinball's feet, the
Chick's chick's feet. I see the scabs on the faces of Keziah's
five-year-old knees.

Maybe it will inherit. Maybe the new feet will do things
differently, praise Be. Doing feet, going here-and-there feet.
Feet full of *I belong here.*

No.

'What no?'

There are no more feet.

The mouth of my scissors gapeth open.

Little jacket pants booties a hat with pom-poms. All red the
Chick's instructions from a 1950s pattern book, she likes the
old-fashioned things. So I knitted and sewed and snipped and
blocked and laid them out to admire.

What good is such an outfit without a baby to put inside it?

So I bought a baby. I went to the toy store I found one the
right size. I took her home I dressed her in the red outfit, she
held out her arms to me. Not me, stupid. I made the arms to
go down I wrapped her in tissue paper I laid her in her box.
Brown paper Scotch tape string. I handed her over to Arthur.
'Air Mail,' I instructed. 'Special Delivery.'

Baby Tears, pih.

*

Rock rock her cradle is filled with doll. The Prince's heart is filled with red wool.

'It doesn't matter it doesn't matter it doesn't matter,' says the Prince.

'You're repeating yourself,' says the Chick.

Rock rock.

'Look, the baby is neither here nor there.'

She looks. What is he talking about? It's right there swaddled in red. She goes to pick it up the Prince stops her with his groaning. 'Keziah, my love, that's a *doll* for God's sake. Please.'

'Please what?'

'Please distinguish.'

'What from what?'

'Flesh and blood from rubber.'

'But it cries and so quietly.'

He does not say no. 'Listen, we'll try again. It's not the end of the world.'

Wrong again. She goes to the window she points to the nuclear power station across the estuary. 'What makes you think I want another one?' She holds her red-breasted baby to her red-breasted breast (I knitted one for her too). Hers and hers, cables writhing up and down their chests.

'For your information,' she tells him, 'I was going to have it aborted anyway, this is no world to bring children into.'

The Prince's ear tunnels suffer temporary informational damage. He sticks his finger in he jiggles it around he manages to come up smiling. 'Of course it's your body, your decision.'

She's not so sure about that. Her body. Hills and valleys, scrubland swampland sand dunes riverbeds. All these places he knows. He loves them as he loves the earth. He might as well own them. He traces her contour lines he journeys along her veins, he travels her coombs her gorges her ghylls her riverbeds her rain-forests, he scales her mountain passes.

Push him off a cliff! Watch him roll!

She does huddling and whimpering. She does, 'Now you'll

leave me.' She draws pictures in blood with her nails on his back.

'My love ...' He takes both her hands in his. 'I wish you wouldn't say such things.'

'Why? Because I may be right? Because it may be true?'

'No, not right. Not true. I'm not going to leave you. Now or ever. There's no one else in the world like you. I will never leave you. Ever. I promise.'

Pinball's stand-in is on the war-path.

'How can you promise such a thing? How do you know someone won't come along tomorrow and seduce you? *Bewitch* you? Where's your imagination?'

She taunts with spitting he poo-poos with sad smooching. Strange, he thinks, it's almost as if she *wants* me to go.

Almost, pih.

She says, 'Answer me.'

So he answers. 'Seduction, bewitchment, what do these words mean? People use them to explain things they don't understand themselves. Men use them as a way of blaming women, as ever, for their sexual so-called indiscretions. As a way of not taking responsibility for their actions. *I couldn't help myself ... She did it to me ...*'

Nothing to do with you, eh, Boychick?

He shakes his head. 'People fall in love – again so called because they're ready. You have to be willing, unconsciously at any rate. I'm not. I want no one else but you. How can I get that through that thick head of yours?' He raises up her sweater, her turtleneck, yea, all her layers, he puts his lips against her chest, feh.

Looking for a direct line, eh, Princeling?

The Chick takes his dewlaps between her two hands. 'Why?' she inquires.

'Why what?' He is practising his direct-line-in-communications work.

'Why should you love me? What is there to love?'

Sabotage. Cutting communication wires. This we also

learned in the camps. What are you doing, my Chick, the war is long over?

'I love you simply because I do. Do I need reasons? Because you're lovable. You, Keziah. Can you understand that?'

'I understand,' she says, but her heart says otherwise.

Let me tell you about Keziah's heart. Most hearts take in love. That mixed with green leafy vegetables and a grilled lamb chop makes a nice meal for the body. The Chick's heart pumps gristle and dust, hailfrost and flies.

And yet and yet. She sucks up his warmth. 'Do you really mean it?' A corner of hopeful uncontaminated heart still longs to hear these things. This I understand.

The Prince says, 'I do. I promise, I promise, I promise.'

She does not say, You're repeating yourself.

'What about the baby?'

'It doesn't matter about the baby. All that matters is you. We'll do it again, I promise.' The Prince's promissary juices run down her legs, feh. He pushes the hair off her forehead with the palm of his hand. 'Tell me one thing.'

'What?'

'Were you really going to have it aborted?'

Rock rock. 'Wouldn't you like to know.'

I questioned Pinball. 'How did you know?'

'Know what?' She made a tinkling with her feet. Instead of broken veins and bruises she wore a bravery of ornaments. 'Know she'd lost the baby, stupid!'

Her reply was of jangling, armbands and bracelets collided up and down the length of her arms.

'I know what I know.'

Rock rock. 'Would she really have aborted it?'

Out of her nose which had resumed straightness came the sound effects of impatience. A punctuation of nose jewels, one ruby one cat's-eye.

She stretched forth her neck. 'Wouldn't you like to know.'

A miracle I didn't bite it off.

Forty-one

The next thing I know we're standing together at Pinball's grave, a slim Chick a fat Adolf and a bunch of dancing worms.

'Where is the Prince?' I inquire.

'On his way to China.'

The other side of the world.

'A conference. He's giving a paper.'

To give a paper, this is a profession? 'Why didn't you go with him?'

'Because I wasn't invited. Besides, I hate mooching along as academic wife. "And what do *you* do, Mrs Prince?" "Who me, I have miscarriages . . ." Besides it's an opportunity to come and see you. Besides it's a relief to be rid of him.' A lot of besides.

'He went alone?'

'With a colleague.'

'Who?'

'You don't know her.'

'A *her*? You let him go alone with another woman?'

'Not another *woman*,' she corrects, 'a *colleague*. There's a difference.'

'What difference?'

She appeals to the hump of earth that was her mother. 'Look, they've known one another for years. He doesn't even *like* her.'

'What does she look like?'

What does it matter? Skinny! Big eyes!'

'What colour?'

'What kind of thing is this to discuss over my mother's grave?'

'What colour!'

'Cop uniform blue!'

She takes my tissues she takes my arm, her mother is no more. She is no more mother. Tell me, my Chick, why did you have to go walking on water? A miscarriage. Missed carriages, pih. Her nose runs with rivers. Ashes to ashes hot knitting needles to hot knitting needles.

'Aunt Adolf, why are you looking like that?'

'Like what?'

'Like you know something I don't know.'

'Hoo ha, because I do. But you won't believe.'

'Probably not. Try me.'

'Not there.'

'Where? What? Who?'

'The Pin. Shook herself from the dust.'

She feels for a crazy hot forehead I look to the sky saying, 'Risen.'

'Oh God I don't believe this.'

'Believe,' I recommend. 'Like a fancy bird. Picture it.'

So she pictures so she shows the parting of her pearlies so she says, 'My mother the mythical bird.'

Hoo ha, she calls her the Phoenix she does not mean Arizona.

Forty-two

'You only just got here.'
   'I have to get back.'
'What for, the Prince is in China?'
'He'll be back by now. I want to be there.'
Two hours later the phone rings, hallo? It's Keziah calling
from the airport. Her plane is boarding the lights are flashing.
'I just called to say goodbye.'
   'Goodbye.'
'I have to go now.'
   'Go.'
'*Smack smack*,' she kisses her instrument.
   'You'll get germs.'
Final boarding call for all passengers to London Gatwick.
Still she doesn't hang up. Will I be all right she wants to
know. 'Don't worry about me, I have my birds I have Arthur.'
Pinball, hoo ha. 'What about you, are you feeling all right?'
   'Yes, I'm fine.'
'You're not nervous?'
   'About what?'
'Flying.'
   'It puts me to sleep.'
'How about the Prince?'

'What about him?'
'He'll be waiting for you when you land?'
'With any luck.'
'What's it got to do with luck?'
'Flights from China are very unpredictable. But I hope so.'
'I hope so too,' I say.
What Pinball says I do not pass on.

The ground under her feet is rubber she is a slow-moving story. She carries her wherewithal over one shoulder. Under her other arm is an album the contents of Pinball's Disaster Drawer every item neatly pasted by the slow and careful child. She sat at my kitchen table we talked we ate. I made her blintzes, 'Too sweet' she complained. I banged my frying pan.

The conveyor belt finishes, the end.

She picks herself up she makes her way to the departure bay. A long line which she calls a queue. Couples in front, couples behind. Tall ones, short ones, dark ones, light ones, mixed-up ones, a regular Virgin Atlantic Noah's Ark. The woman behind her is holding a new offspring in her arms. The Chick takes a swipe at the soft cheek, the mouth begins to howl. The Chick says, 'Oh god, I'm sorry. I seem to have that effect on babies.' On the whole world. The mother says not to worry. Her finger fingers its way into the offspring's mouth, the offspring goes quiet. The Chick wonders what hers and the Prince's would have been. Woe the harvest is fallen too soon. I am a free person. A non-travailer. Alone in the world. A remnant small and feeble.

Keziah, my Chickadee, listen to me. We are all alone in this world this is a basic fact your mother and I learned it when we were girls when the train gathered speed. What's that rumbling noise? The doors flew open, it was like Mr Noah's Ark in reverse, two by two the people who were our parents and grandparents got pushed out into a sea of grass, red with blood and such pretty poppies.

Anyway, what kind of alone? You have me. You have the Prince.

Pinball's snorting is legion.

The Chick walks a gangplank into the plane's belly. She climbs over two sets of knees, her seat is next to a window. She reaches down she unlaces her sneakers. She puts on the green and white tweed booties I knitted for her, stretchy with pompoms, may your feet rise up like yeasted loaves. Left foot right foot a perfect fit, they took me no time to make. She called me creative. I called her ointment.

The stewardess pulls on her toggles, the Chick does not watch. If they crash they crash. A great heaviness befalls her. She puts her seat back her head follows. She thinks about the Prince her husband in China. She sees him bending banana-backed over his sugar-pea students. She sees him taking pictures of early spring flowers. Going to archaeological sites, walking on the Great Wall, pushing strange foods politely around on his plate. Smiling his lamb-chop smile. Wishing he could get home to his poor twice-bereaved wife.

Pih, she does not see what Pinball sees.

'Don't see!' I warn her.

She can't help it, it comes with the job.

'Is it worth it for a fancy get-up and a bunch of trinkets?'

No choice she claims.

Peradventure it's not always so much fun being a prophet. It's even worse being sister to one.

Witness a place called Chengdu. The Prince stands up in front of an heap of skinny students in baggy blues, he is about to deliver his lecture. Outside the rain is soft. Willow trees with their long catkins hanging down, also stone lions with red pop-eyes. The Prince grows more impassioned, more spontaneous in his delivery, he scratches his hairs.

I say to Pinball, 'There's something going on here. He looks somehow different, filled out, wrinkle-free.'

'Yes.' My rocker stops its rocking.

'Excuse me,' the stewardess leans over to the Chick, 'but would you mind putting your seat in an upright position.' It is not a question.

My question is a question and it is this: 'What happened to the holes in his elbows?'

They are no more.

The students clap his hosts clap. Everyone is clapping except for his colleague.

'What is she doing?'

'Doing.' Outside the world is soft and the colour of jade and it smells of sap and spring.

Prepare for take-off.

You see those winking coloured stars? The Chick presses her nose to the glass. More germs! Not that she ever catches colds she only catches miscarriages and death.

Her nose and the glass achieve separation. She presses a button, the chair back and her head become intimates.

'Can I get you anything to drink?' asks the stewardess.

'I'll have a gin and tonic.' Two little helpings of Chinese wisdom. 'Thank you.' The Chick pours, one from bottle A one from bottle B. Aunt Adolf, what makes a good wife?

How should I know? I was no wife. I was not given the chance. Arthur and me? Pih, maybe I got the better deal, maybe I'm not sorry, maybe we were not cut out for marriage your mother and I. A lot of maybes. Pinball was no wife. Pinball was a cage full of crazy birds, you opened their door you said Go! Fly! and they jumped on top of one another an heap of cheeping.

Why did she stay with Solly?

Not long.

Long enough.

Maybe because Solly was damaged. She would not have stayed with a normal man. This way she was free. Another point: such a man would never leave her. Or so she thought.

Why do you stay, my Chick?

She closes her eyes. Me? Because the Prince loves me. Because he'll never leave me. Because – hoo ha, listen to this! – because I love him.

Pinball's rocker rocks a rocking so fierce it causes a great wind and terrible, this I have not seen before.

'Annie, what is it?'

'The Prince.'

'What about him?'

Don't listen! Fill your ears with headset! Twiddle your dial to Tchaikovsky's Piano Concerto No. 2! Have another drink! Make it a double!

She hath filled his brow with wrinkles and for that . . .

Pinball is concentrating so hard her headband snaps. More rain more lions with jewelled eyes and overactive thyroids. These things she sees. More drippy willow trees. More applause, a great clapping. Hugs. Embraces. Kisses on one cheek, kisses on the other. We are so proud to have you. Honourable and honoured guest from England, come with us into dinner and eat of our strange foods, slimy and unkosher and with many tentacles, feh.

His English colleague Helen raises a glass to him, 'That was absolutely marvellous.' Her eyes are the blue of a Milk of Magnesia bottle. His are like the milk inside: warm, half-curdled. He drinks to her, they are surrounded by a sea of friendly strangers treading water.

Dinner is over the Prince excuses himself. He goes to his room he does his ablutions. He tucks his stripy pyjamas tops into the elastic of his stripy pyjama bottoms. He climbs into his narrow dormitory bed, there comes to his ears the sound of knocking. Who can this be?

And I say to Pinball, 'Stop right there.'

Too late. For the time it takes for the Slimy Fish to slither across the room and into the Prince's bed he imagines his poor bereaved Keziah on her way home to him in an airplane. And then he does not.

The Chick conks out. Sleeps through the duty-free hoiking through *Terms of Endearment* through people climbing over each other through having her dinner set down in front of her and taken away again through having her upper arm poked to make sure she's still alive.

Forty-three

The Chick switches on her overhead light. A groaning and a
hissing from round about a burying of heads under smelly
airplane blankets. The offspring makes wailing noises. All this
she ignores.

A black leather album its covers dull and pocked like the
surface of the moon. She rubs it with the palms of her hands
please God not yet. Who will protect her from its contents?
Yellow torn wavy with glue each page coated in plastic smooth
smooth. She knows for she has made this memorial herself
even put it in alphabetical order. Be brave my Chick open
sesame. She parts its wings a choirgirl about to sing. Some
song, pih.

Abortions
Accidents (Misc.)
Adulteries
Bombings
Burglaries
Butcheries
Cancers
Cataclysms (see Nat. Disasters)
Chemical Warfare

Child Abuse
Crashes
  (Air, Road, Sea)
Crazinesses (Misc.)
Defenestrations
Disappearances
Drownings
Drug Addictions
Drug Overdoses
Earthquakes
Explosions
Fall-out, Nuclear
Famines
Fires
Floods
Frame-ups
Freak Accidents
Guerrilla Attacks
Heart Attacks
Illnesses (Other)
Kidnappings
Maimings
Miscarriages (of Foetuses; of Justice)
Molestations
Natural Disasters
Nervous Breakdowns
Political Imprisonments
Rapes
Shootings
Stabbings
Starvings
Stranglings
Suicides
  (by Asphyxiation, Hanging, Shooting, etc.)
Terrorist Atrocities
Tortures (Misc.)

Unclassifiable Disasters

O song of songs with a tune like a fishbone in the throat.
  O song of songs which is Pinball's which is also the Chick's.
  The only one of her mother.
  The inheritor of the song.
  Humbled humbled.
  Choking on the tune.

  Do not look upon me for I am cursed.
  I am comely as a crater.
  The sun does not look upon me.
  I am the rotten grape.
  I have no vineyard.
  I am not suitable material for gardens.
  Soon I will be cast out.

Woe woe! This is her song and her mother's song and her
mother's mother's song and its chorus is:

  You will lose.

She closes the black leather cover with its holes like the
surface of the moon. She puts on her headset she hears a song
it goes like this: *You will lose ... you will loow-ooh-ouse.* A
familiar song a catchy little tune.
  She slides the portfolio back under her seat. The airplane
flies smooth smooth right-side-up. She flies belly to earth. She
experiences turbulence. A juggling of internal organs. A
heaving a stretching a humming a vibrating. A labour in the
throat a speech travail. She opens her mouth a spreading of
lips.
  'Enough.'
  'Pardon me?'
  'Sorry, nothing.'
  Not sorry! Not nothing! Enough!

Enough losing. Enough eating betrayal by the slice.

Eat smoked salmon! Drink champagne! Celebrate winning!

Pinball is dead my baby is no baby what more can go wrong? Now I can live. Look I'm flying. Back to my backwater back to my long-legged sea-birds back to my long-legged Prince.

I am the only one of my beloved.

I am! I am! I am!

You will lose, poo.

She raises her window shade the run rises once in a while over England. Green fields cockeyed with proximity tilt beneath her. Her mouth also tilts, make way for teeth.

She fastens her seatbelt she opens her book she reads a little of its contents. *Gaudy Nights* by Dorothy L. Sayers. Ho hum, she thinks about the hero Peter Wimsey she offers up a sigh into the disgusting airplane air. Peter Wimsey! So learned so competent so discreet so romantic so musical such a defender of woman's rights. So smooth so cultured like buttermilk he would coat the six sides of a glass holding a candle for the dead. Boy oh boy wouldn't it be wonderful to have a man like that! Oh it would it would. And then she thinks—

I HAVE a man like Peter Wimsey! Even better!

Hoo ha, a revelation.

She climbs over the people in her row. She goes to the toilet she puts on eye make-up even cheek blush and lipstick. No more rotten fruit.

She lands with a nice plop she walks the gangway into the terminal. No more terminals no more endings this is our new beginning.

'Live ye!' yells Ezekial otherwise known as Adolf.

She stands at the baggage carousel she watches her bags go round and round. The second time round she catches hold. She walks out through the green exit, NOTHING TO DECLARE.

The Prince is also smiling his head is tilted back to reveal nose hairs. The grin gets bigger and bigger until he looks like a demented airplane. He taxies towards her his wingtips rigid.

Instead of folding her up in the arc of their love he runs straight over her. She's left lying in the terminal crushed and bleeding.

Isn't it amazing what jetlag can do to a person's imagination?

Forty-four

His right hand is under my head his left rests on the round goblet of my navel. More like a punchbowl to serve an army. Arthur is left-handed.

Who let my birds out?

Arthur's hands are on me, I am filled with his hands his hands are filled with me. We do not make love in the ordinary way for we could easily crush one another to death.

The thirty doors of my heart are opened, birds fly around our heads.

We are close very close. We are grace we are a ballet, *Love for Two Behemoths*.

The winged ones want to play too. Come! Join us in our celebration! So they do. A mouthful of feathers a forehead full of splats. 'Where am I?' asks Arthur. 'Heaven,' I inform him. He says he's having trouble breathing maybe the air is too thin.

So I climb off him, I arrange my bulk on its back I wave away my birds. Enough, Arthur needs his rest. He comes to me for peace he does not need thirty pairs of wings beating around his head.

Peace, pih. 'You'll soon be getting plenty of that, Arthur. Enjoy the activity while you can.'

'Letisha! Get those fucking birds off my head! Do you want me to leave here a man with no eyes?'

'Don't excite yourself, Arthur,' I chide, 'it isn't good for your health. These are no wild birds they are only playing with you.'

'Playing my foot!'

But it wasn't his feet or his eyes they were interested in it was that head of his, so smooth so sweet and shinier than a blessing. Look! A mirror! Peck peck! Well you could understand the temptation.

'Hold still,' I told him. He held the little bottle with the skull and crossbones in his fleshy hand. I poured iodine on to his pecked pate he yelped like the virgin of Israel.

'Faint not,' I advised, quoting from the Good Book. 'To them who have no might he giveth strength.' I slapped a nice blue Band-aid across the shininess. A going down of the sun, amein.

The telephone rang, I ran to answer it.

When I got back he was not there.

According to Pinball he was no more.

'I don't believe you.'

'Believe me,' she inisisted.

'What is this some kind of epidemic?'

'Logic.' She did not look logical.

But the evidence was on her side. My birds pecked like vultures at their cuttlebones they shrieked like sea-birds. They balanced on one leg they sang not. Where is our bald head to peck? Where are our Othello crumbs?

Dumb creatures suffer loss too!

Speaking of dumb creatures his wife called me up she said, 'Arthur is dead I thought you should know.'

A generous spirit stacked on top of a pair of legs. I was dying to ask her if she still wore black stockings with seams even though they went out of style years ago but it didn't seem the right moment.

'When did it happen?'

'About an hour ago.'

'Just like that?'

'Just like that.'

I thanked her for telling me. She said it was quite all right. And then she said, 'I knew.'

'Knew what?'

'Well, you know. About you and Arthur. Your days together.'

I said, 'We ate Othellos.'

'You're welcome to come to the funeral,' she invited. Again I thanked her.

'Don't mention it.'

'I didn't.'

'What?'

'Nothing. Tell me,' I inquired, 'how did it happen? And where?'

She knocked on her breast twice saying, 'Heart.' I heard knuckle on bone. I tried it myself it sounded more like a plumping up of pillows. Apparently he was in a cab on his way home. No briefcase no briefs, only a box of chocolate Othellos on the seat beside him. (Thief! My Othellos!) He said he didn't feel too good so the cabbie pulled over he fell out the door. He sat on the kerb he held his heart he was not saying the Pledge of Allegiance. He was no more.

'Imagine that,' she said.

I imagined the Othellos, what happened to them?

'I mean,' she went on, 'a big man like Arthur, millions of people stepping over him. Such a dirty place. Probably garbage all around him, you know how it blows along the kerb. Beer cans, newspaper, even dogshit because not everybody pooper-scoops these days, you know?'

I said I knew.

'I'm sure he would have liked you to come to the funeral.'

'Thank you but no thank you.'

'Don't you want to say goodbye?'

'I'll do it my way.'

'Isn't that the name of a song?'

'I wouldn't know.'

'So what way is that?'

'My way is my way.'

She suffered a loss of air. 'Y'know, the doctor told him he had to lose weight but would he listen?' She answered her own question, 'No. He liked his coffee and cake too much.'

My fault! I encouraged him to bring me Othellos, I let him eat them, I fed him heart disease. Murderer! He was probably on his way from me when he died, the evidence was in the cab . . .

I hung up. I went to look for a greater intelligence. My sister or my sister's spirit or whatever she was was busy rocking. 'He's dead,' I informed her.

'I told you.' Her pearls were pearly in the moonlight.

'Shut up. Nobody likes a know-it-all for a sister.'

She twirled her ankle in my direction. Then she held out her arms to me.

I woke up on the porch floor with the taste of Pinball's lap in my mouth. I thought of Arthur I thought of chocolate. Comfort me with Othellos for I am sick of death.

Dark chocolate.

I called the sweatshop. 'I won't be coming in today.'

I slipped out of my slept-in housedress I put on a little black number, size 22. I rolled garters to my knees the fat hung over. I went out on to the streets in search of Othellos. I took two buses I found a bakery in Sheepshead Bay, not the original maker of Othellos but what you might call a reasonable facsimile thereof.

Legal language, pih. Arthur was a Big Man because I put him through law school. I was a Big Woman who did piecework for a living. Justice, poo.

I took the reasonable facsimiles thereof home I sat at my kitchen table I had my own private funeral, a very enjoyable occasion. I put out two plates, one for me one for Arthur for old time's sake. I ate his Othellos I ate my Othellos I ate enough Othellos to feed the Supreme Court.

Forty-five

I swam across the Atlantic by numbers, this was no water ballet. Thanks be I reached shore I heard a cockamamy English dialling tone, *bloot bloot*. I was ready for the Prince but it was not the Prince. A voice without form and void.

'Hello hello? Keziah is that you? Are you all right? Say something.'

Somebody was strangling her.

'My God what's going on there are you sick laryngitis what? Tell me!'

'Can't. Will write.'

'What are you, a telegram?'

A nothing.

'You're drunk. Somebody drugged you mugged you you fell down and broke your hip. You had a breakdown.'

Still she could not would not say.

'Put him on.' Him.

A tinkling of bells Pinball shook her head.

Her daughter said, 'No.'

'He beat you up I'll kill him.'

She did not laugh.

'He's dead he had a head-on collision a heart attack. By the way, Arthur is dead.' This she did not hear.

She said no to all these things.

'There's only one thing left.' So I spoke what Pinball had already spoken. My telephone was filled with weeping my mouth with gall. 'He won't get away with this! My sword is sharp the knife and scissor man came to me this morning!'

On my kitchen table was an innocent milk container. I lifted up my blade I aimed at Elsie the Cow. Stab stab I went – 'lice! locusts! thunderbolts!' – right between the eyes. The sacrifice of an innocent in the pursuit of justice.

Hoo ha.

My feet ran with milk.

Forty-six

'Don't blame him,' she writes. 'It was all my fault.' Her words are nailed to the page. I see holes I smell blood I appeal to the one who was her mother, 'How can she say these things?'

'She can say,' says Pinball who is even more annoying in death than in life.

'Look what he did to her.' Judge for yourself as Arthur would have said to the Ladies and Gentlemen of the Jury.

China, a faraway place. Pinball got it in one. Hats off to Pinball.

The Prince walked in the door he took off his hat. The Chick greeted him with the shyness and solemnity of one suffering a renewal of love, woe woe. She said, 'You don't wear hats.' He looked at his hat. 'I do now.' A Chinese cowboy hat. She laughed as she once laughed at his red glasses only this time his look said, Watch out I am no longer a man to be laughed at.

Next came his shoulders, they'd grown three inches in each direction. She put her arms around his neck she felt a tree. She slid off him, where was her sapling? Why was he smiling like an Hittite?

'Did you have a good time in China?'

He put his hat over his crotch. 'Very.'

'Tell me all about it.'

So he told. How the people enveloped him the mountains told him faraway beckoning stories. How the Temple of Eternal Tranquillity whispered to him of a past uncontaminated by doubt. How the temple shone with promise and hope, the animals bowed down before him smiling. How the crane raised its beak to the sky how it flapped slowly away into a sky bruised as lovers' lips. How the soles of his feet ached.

A selective telling.

The Chick's eyes filled with tears. A Prince a poet. 'How was the travelling?'

'Air France lost our luggage on the way out.'

'Where was that?'

'In Paris.'

'What did you do?'

'Helen speaks French. She was able to negotiate with the Embassy. Eventually we got them back but not for a week.'

'What did you do until then?'

'Air France gave us blank cheques to buy essentials to tide us over. Helen bought an ivory bracelet.' He bowed his hairs.

'An ivory bracelet doesn't sound so essential.'

'No.' He tried to look disapproving but his sliver of lip could not stop itself from quivering. Oh pack me in oil let me join schools of carefree profligate fishlets.

'My baby is dead,' said the Chick for some reason.

His hands wanted to juggle. 'I'm so sorry,' he said. Hers floated like foetuses.

'Would you like something to eat?' she offered. He allowed of a light snack. 'I'm not very hungry these days.' Or nights apparently. She put out bread and cheese on a cheeseboard. Soft Brie, smelly blue, holey Swiss, the Prince was a lover of cheeses. She uncorked a bottle of cold white wine. The table shone, the sun was on its way down.

'I've stopped eating cheese,' he informed her.

Correction: The Prince was *once* a lover of cheeses.

'Since when?'

'Since China. Helen doesn't eat cheese. She's on a vegan diet, no dairy products, so I thought I'd try it too. And I feel much better for it.'

This she saw. 'But Helen has a reason for giving up cheese –' fish skin, feh! – 'you don't.'

'Well, that's not quite true. According to Helen cheese is mucus-producing. It's not particularly good for anyone. And I do feel a hundred per cent better.'

'So I see,' she saw.

'You're in love with her,' she told, it was no question.

His eyes were gooey with consenting. 'How?' he asked.

'Hownowbrowncow,' said the recesses of her mouth.

'What? I meant how did you know.'

'You can't stop saying her name.'

He looked down at his lap, he smiled at it.

The Chick went round to his side of the table she lifted up his chin. She pulled his legs apart she inserted herself between his not-so-poignant poignancies. She looked like she was about to perform a wisdom-tooth operation. 'Knowing you–' she squeezed his jaw with one hand – 'I bet you didn't go to bed with her. Too principled! Too pure! Too scared! Am I right?' He could not speak for jaw-crushing.

'Well, am I?'

He unclamped her hand – gently gently – a freeing of teeth a flapping of factual tongue.

'No, as a matter of fact, you're not.'

'It doesn't make sense,' I take my case to Pinball. 'Two weeks after a misscarriage her husband tells her he's in love with another woman and she says it's her fault.'

'It is,' she bangs.

'How?'

'Hownowbrowncow.' The only mother of her daughter.

'Please.' A rocking and a banging.

'She knew it would happen, it happened.'

You will lose.

Woe woe.

She sits on the floor her legs in a V. Her gravesticks are brown and baggy in their track-suit bottoms. No fire burns in their fireplace. She stares at the space between her legs like a child who has lost her pail and shovel.

V for Victory, pih.

She leans forward she puts a hand under each chubcalf she tries to lift them. One two, two inches and two inches, all fall down.

Hei, here comes the Prince. 'What are you doing?'

'Yoga,' she says. It sounds more like housewrecking. He does not believe her. Neither do I. Neither does Pinball.

He says, 'I'm sorry.'

'You're sorry,' she repeats.

'Look, I know this is all terribly unoriginal but . . .'

But what, O Unoriginal One?

'But it just couldn't be helped.'

'You're right,' she says, 'it is unoriginal. Tell me something new.'

So he tells her, 'I'm going to have to let you go.'

Back into exile! Ho ho, heave ho!

And what does she do?

Left leg right leg, moving parts for the purpose of going out from the place that was her home. As You Wish My Lord. The beast of burden who was his wife wears a backpack filled with fillings.

'Come come, I didn't mean it *literally*,' says the Pharaoh of Greater-than-Literal Generosity. 'You don't have to go this minute. In any case if you like I'll go.'

She does not like. For it seems to her somehow right this way. Familiar. Peradventure you have been rehearsing in your dreams, my Chick?

'Where will you go?'

She names a friend. She grabs on to the doorknob.

Your own house! You painted walls, scraped floors, laid carpets!

She turns for a minute, looks at the Prince who was her husband.

Smite him! Peck his head to pieces! Snip off his nose! Snip off his thing!

She is in no condition for snipping.

Blast him with cursing! Drown him in his iniquity! Sink him in the mighty waters of your leaving! GOOSE HIM!

Her toothbrush also goes with her.

Go out with an high hand!

Her hands are low at her sides her back is an hump. She opens the front door she is removed like a cottage.

Forty-seven

The Prince crept into the kitchen he nibbled up the despised and rejected Brie. And Swiss and blue. He went to his bed he groaned into his pillow. (And may he have nightmare upon cheesy nightmare every night for the rest of his life!) And in the morning he was sore of stomach and also spirit for he saw he was in danger of losing both the Fish and the Chick. (Old Chinese saying: Take out big insurance policy before setting fire to house.) In other words, what if he threw Keziah away and then the Slimy Fish decided not to leave her husband and children after all? So after sitting for a long time on the pot he made a decision.

The Chick spent the night curled up on her friend's living-room floor, no carpet, comfort me with further misery. Every ten minutes she woke up. She crawled to the toilet bowl like somebody looking for something precious they'd flushed by mistake, hoping it might by some miracle come floating back up again. It didn't. She opened her mouth but no substance of any substance came out except for a trail of spit that got longer and longer and hung and hung from her bottom lip and she stared at it and was as one hypnotized. She hung and the spit hung and her arms hung and even her hair which was not hanging hair hung. Yea, and it was good for she could breathe she could forget she could just hang there a limp thing staring at her own pretty shiny spit. But eventually the spit broke and the invisible hypnotist snapped two fingers saying 'Wake up' and she woke up and remembered and once more resumed her pukeless puking.

In the morning her friend stood in the doorway watching her. 'I hope you realize the symbolism here. I mean, you obviously can't swallow what he's telling you.'

The doorbell rang. The Prince held out his arms in a horizontal position. The Chick held on to her toilet seat. 'What?' she asked of him and he replied, 'Come back and try again.'

She thanked her friend for her hospitality. She got in the Prince's car she let him take her home to try (try what?), yea and it was very interesting.

May you live in interesting times. A Chinese curse he brought it home to her a present among presents. Chinese brushes, Chinese ink, how interesting, what am I supposed to do with these? 'Paint,' he told her. 'You always wanted to do Chinese brush painting.' 'I don't now.' Her voice was shredded scrollwork she picked up the ink stick it was heavy she dropped it, the Prince hopped out of the way it missed his foot but only just. *Bird gives wide berth to wounded animal.* Another old Chinese saying, I just made it up.

'What happens now?' she asked. 'What should I do?' Doing for love, pih.

The Prince had recently seen a thrashing of tails a raising of legs a parting of ways (no instruction manual required in fact let me show you a thing or two) – and boy was it good!

Whereas Keziah his wife sat quiet as a fortune cookie (*Wife who box with Slimy Fish always lose*). She wore the same stretched-out-slept-in puked-in brown track suit from the day before. She had a prematurely disqualified look. Still the Prince went down on his knees before the wife of his youth he buried his nose in her lap which was not fresh saying, 'Fight for me.' It was torn from his throat like a piece of burnt chicken skin.

Fight FOR him? HAH! Fight HIM! Lift up thy rod and break his head! Make like Jael! Pick up thy pointy gifty paintbrushes and make holes in his temples! Crush his feet with lead weights! Stomp on them with hobnailed boots! Make the tarsals and metatarsals and all the tarsals' tarsals to cry out in agony!

But she did not.

For although she knew she did not stand a chance (which was *why* she did not stand a chance) she also felt she had nothing to lose (everything to lose!) and maybe the smell of blood was better than the smell of her old track suit.

Feh.

On the other hand, the blood you smell may be your own. So Pinball say.

Listen to your mother!

But she did not listen for the Prince was busy arranging her limbs, left arm here right arm there. 'Hold me,' he says. So she holds, for dear life she holds, don't leave me don't throw me away.

Dummy! That's not what he wants! He means wriggle, thrash, open your eyes! Open your legs! He means love he means sex you know what he means. Move! Do! Make like a floozy not like a baby monkey!

Oh *that*.

The Chick is not stupid. She knows shrivelling when she feels it.

'Wait right here,' she tells him, 'I'll be back in an hour.' She drives to town she buys a one-piece white lace body thing with snaps at the crotch. She drives back home again she soaks herself in perfume oils she reeks like Esther and all her serving women put together. She puts on the lacy thing it makes her to bulge out in strange places. (*Aunt Adolf say fat juicy woman better than dried-out kipper any day.*) On top of that she hangs a loose kimono. Her hair she brushes out like the burning bush sprayed with sparkly things. Earrings she hangs from her ears, Pinball says if she's not careful all her bulbs may pop at once. I tell her look who's talking.

The Prince is reading his newspaper.

She goes into the kitchen she concocts a concoction of eggs and cream and half a bottle of brandy which is twice what the recipe calls for. She heaps a bowl with salty nuts. At last she has everything arranged in front of the fire, even the food and the eggnog and her arms and legs and face (smile!).

The Prince peels the paper off his face.

He sees the Chick's eyes painted round with black, he has trouble looking at them.

They sit on cushions facing each other. 'We need to talk,' she says. Talking this she likes. Little Golden Books, open covers, spread pages. Tell me a story. The Prince flings down his paper. 'What do you want to talk about?'

'Anything. Everything.' Fifteen years together is not pih.

'Do you remember that concert we drove to in Davis?' He remembers. A hot night a cool Dutch harpsichordist. On the way home he confessed to being in love. A California blonde big as the Grand Canyon. Unfortunately she did not return his affections. 'So love somebody else,' advised the Chick. 'Love isn't like that,' he objected. 'Who says?' said the one beside him. 'You learn to drive you learn to love. And then maybe it lasts longer.'

Who sprinkled rosewater on my neck? Cool cool, he stopped the car he took her in his arms. Hoo ha, a prophet this he liked. Happily ever after.

'You were right, of course.'

'Was I?' She pours more eggnog into their glasses.

'Whatever happens,' he tells her, 'I've loved you more than any other woman in the world.' She puts down her glass her moustache is creamy. 'Even the Big Blonde?'

'Even the Big Blonde.' He does not blink.

And now, 'Even the Slimy Fish?'

Pinball says she's pushing her luck but for once she's wrong.

'Even she.' He does not hesitate.

Both their faces are wet. She is touched by his words, he is also touched by his words. They are both touched by the eggnog, half a bottle of cognac, hoo ha.

'Do you remember that movie?'

The Chick laughs, 'What movie?' for they spent the whole time studying love under a cape knitted for her by Guess Who.

And now she stretches out one foot. The Prince tilts towards it.

And God held out his index finger to... Well I haven't seen the Sistine Chapel ceiling but I've seen reproductions. Anyway the Prince stretched forth his index finger towards the Chick's foot and when the tip of his finger touched the top of her big toe lo! a spark sparked and it was something different.

'Can you think of all the places we've made love outside?' she tested.

'Up in Tilden Park that time,' he began.

'Oh, and on that dry hot hillside in Marin overlooking the Bay, remember?' He remembered. A plane flew low overhead, the Chick waved her legs. All over the hillside she imagined couples hidden in the golden grass also doing this thing.

'The beach on Skye,' he remembered.

'It was so warm, like the Mediterranean.'

'Gorse bushes against the blue sky.'

'Then there was Crete.'

'And the Japanese hot tub up on the mountain in Santa Fe in moonlight.'

'And in our sleeping bags under the stars: Yosemite, Monument Valley, Big Sur...'

'Death Valley.'

'Hoarfrost on cactus in the morning,' she embellished, 'with the sun shining through.'

'The Coniston shore.' He leapt to another country. A hot freak February in England.

Enough. Her husband takes her by the hand. He pushes her ahead of him up the stairs his arms around her hips, O lead me in love for I am sick of being your rod and your rabbi! Halfway up they stop he reaches forth under her kimono he finds lace he finds snaps he finds the moon nice and gooey.

He rises up like a great wave from the sea for there is still much attraction between them. (A little extra chubflesh does not deter him, the Prince is an appreciator of women's bodies.) She holds him between her legs he carries her to the bed thinking it was nice with Helen while it lasted but this is for real this is for ever.

The Chick has caught his enthusiasm. She sweats and pants and digs her nails which are no nails into his back. (The Prince pushed the words 'trying too hard' from his mind as well as 'this will not last'.) And so the night goes on with flip-flops and squashings and goings and comings and slidings and more comings and even comings together, yea and it was really something.

And then they slept. Or rather the Prince slept and the Chick held on phumphing silently into his backbone, 'I won I won I won.' All he knew was a rather pleasant tickle of lips.

'Sleep now, my love,' he advised.

In the morning they began over again just like a honeymoon couple, sex on top of sex, feh. Only this time the Prince yelped with pain, he withdrew like a distressed gentleman. The Chick looked down she saw a rawness a soreness an overused Chinese penis.

He who humps himself silly gets infected willy.

And then she saw his eyes. She saw the Great Wall.

Fight for me, pih.

This was the end of April, a nice month over in England. A month of thawing and of springing, of berries and catkins and cats, of rabbits lying on the road without eyes. Of crawling away to die.

She is her mother's daughter. A dragon's breath a panda's eyes a baby's mouth. No teeth no bite, Adolf say.

She hung her head over the side of the bed, she addressed herself to yesterday's socks, 'You better go to her.'

He did not disagree.

Forty-eight

'May I stay one more night?' beseeched the Prince. 'I'll sleep on the sofa if you like.'

'I don't like. This was your idea, remember?'

'You know what I mean.'

She knew. She let him stay for her plan required the overnight presence of the Prince and his flesh.

I did not like the sound of this. 'What plan?' I asked her mother the Risen One.

'A plan.'

'Tell me.'

She handed me a bottle of toenail polish the colour of fresh blood she stuck her foot in my lap. I charged her with not knowing. I called her a crone with fancy feathers. 'Seer's senility! Cassandra with Alzeimer's!' Vanity always was her weak point.

'Murder,' she came clean.

I threw her foot away. 'What do you mean, *murder*?'

'You asked.' She grabbed the polish

'Don't be stupid.' I grabbed it back.

One thing my sister wasn't was stupid.

It was a quiet night outside their cottage not a creature was stirring except for the owls the vultures the bats. Meanwhile inside the Chick was busy in her kitchen admiring her family of knives: father mother plus four kiddie knives, all in a row size place in their maplewood rack imported from America.

One by one she slid them out she caused them to lie flat on her marble chopping board. She set them to spinning with thumbspins. She lit a candle she worshipped the flashing of blades.

She lined them up she tested for sharpness, her thumb was striped with testing. She sucked her wounds her teeth were as newborn lambs gory with their mother's blood.

And I said to Pinball, 'Mad.'

'The night of the sharp knives,' she reminded.

I said, 'What does one thing have to do with another?'

'Everything.'

'What if she ends up in prison for the rest of her life?'

According to Pinball all life is a prison. At least this way she's *doing*.

A sliding of knives a shedding of bowels, surprise him with smiting. Catch his blood in a pail take it down to the kitchen add milk and eggs whizz it in the blender pour it into a mug and drink it down.

Strawberry eggnog delicious.

The Chick is a slow and careful butcher. She chooses the filleting knife not big but thin and shapely, perfect for disembowelling purposes. She climbs the stairs. Only her chubknees suffer gravitational doubt, are we really doing this thing?

Yes.

Her knees and her knife move forward.

The Prince her husband. Look how he sleeps on his back. In his own bed. Her bed. Look how his chest goes up and down how this thing also rises. Double feh.

And look how his pyjama bottom is tied in a heartbreaker of a tidy schoolboy's bow. This she undoes with the delicacy of a fishmonger with a higher degree. She parts his flaps she perceives a swordfish standing on its tail smiling up at her (hoo ha, a lot of imagination, not a lot of sleep). She considers the thing from all angles (how to do it nicely?). And I say poo on nicely, just Do! No time for butterfly cuts! Chop! Slice! Slit! Off with its head!

She rests her blade at the base of his merchandise. The Prince feels a coldness in the testicular region peradventure he needs to pee. He opens his eyes. 'What are you doing?' he inquires. 'Cutting off your penis,' she informs him. He slides his hand around her hand he squeezes with a terrible gentleness saying, 'I shouldn't do that if I were you.' The knife falls to the floor the Prince falls back to sleep.

Pinball collapses into her rocker I think she has been sick in the toilet. When she wakes up she says she has dreamed a dream. 'Tell me.' So she tells.

'Once upon a time an old woman went on a pilgrimage. She was on her way to visit the sun to ask his advice for herself and a few others who were in trouble. Now she happened upon a rock which for many years had been hanging, not falling and not *not* falling. Such an unhappy rock! "Please," it begged the old woman. "Ask the sun what I can do to stop myself falling and so be at rest and passers-by be free from fear." So the old woman took pity on the rock and went to the Sun and asked the rock's question and the Sun said, "This rock must fall and bring a person to death and thus it will be at ease."'

'No!' I protested for I knew what this meant.

'Yes,' she said.

The Prince rumbled in his sleep.

Pinball was sick between her feet.

The Chick runs to the bathroom she locks herself in. She sits fully dressed on the open pot she holds the filleting knife to her wrist. She looks up one last time and there it is, hosanna! the Prince's bathrobe which he calls a dressing gown hanging on the back of the bathroom door. Blue and white stripes. Also a blue and white striped cord which trails to the pine floor which they sanded and sealed together till death do us part.

She frees the cord from its loops she wraps it around one chubfist and then the other and she goes forth, oh wrap me round with stripy solutions.

A wise man once told his flock, Wear nothing around the neck for there must be no break between heart and brain.

Except in the case of an adulterer.

'A tricky thing to pass a cord between head and pillow without disturbing the head,' observes Pinball.

The Chick works the cord from crown to neck. Slowly slowly do not rush for a life depends on this. At last the cord is in place behind his neck, all she has to do is squeeze.

Now!

She lets out breath his nostril hairs pick up the stink of final solutions, feh. They wave they tickle him into waking. 'What now?' He is bored with games of murder. He yanks the cord from her hands I wipe the vomit from each of her mother's ten shiny toes.

Forty-nine

'Shall we go for a walk?' asks the Prince. It is morning. The Chick thinks maybe the day will never end we will walk together for ever and then go back to the house and he will forget to leave and the Great Wall in his eyes will crumble and the doves will be reinstated, *coo coo coo*.

'Yes,' says the failed murderess, 'that would be nice.' Her voice is as flat as her mother's chest. Pinball is without breasts but her mouth is enlarged with sadness. What can I do for my sister?

'Where would you like to go?' he asks.

'It doesn't matter,' says the crushed one, 'you choose. Maybe somewhere flat.'

The Prince of Rocks thinks of his Slimy Fish rising up from the waters singing and dancing, Let's go here let's go there, and of rolling and bouncing in her wake not having to do or not to do and just the thought makes his shoulders to jut out and his eyes to glint with glinting but he knows the Chick is looking up at him waiting for him to tell her where they should go and now he's thinking, How is she going to live without me telling her what to do? But that is a thought unworthy of a brave and righteous rock so he replaces it with, She will live. Somehow she will live.

To bring its own ease the rock must learn to crush.

Ouf.

They walk along a wide and bending river to the grounds of a stately home. They walk through the gardens and through yew bushes cut into fancy geometrical shapes. Beyond this is an open field with many cows and the many cows are looking back at them. The Chick is trying to figure out why the cows don't come into the garden to trample the flowers and deposit cowpats on the tidy paths. 'Why is that?' she asks the Prince for he is still as One Who Knows.

He takes her by the hand as he would a daughter. He walks her closer so she can see the ditch which separates them from the cows and he explains, 'It's called a "ha ha".' And she looks into the ditch and she says, 'But you promised. You said you would never leave me, you said for ever', and when the Prince says nothing she looks at the cows and the cows look back at her and so it comes to pass that now she understands.

Hoo ha, a *ha ha*.

Fifty

The eye and the fat head and all the other parts of the adulterer wait for twilight to say bye-bye.

So it was that the Prince passed backwards out the door like a man afraid for his rear end. He carried a big blue suitcase. He shut the door behind him, an eager but also a reluctant man. A shutting of shuttings, amein.

The Chick watched the door in its closing the Prince in his backwards parting.

'Bye-bye,' he said.

She played the scene backwards like this. *The door reopens, the Prince plonks down his suitcase he comes towards her, Oh welcome back my rock my fortress my deliverer my high tower and my refuge!*

But he did not do this.

She stood looking at an upside-down strip of wallpaper little green flowers on a creamy ground until she could not distinguish right-side-up from upside-down. She said to herself in the language of received wisdom, Pull up your socks. She wore no socks. She heard a bird imitating a telephone, *bring bring*, she ran to answer it there was no one there. She heard laughing. Birds sheep cows horses deer, even the sea worms stood up and laughed, Oh to see such sport! as the

Prince ran away with his big blue suitcase.

She took hold of the knob of the pine banister behind her. She waited for the earth to shake and tremble for the foundations of heaven to be moved by His wroth for the Prince's car to be devoured by fire for darkness to ride under his feet, and so on and so forth, dark pavilions round about him, dark waters thick clouds lightning and blasts of righteous destroying breath, etc.

But all that happened was that the door of their cottage (shiny nursery blue) was pulled to and the Prince got into his car and drove off leaving a trail of exhaust fumes hanging in the air.

PART SIX

Behold I will do a new thing.
Isaiah 43:19

Fifty-one

I lift up my voice and cry, Him!

I holler to God saying, Lord of the world you see the humiliation of those who have been humiliated you see my Keziah's crushed heart. Give me light give me a sign give me a clue. Tell me what to do, Lordy.

He tells nothing.

I rent my housedresses every one of them, even six and as big as tents. I sprinkle salt on top of my head facing heaven. Still nothing. What am I to do? 'Put shoes on thy feet and Do.' What voice is that? A voice. 'Do what?' I ask of it.

'Go forth.' Pinball's rocker rocks forward backward backward forward. She raises up her paddles to the stars the stars wink back. Golden toerings she is no more adorned with gravedirt. Her posts are sunk into the ground she swings on her gate like a girl.

'Go forth do what?'

'Put arguments in your mouth. Put toothdust in his. Rescue the remnant deliver the Chick. Take away his nose and his ears fling the giblets on the fire.'

Hah! This I like! I smite my hands together. 'He shall be no more remembered.'

My heart makes a noise in me. 'Heart poo,' says the Pin,

'you ate a whole pot of butter beans.' She holds on to her nose I hold forth the finger. But she's right I have as it were brought forth wind.

'My bowels my bowels!' I cry. What help for Keziah I cannot help myself?

My sister is a slit of eyeball. She points east across the water saying, 'Go! Help! Fly upon his shoulders!'

'What am I an airplane? An outsized fiery flying serpent? This thing I cannot do.'

'Do!'

'How?'

'Fart on him!' She rocks with the sweet jerkiness of doing revenge. Smoke rises from her mouth's place, soft fluff falls from her once-were feet they rub together in glee. She smells a lot better than I do.

I am a bath toy in her hands. Squeeze me, O my sister, my servant my sidekick. I spout my willingness up to heaven. I wag my tail I flip my flippers my mouth curves in a stupid grin. 'Just tell me how.' I bat my false eyelashes. Maybe I could get a job in Disneyland.

'Swim who cares.' In death she can Do, we can all Do. She could conduct the London Philharmonic in wetsuits under the Atlantic.

'Go by boat.'

'*Boat*? What about the *Titanic*?'

'What about it?'

My sister has no more Disaster Drawer she has no more disasters.

'How could you forget one of your favourite clippings? Shoes,' I remind her, 'how can you forget the shoes?' Found by a deep-sea diver in the bowels of the sunken ship. Little children's shoes women's shoes men's shoes. The clothes got eaten the skeletons got eaten but the shoes were left, fish do not care for tannic acid.

'Then fly,' she says, 'it's quicker.'

'What about the PLO? What about the poor people who

were hijacked who were made to walk through rivers with crocodiles? What about all the people who were crushed by birds falling from the sky over Africa . . .'

I see smoke I see a curling lip I see two sisters one alive one dead rocking their way through the rest of the day. I hear Not Interested in Excuses. I hear Africa Is Not on the Flight Path to London.

I see that I am going.

My Chick, let me tell you something about your mother. Your mother was once a straight tree beautiful in her smoothness and in her multitude of thick branches. Not like me a hairy stump. But she was plucked up by the men in uniform who devoured her fruit and she became broken and withered and her branches became things for trailing over the arms of her rocker. Let me stop there.

All that is over. And yet not over. It may be too late for Pinball too late for me but not for the Chick.

Revenge upon the one who seduced our Keziah saying for ever for ever and she was stupid enough to believe him and she was polluted and she was alienated from us. And there was no forever.

Revenge upon the one who discovered her nakedness and having discovered it said, *I say, you're naked*.

Revenge upon the one with the holes of holiness at his elbows. A man who did spoiling but was not spoiled. A man of privilege who claimed the way was equal.

The way is not equal! Not of gods not of princes. Not!

Therefore let us judge him.

Let us be no more dumb.

Let him hear the noise of my roaring and my sister's howling and all our roarings and howlings.

Let us raise up our voices and cry, 'Tail!'

Overturn overturn overturn.

Enough. It is time. Time to Do. For Keziah for Pinball for me throw in Queen Vashti while we're at it. She was the one who refused to come when King Ahasuerus crooked his fat little finger saying 'Come.' And she did not come so he kicked her out and replaced her with Esther.

I will do against the Prince and Arthur and Moosa and King Ahasuerus.

Watch out Dog Prince here comes Adolf the American Beauty. A face of whiskers and more whiskers. A wherewithal full of scissors and knitting needles for poking and slicing and stabbing the caul of your heart. A beast from a far country and her beautiful sister from the end of heaven with weapons of indignation just for you, Sweetie-pie.

You.

I am sent. We are sent.

A mother does not forget her sucking child even after she is planted in the wilderness.

'I'll phone to let her know I'm coming.'

'Don't.'

'Why not?'

'She will not approve of this thing. She will get in your way. You must do this thing alone.'

'Oh that I knew where I might find him! That I might come even to his seat!'

'You will find. Even to his seat which is a high seat but also a low seat.'

'Haha haha! My face will I turn to him!'

'Your belly also. This will cause his bowels to turn to *schav*.' This is spinach soup. This is Spoken.

I rock. Pinball is right. Who else will wipe the nose of the dog in what he has done?

Let me obey.

Let me go.

Let me not shake like *ptchia* which is calf's foot jelly.

'Be not afraid,' says my sister the rocking one.

I put off mourning I put off sackcloth. I put on a green dress with parrots I put Scholl's wide as ships on my feet. Queen Adolf rolls down the Highway of Kings, righteousness in her girdle also Playtex. I go to High Flyer Travel I find my spurious sister hanging around the doorway. I say to the girl at the desk, 'One ticket to London, England.'

'When would you like to travel, madam? If you go before the end of April it's still low season.'

'Low season.' I smile with all the spaces between my teeth. Fee fie fo fum I smell the blood of an Englishman, poo. Pinball's wings stretch upwards.

Here we come.

Fifty-two

The airplane came down with a vengeance upon the landing strip and I vomited into my vomit bag. May the pouches under his eyes decide to droop. I sat and I sat. I sucked on sucking candies. I saw rain. What am I doing here?

The whole plane emptied yea even the pilot with his Adidas bag. A stewardess came to me saying, 'Do you know where you're going?' And I said, 'I am going. I am sent.' She directed me to a Tourist Information Office.

At Euston Station there were no chairs for the consideration of jet-lagged avenging angels so I stood among the many until a voice said unto me, 'May I help you?' And I said, 'He is the one who is going to need help when I'm finished with him.' I bought a ticket. Return. 'I plan to return,' I told.

I walked with my wherewithal and my rolling ship's feet down to the last platform and there I lifted my chubclubs into a car saying First Class Only, nice and pink. Warm. A man in a uniform took my ticket. 'I'm afraid you can't sit here it's first class only.' I said, 'You *should* be afraid.' Hoo ha, he punched my ticket. I took off my Scholl's I put my feet up on the upholstery. I snored through my holes.

One hour and one hour and one hour, add them up. A long time. My merchandise was not fresh stuff. Never mind. I picked it up I turned it sideways Justice doing a shufflestep down the aisle. I saw a door behold no handle. I kicked with my feet, oh let me out. 'Use your head,' says a voice, I know that voice. So I slide down the window I stick my head out I turn the handle and lo! a sack of old woman tumbles out on to the platform. Welcome to England.

Men in blue run to me from all directions.

'Hot sweet milky tea, there you are, madam, drink that.'

Where's the lemon?

'Drink up, there's a good girl.'

Girl? Listen, my bones and sinews may be bruised but my fist is still fat.

They take defensive measures. Three of them it takes to lift me up.

'Oopsa, easy . . .' I'm on my feet. Hello feet.

'Do you know where you're going, madam?'

I know where I'm going and I know who's going with me. Pinball are you there?

'Are you sure you're all right, love?'

'Love, feh, take me to a telephone.'

I dial the number of his department. 'Hello?' I say (the voice of the turtle is heard). 'This is Dr Lodz from Poland speaking a colleague of Dr Prince's.' Hoo ha. Pinball's cheerleading warms my cockles also the small of my back which is not small. 'He is there by any chance?' I hold my breath I hold my goose-bumps, this is a cold place. According to my calculations which were the Chick's calculations the Prince is still away on his vacation which was once upon a time the Chick's vacation but is now being enjoyed by the Slimy Fish, feh.

'I'm terribly sorry but Dr Prince is away on holiday.'

'A shame.'

'If you'd like to leave your name and where you're staying, I'll get him to contact you when he returns.'

'When do you expect him back?'

She consults his diary. 'Day after tomorrow.'

'Thank you.' Honey and milk are under my tongue. 'I wonder if you would be so kind as to give me Dr Prince's home address, I seem to have misplaced it. I should like to put a note in his mail box to let him know where I am staying.'

'That won't be necessary, Dr Lodz. I'll make sure to tell him as soon as he comes in.'

'That is very kind of you but perhaps he comes to his house earlier than to his office. In which event it would be better to leave the note at his house. You don't mind giving it to me I am not from the secret police?'

'Well, as I said, I don't think you need bother but if you insist . . .'

So she gives so I thank.

So he shall know I am in the midst of England.

I say bye-bye to my admirers in blue.

A taxi is waiting outside the station a nice-looking lady driver. 'Take me to a butcher.' She takes me to a place called the Covered Market, very historical. Also very chilly but it has what I need. I get back in the taxi we drive up a long steep hill at the top she stops.

Where is the house of the prince? asks Job. *Where is the dwelling place of the wicked?*

'This is it,' says the taxi driver.

I look around. 'A nice neighbourhood.' Now I am here I am in no hurry. 'Crawling with academics from the university,' she tells. I see hookworms and palmerworms whatever they are and cankerworms and most of all heartworms, feh.

'A nice view.'

'On a clear day you can see the Lake District.'

'Harrison's Tickle, my niece told me all about it.'

She laughs. 'I think you mean Harrison *Stickle*.'

'What's that smell?' I ask for it is disgusting.

She says, 'The Smell. Nightingale Farm,' she explains. 'Just over the hill next to the slaughterhouse. They melt down animal carcasses and such like. On hot days it makes you sick just to drive through.'

I have made the stink of your camps to come up unto your nostrils.

'Thank you.' I give her a big tip.

I stand at the front door with my wherewithal in one hand my shopping bag in the other. I look up, the stone face of the house looks down. A grey face a cold face a rising-up face a slab of judgement. Up up up such a house I have never seen. Pinball says it must be a prison. All houses are prisons to Pinball. No, I tell her, this one is not for locking up, this one is for letting out. A running-away-from-wives house, a starting-over house. How does a person visit such a house?

Pinball has the look of one who is about to smite with blasting. Wait, I say, but she huffs and puffs and pretty soon I can feel the ground tremble, *may it develop a crack even unto its foundations* ... I hold on to the wall and I do chatter like a parakeet. Mine eyes begin to fail, do I see what I see? For there is now a great crack up the nose of the house. Will it fall down an heap of stones around my feet? I hold out my hand. 'Do me a favour,' I beg the Pin, 'not yet, there's work to do first.' Pinball says don't worry the crack will do its work in its own sweet time.

So now we go around to the back door where I look with my eyes and I see a doormat for the wiping of shoes even fancier than Arthur's Florsheims. I bend down I pull a piece of cold rod out from under the mat. A sister to dragons a listener to the professional secrets of a pinball prophet. My sister Annie couldn't get out in life but in death she has a talent for breaking and entering.

A key.

The smell of fresh wood, just-dry varnish. A kitchen of golden flooring squares of cork so shiny I can see my face in it which is no blessing. A kitchen of such starting-over-again-ness I want to do it an injury. But I have more important things to do first.

I have come prepared.

I am ready.

I am ready to cut away the thickening around the Prince's heart I am ready to crouch behind doors for seven days and seven nights I am ready to fall on my whiskery face. Pinball counsels, 'First gather your strength.' So I do. I sit down I nibble a cookie called Digestive. I sip English tea with astonishment, the Prince keeps no lemons in his love nest.

I am tired. My teabag dangles my cup runs over with stupid smiling green painted frogs. A plague of frogs on his head! Into his porcelain sunken sink and into his two-tone plastic electric kettle and into his German-imported dishwasher. May they come up his house an army of hopping frogs even into his drainpipes!

What is this kitchen? I see dark-blue cupboards an openness of shelves an army of glass jars filled with different colour beans and rice and nuts and raisins and tea, yea even up to the ceiling.

Lights shining down on my head sneaky spotlights sunk into black holes. Hot and dazzling. Who-goes-there lights. Lights to make Adolf sink with her chubknees on to his glazed floor where she can see her own face a terrible face a face that has flown thousands of miles that may have left half its features in the clouds.

May his gaily coloured beans leap from their jars his cheese grow bruised-looking fur in his refrigerator. . . .

Pinball, what are you doing?

Doing. Scattering his beans all over his floor, may he break a leg.

Two legs and a hip.

Beans, pih. Enough. The time has come for me to Do.

Up the Prince's staircase. A wideness of white a glossiness of paint a carpeting of gall green a curving of banister a sprigging of young leaves on the walls. *I dreamed I broke into a prince's house in my 42-E specially constructed feedbags.* Hah! Inside my breasts are great and nearly as ugly as my face. They say if Abraham Lincoln ran for president of the United States today he would not be elected. It's a good thing I never wanted to be president. One flight two flights yea even up to the Prince's tower bearing my shopping bag with me.

'Will there by anything else?' asked the butcher a nice man peradventure I'll pay him a visit on my way home. 'Could you by any chance sell me a little extra blood?' A wideness of teeth a twinkling of gap. 'Blood pudding,' he said, 'nothing like it in the world when it's made right, the wife never uses enough blood in my opinion but never mind.' 'I also like a lot of blood,' I showed him the tip of my tongue. 'As a matter of fact I always use more than it calls for.'

He gave me an extra pint, no charge.

Toodle-oo.

Fifty-three

A nd now—
 Howl ye. (For the day of Adolf is at hand!)

I come to spoil houses (safe and steep!).

I come with fire in my bones and the tools of my trade (hah!) in my shopping bag.

I come with a bosom of loose boulders.

With the feet of a golem. (Also the feet of a chicken!)

With a born-again dragon called Pinball breathing down my neck.

I come.

The Prince's study, it waits at the top of his house. 'It can afford to wait,' says the dragon.

Up up and more up, a lot of stair carpet he has here. Please. A rest. Two minutes. My fatness my fatness, woe unto me!

'Up, Adolf, up!'

What, am I a dog? Throw me a bone? Better yet, throw me *him*! My chubsticks could make butter with so much churning!

'Lift thy tongue from the floor!'

'Shut up, I'm coming.' I reach for the banister I grab on. Praise be She sends a lion to rumble his tower (who will not fear?)—

Rumble rumble rumble!

The Prince's study is a fine thing. A runway of white desk an avenue of machines a wall of books and high. Over the desk a sloping roof and in that roof a skylight and through that skylight a prancing of clouds.

I collapse into his desk-chair it tilts me back to an angle of reposeful repose. I remove my Scholl's I place my feet like a calamity upon his desk. Oh let me to lie back and dream of Othellos and bringers of Othellos. Of birds of sisters of rocking rockers of. . . .

'Later,' says Sergeant-Major Pinball.

'Leave me alone.' I put forth my middle finger.

'UP, FATSO, UP! NOW! GET TO WORK!' A bubbling and smoking, her cheese boils over and pinkly. 'Have you forgotten what you came to Do?'

Doing. I am reminded.

I have come to make him a miscarriage.

To recompense him for his iniquities and the iniquities of his father and all his fathers together which have blasphemed against us with all the length of their woolly green socks.

Toenail I call him.

Worried I call myself.

How shall I do this thing?

In the airplane there sat a man beside me I said to him, 'How do you do?' He said he was in computers. 'Very interesting,' I said. He showed me disks he explained how they work. 'And people use such things for writing books?' I inquired, already I was an Englishwoman my tongue was a paddle for cream mixed with peach nectar and more cream. 'Whole books,' he explained, 'can be reduced to the size of a floppy.' Floppy, I liked floppy. 'You don't say,' I said. And he said, 'Of course it can also be a hard disk.'

'You don't say!' He didn't even mind me repeating myself.

'State of the Art,' he replied.

'But tell me,' cooed the turtledove, 'can these floppies be . . . destroyed somehow?'

'Erased. No problem. You can wipe these things out just like that –' and he made to snap two of his chubfingers but they slid rather than snapped because of being smeared with American Airlines chicken grease. And I said to him, 'Now how would a person do such a thing supposing a person wanted to do such a thing?'

And he said, 'Nothing to it.'

'HOW?' His tray rattled his fork which was upside-down in his mouth pierced his tongue. I gave him my napkin. And his answer came forth bedewed with only a few drops of blood. 'A magnet.' And I said he would be blessed.

Fifty-four

I sit at the Prince's desk and what do you think I see before me?

How did you guess?

I take them out of their plastic boxes I line them up one beside the other. I make them to stretch out like little black boxcars of a train chugging across a white landscape. I see wheels revolving through snow I smell smoke I smell burning bones. (How should I forget these things?)

I unwrap the magnet from its tissue paper. 'A gift for my son-in-law,' I told the man at the hobby shop. I touch it to my lips. Cold. Here, let me warm you up. I drop it between my breasts.

Oooh.

I open the first flat plastic box the disk slides into my hand. Two beady eyeholes a magnetic nose a white plastic mouth saying 'O'. Prepare yourself, O Floppy One, for you are about to be wiped clean yea even unto innocence. My cleavage is hot so is my magnet. I wave it over this and all his other disks—

Once.

Twice.

Three times—

It is Done.

I pull a peach from my wherewithal I sink my teeth into its flesh, juice dribbles down my chin. And now I spit the pit at the Slimy-eyed Fish whose picture is tacked to a bulletin board above the Prince's desk. *Thuck*.

What now?

Look around.

Adolf, a seamstress, the wife of nobody – have I done this thing?

'You have Done,' says my sister. 'But not enough.'

'Have a heart (ha!).' Her spangly winglets flutter all about me.

'To work, Adolf! Time!'

Time, pih. I am weariness I am hot fat poured out (hot Adolf!) congealing fast. Cold lard, feh.

Oh let me rest. Let me wrap myself up in princely blankets Sleepy the Dwarf of exceeding proportions curled up upon his floor, thick carpeting praise be. Let me snooze let me dream dreams.

I'm coming, my Chick. Soon I will hold you in my arms and the heat of my breasts and belly will be as a womb in their warmth and in their holding and when they open and let go you will slide out as one reborn. And then I will give you suck and dandle you upon my chubknees. As one whose mother wasn't so good at comforting because she had other things on her mind, so will I comfort you. And when I tell you about what I have done to the Prince and all his floppies you will rejoice with your feet and your teeth will laugh and all your bones will dance in their sockets.

I always wanted blonde pigtails. Little Mary Janes on my feet, one strap two straps ankles narrow as new trees.

Goldilocks me, tee hee.

Skip skip skip to my Chick.

Oh but I have come such a long way! And now I must rest. But what's this? Bless me, a king-sized bed!

Goldilocks oozes in and snoozes away but pretty soon (do

you guess?) in lumbers an angry Prince of Bears. 'And who is sleeping in MY bed?' Rumble rumble. He hearkens diligently with much heed and cries: 'BEHOLD A LION!'

But it was only a dream.

Fifty-five

Morning. Light like a pearl prised from the unwilling mouth of an oyster. Poetry, pih. I am tired I am old I am not unacquainted with grief. I do not want to do what I am about to do. My legs are stumps with many rings, I have to bribe them to go back upstairs. Soon soon I promise them the mountain before ye shall break into song, you will become light as teabags you will fly up like the limbs of a young girl. 'Tell us another one,' says Pinball. 'When you were a girl your legs were even worse than they are now.' The marches didn't help. I look down I see the front half of an elephant.

'Soon they shall rejoice,' she promises.

'Easy for you, Twinkletoes, me I have to walk every step.' One foot two feet three feet four.

'Lift up your eyes on high, what do you see?'

'Stairs and more stairs.'

'And at the top?'

'The Prince's study.'

'Good. Go to it. Do what you need to Do.'

Annie, what are you telling me to do?

OK I know. I have been playing story books I have been making small mischiefs. A melting of disks a flinging of beans.

Enough it is time.

I feel a weakness coming on.

'Faint not,' says my winged counsellor. 'The sun shall be turned into darkness the moon into blood.' (My sister prophesies an eclipse.) Up and down the stairwell flowers cry out of their wallpaper.

Prepare thyself, Princeling, I come to bring illumination.

Tee hee.

Hard copies. This is what the man on the airplane called them. It's no use wiping out disks he said if there are still hard copies around. So I gather them up from his desk from his shelves from his file cabinet from the four corners of the room. Papers upon papers letter upon letter note upon note bibliography upon bibliography curriculum vitae upon curriculum vitae manuscript upon manuscript, an heap as high as the skylight.

I am a dwarf before it.

'You are a veritable lion and don't you forget it.'

Veritable, I like veritable.

Such important writings.

'Pork scratchings.'

Amein.

It is time.

Let his roots be plucked up.

Let the lies of the defiler be consumed and let ashes only remain under the soles of his feet.

My matches are hot.

My chicken is dead.

My blood hoppeth around in its container.

'Stand,' commands Pinball. So I stand upon my feet which are the feet of a great clay thing, my bunions twinkle in their stockings.

'Off!' howls the voice that was my sister's.

What off?

'Strip! Undress!' Pinball slides across the skylight. The One Who Has Been Eclipsed passes over the moon.

We are ready.

I roll down my stockings my garters come too. I unhook the great contraption of my brassière my breasts are loosed, Beware of Falling Rocks!

The beast opens her jaws, out of the cave a roar so hot it shoots forth flame.

Toe, you are torched.

I hear howling I hear crackling. Hot hot rivers run down between my breasts.

My chicken sprawls across his desk. I grab its beak I stick its neck between my teeth. I bite I tear, off comes the head, *ptheh*. I pluck away its crop I cast it beside the altar on the east side by the place of the ashes. The rest of the head I toss on the fire.

'Don't forget the salt!'

All around I sprinkle salt. (Spice it well and let the bones be burnt!) And now I dance I swing my chicken round and round I fling the extra pint of blood given by the butcher. A splattering of walls a sizzling a jumping of fire. Pinball, what do you have to say? I think I see her doing the shag.

Sometimes life is fun even for a prophet!

Our duet is great, it goes out from the skylight it fills the sky. Around and around, swinging and flinging, going and weeping, doing and singing. My song is the roar of a lion, Pinball's is a dragon's howl, somewhere I hear the glad yell of the dragon's whelp. An astonishment and an hissing. Woe unto him.

The fire burns. My legs, as Pinball promised, have become as grasshoppers'. Up and down go my poignancies. Hoo ha, I am hopping I am swinging.

Around and around.

Pinball hands me a bottle, what bottle is this? An opened bottle. A bottle from the Prince's wine cellar. A putting down place a rack of racks a crusty nest of faith in the future. A bottle growing mould and moss, a label as unreadable as human behaviour. Now I lay me down to sleep I pray the Lord my claret to keep.

With one hand I fling blood with the other wine.

How much better is thy wine than thy love, eh, Princeling?

His words are charred screws.

His disks are become floppied unto melting.

Judgement runs down my chin, it drippeth off my ledges. It also drips down his walls.

Ho ho, what would he say if he could see me now?

And he hearkened diligently with much heed and he cried: A lion!

But this is not what he says. (For, yes, he stands before me.) 'Adolf,' he says conversationally. Only the hole of his mouth standing open reveals anything unusual is going on here.

'YOU!' My voice is terrible my face is even worse. My teeth are blunt and staggered my claws reach out. I am ringed round with fire. (Did he flee from the Chick and a lion met him?)

Again I cry, 'YOU!' A fatness of fury feeds my flame. Who can stand before my indignation and not fall over?

The Prince tilts not even an inch.

'IT SHALL BE WHOLLY BURNT!' My face gathers blackness the ceiling above me also gathers blackness. Blackness upon blackness swirled with red, my eyes see these pretty things. Round and round I spin, my chicken also spins I stretch forth a finger I open my mouth against him saying, 'AHA! AHA!'

And then I fall upon his feet. English leather, not nice to nosebones.

Fifty-six

'The Torah is called a fiery law.' A charred voice. Mine, it crawled out of its burnt hole.

'So I gather.' A voice from on high but deeper than Pinball's.

'Is that you, Arthur?' I sniff, something smells terrible. Me. Am I an offering? 'What is that?'

'Don't try to talk.' A feather caressing an unidentifiable body part.

'Where are my eyes?' Fried eggs over well, see how they curl around their edges.

'The lids are rather badly burnt,' says the Voice. 'They're swollen shut.'

'Am I blind?'

'I think not, though it may be some time before you can see out of them. But I can tell you you're lucky to be alive.'

'Who's telling me?'

The one I call Prince.

'Don't be stupid. I burnt his house down. Stubble and smoke, melted floppies, splattered blood and wine. What a mess!' My tongue filled my head, a cow's tongue is also black. 'He wouldn't dare come near me after what I did. Besides, he's still away studying the joy of fish. May he choke on the bones.'

The voice chokes. 'Fortunately I came home a day earlier than expected.'

'Whose fortune?'

'Another few more minutes and you would have been dead of smoke inhalation.'

'I did it for Keziah.'

'I know.'

'Where is my Chick?' My clothes were always too small for my body, now my skin is even smaller.

'I gather she'll be here any minute. I'm afraid. . . .'

What is this man so afraid of?

Once upon a time he opened the front door of his house, he smelled smoke he ran up to his study three steps at a time. There he saw something the shape of an overstuffed armchair, flames leaping from its cushions also curses. The armchair was me. He put his arms around it he dragged it out of the room, the skylight exploded into the night.

I am toast.

'I must go now,' says the rescuing hero.

'Why did you come?'

'To make sure you were all right.'

Hoo ha, a man schooled in forgiveness. A wonderful thing to behold. He turns to leave. If I could move my right leg his nose would be dust.

'The point, Princeling, is that I destroyed your hard words and your soft words. I turned your tower into a red sea. At least sue me for property damage.'

He shakes his head. The Earl Grey smile (oil of Bergamot, feh) I did not need eyes to see. 'You're rather the worse for wear yourself, so I reckon we're even.'

He reckons. The black hole opens the tongue of the cow will not rest.

'Who the hell are you to reckon?'

'Letisha, please,' he shushes.

Please what? 'If you are God who am I?'

'Really, Letisha, this righteous indignation is a bit much.'

'Louse! Boil! Harlot!'

'Look, leave it alone could you? You're in a fragile physical state not to mention a rather volatile emotional state and. . . .'

'BLOW IT OUT YOUR NOSE!' Thus speaketh the preacher in the doorway, the preacher is Keziah. O sprung daughter of Jerusalem, come to me!

The Prince turns he sees the wife of his youth. No more.

'I've come to see my Aunt.'

He does not step aside. 'I must warn you she's not a pretty sight.'

'She never was.'

She sits on my sheets. 'Look at you,' she says.

How? I am cooked I am stubble I am blind.

'You look terrible.'

'Tell me.'

'You really want to know?'

I want.

She examines she tells. 'Well, first of all there are black tracks down your cheeks. Also some kind of black crust around your mouth and nostrils. Your eyes are all closed up – I guess you know that – and the lashes and eyebrows burnt off. The rest of you is mostly covered in bandages.' She reaches out. 'Your hair is, God, matted like some old wool sweater that's been put in the washing machine by mistake. And – this is the worst – you smell terrible.'

I don't smell a thing.

'Aunt Adolf, what have you done to yourself?'

Hoo ha, what I have Done.

PART SEVEN

Then lifted I up mine eyes, and looked, and behold, there came out two women, and the wind was in their wings ...
Zechariah 5:9

Fifty-seven

She was busy with her griefwork. Three hours and three hours she sat each morning on her floor and wept. She went forth to her kitchen she boiled water her teabag dangled down. Camomile tea and mashed bananas, feh. At least add soured cream I advised which is protein which is fat. She shook her ears, 'It's good for me to come here. It gives me a purpose. You are my medicine.'

She was right. Twice a day she visited me in hospital. She wore desolation she wore the same stupid brown track suit. If I was toast she was crust. The one left behind. The one torn off. Remnant of her people.

'Don't give him the power,' I told.

'He's got it. He took it.' Hoo ha, the big blue suitcase.

'Take it back.'

'How?'

'You'll find out.'

'When?'

'Soon.'

They let me out of hospital. She took me home to her cottage which was once their cottage. (Good! All yours! Claim rights! Claim furniture! Celebrate freedom!) She fed me she washed me she did doody duty, double feh. She dressed my burns they looked more presentable than she did. The slow and careful child worked for a month on my hair.

And still she mourned and faded away and drove a yellow library van and languished and faded and saw to her Disaster Drawer and what was I Adolf the charred to do?

I watched and I waited. I rocked without a rocker.

I exercised feet I exercised skin. I learned to blink I learned to smile. Adolf the merry-hearted, pih.

Her teeth would not smile.

Walking. Learning to walk. This we can Do together.

Let not the skin of one thigh rub against the skin of the other. Left foot right foot arms hooked not-so-merrily we roll along, a blistered behemoth and a cracked cork. (O flotsam, floating in the mighty waters of his leaving!) The way is holey the way is slow, four gravesticks in a row. Mine are growing new skin Keziah's are sprouting new hairs. Hoo ha, another whiskery old woman in the making.

Whoa, cowlady needs a rest. No kind of walking is easy for me this is not easy walking. Limestone pavement she calls it. Soft stone worn away by rain. It's like walking in Goliath's mouth he hasn't been to the dentist recently. I stare down between two molars I see green fur. Moss ferns lichens she informs. It makes me dizzy. 'Don't look down,' she says. So I look up to the sky I close my eyes I see fire. In my sleep I also see fire.

Keziah sees the Prince walking out the door backwards carrying his big blue suitcase with the leather schoolboy's belt around it. He raises his Chinese cowboy hat he trips on the doormat in his urgency. Over and over again she relives this scene.

My scene is otherwise. The Prince walks *in* not *out*. He faces forwards not backwards. He drags his cargo (yea a great and a lumpy thing) wrapped in blankets down a staircase. There comes forth smoke from its nostrils. Stairs and more stairs bump bump bump a classy removal man's work is never done.

Everlasting burning pih.

What I have Done. What I have *not* Done.

Annie, forgive.

Keziah, forgive.

My mouth is tired of mourning my throat is dried I could drink up a river. My stomach rumbles (so much walking!), beware a blasting of the terrible one. I go and stand by the stove which is called a cooker. 'Something to eat,' I say. It is no question. She puts one hand to her stomach a nothing stomach. Her throat still refuses passage. A closing down of holes.

Broth I name she does not say no. So I put things in a pot, vegetables onions carrots celery butter beans barley garlic seasonings. I let it cook the smell fills the house. We sit beside a fireplace painted a colour which is not grey not blue. Slate she calls it.

I place a bowl white with a blue rim on her lap. 'Be careful it's hot.' I wrap her fingers around the spoon. A heavy spoon a long journey from bowl to mouth. 'Blow, it's hot.' She makes a small disturbance in its surface. 'Eat!' I order. She puts the spoon against her lips but the lips do not open the mouth does not receive. This I have seen before in her mother.

There is only one thing to do.

'Aunt Adolf, what are you doing?'

'Doing.' I do not wait for objections. I tip a tipple of soup into her mouth it stays there it settles around the teeth the tongue but it cannot stay there for ever.

'Now swallow.' A noisy gulp an obedient child. 'There was that so bad?' Broth watered with tears, pih.

Fifty-eight

Once upon a time it was the Prince's birthday. What thing does he love best? Maps! Keziah his wife went to a special office called Ordnance Survey and she marched in saying, 'Give me the biggest map you have.' And they said, 'I beg your pardon?' 'The biggest map you have.' Still they did not understand. 'How do you mean *big*?' They tried discussing a thing called 'scale'. She would not discuss. 'No no I mean big as in BIG. There!' she cried pointing to a red leather binder with gold lettering and as tall as a building. 'What about that one? That one they told had every map in the country, large scale special edition paper she couldn't possibly afford it. She said, 'I'll take it.' ('Hallo? Aunt Adolf, can you wire me some money quick, I'll pay you back.')

He knelt down before her she held it out to him. For a moment they were joined by that flat red sea. 'What is this?' 'You'll see,' she said and so he Saw. 'Where on earth did you get these?' 'On earth,' she replied. His Ordnance Surveys runneth over. Beside his Book he was a stick figure as it were jumping up and down yea he was pleased with his present.

But now—

Do I hear crackling? rending?

Five in the morning. She sits in the middle of the living-room floor pulling her poignancies to her. Rock rock back and forth back and forth she does it without a rocker. Now she puts the soles of her feet together her knees drop open. Two divided thighs two open broken wings. She gathers them together sticks them straight out in front of her. Beat thy kettledrums with heels. She is ready.

She lays the Great Book across her lap it reaches to her feet like a skirt. She opens its red leather covers. She removes the first page with tearing. She does not look to see which part of the country it represents. She spends the next hour tearing up and chewing up and spitting out the entire United Kingdom, page after page, *feeyuch*.

The room is filled with crumply waves.

Back and forth back and forth.

I go to her in her rough sea I pick up one of the paper waves. Lines and signs a pictorial representation of every square inch of country, the Prince was a man who never got lost although he was known to remark on occasion, 'We're not exactly found.'

She drools she spits paper, fury has paid a visit to her bones and sinews at last thanks be. If she can't tear out his heart at least she can tear up his maps.

This she is Doing.

'Haha haha! Do more!'

So she Does so we Do. Snap crackle pop get your red hot Ordnance Survey Popcorn Balls! We toss we juggle our balls are hot so are we. Pop pop on the fire. Popcorn to popcorn ashes to ashes, amein.

And now—

'Oh God what have I done?' On her belly she swims in that tear-popped sea.

'What you have Done.'

Doing, pih. She is more torn than maps her fury has deserted her as he has. 'Shit,' she blubbers forth, 'now I have to clean up all this mess. What the hell did I do this for?'

'For Doing.'

Scrunched-up ball by scrunched-up ball I throw the remainder of the Prince's ordinances into the fireplace. This is fun! This is good! I try puting one of the map-balls into her hand but her wrist is without power of propulsion it lands between her legs.

She is flopped she is played out, her head lands in my lap. Her forehead is a hot forehead her words are cold words. 'Christ, what a waste. What a useless exercise.' This I deny. 'The sad revenge of a discarded wife,' she insists. 'Stupid, empty, meaningless, *petty* act. I feel so ... helpless,' she wails into my lap. 'What did it accomplish?'

'It accomplished. He is no more the owner of a special thing.'

'Big deal. Now I'm the owner of an oversized empty map binder, what am I supposed to do with it?'

'Smack him with it! A menstruous cloth on his head!'

She tries to laugh her success is only so-so. She reaches for my chin a whiskery thing. 'Oh, Aunt Adolf.'

'He won't forget,' I tell.

She tells otherwise. She sits up a straight thing on her spine. 'For once you're wrong. He'll forget. I'll give him back the folder he'll start a new map collection. By the end he won't remember my name.'

Reproach has broken her heart as revenge has broken mine.

We are popped popcorn.

Prophecy, poo.

If only she were wrong.

'Do you remember,' I ask her, 'when I beat up Arthur's floozie later to become his wife?'

She nods she remembers. 'At least you hurt them, you did it with conviction.'

'I did it with a handbag full of nuts. I let her have it. I caused bruises I caused a broken nose.'

I cause myself to stop and consider.

'Aunt Adolf, what is it?'

'What it is is this. You think I felt so wonderful afterwards?'

She reaches up she runs her finger over the stubble of my eyelashes. 'They're growing back,' she tells. Together we rock, a great rocking back and forth as Pinball and I once rocked only this rocking is without chairs only arms and legs and laps and chests and noses all jammed together.

Fifty-nine

'How long can you stay?' she asks.
      'I can stay.'
'What about your birds?'
'A neighbour is feeding them.'
'How is it without Arthur?'
'Without.'
'And Pinball?'
What can I say? Still with? In a manner of speaking?
'I miss her,' I say.
'Me too.' And then she says, 'What would she do if she were here?' Pinball in little England, hoo ha, this is good this I don't have to think about. 'She'd be looking for a machine to play.'
'You mean a *pinball* machine?'
'I mean.'
'Let's go,' she says, 'I know a place. I always wanted to go there. Very seedy.'
'Where?'
'Not far.'
'Can I go without a brassière?' Elastic straps hooks anything tight this is torture. My new skin groweth back and boy is it tender!
'You can go naked for all I care,' she tells.
'Pih, is that so? You want *these* flashing from your passenger

seat?' Behold a pair of stuffed to the gills hot-water bottles slippery pinky bulby globes, oh what bosoms!

The Chick stares I close my robe on my embarrassments saying, 'I'm sorry.' She comes over to me, 'Don't be,' she says. 'It's wonderful. You're wonderful. *They're* wonderful –' she pokes! 'You look like a fertility goddess.'

So the fertility goddess puts on a size 46 T-shirt saying SAVE THE WHALES, loose shorts no underwear flip-flops on her feet.

'OK I'm ready let's go.'

A lot of people a lot of rocks. Floodbreakers explains the Chick this is a place where waves come up halfway to the moon.

She wiggles her little car into a tight spot. Adolf say too much room for manoeuvre cause panic. Didn't I know her mother?

PINBALL HEAVEN. I stop in the doorway my feet say no more. 'What's the matter?' I don't know. I don't like this I'm blocking the way. (In or out, whalelady, which is to be?) Throw me back into the ocean I'll swim home.

'What are we doing here?'

'You wanted to come.'

'I know but now I'm not so sure. What about you?'

She's trying tough. This is fun this is Being Brave this is Doing. Revisiting the Scene of the Crime! Maternity Unit Pinball syle!

'Was I really born in a place like this?'

'No. Not so big not so dark not so noisy. There was only one lonely pinball machine in a corner of the café. The machine and Pinball. She played all day we couldn't pull her away.'

'What was she thinking about?'

'About not thinking.'

'About not being about to give birth?'

'About not being anything. As long as she was attached to the machine she was attached.'

'Let's go,' she says. A little nudge a little easy-does-it and we're in.

CLOUD 999 ... NUDGE NOW ... CRACK THE NUT ... BREAK OR TAKE ... TOP THE LOT ... NUDGE NUDGE ... JOKERS WILD ... 777 HEAVEN. God help us. Someone. Pinball, are you there? Show us the way. Where do we go what do we do? We are balls (one big fat beachball, one little silver one) we are rolling we have no idea where we're going. Fruit machines, feh. Electronic blips scales bubbling honking flashing lights! Help!

Our eyes fail while we wait for God.

'Look,' she points. FUNHOUSE, ADDAMS FAMILY, GHOULS, SPACE STATION ... a line-up of pinball machines. 'Which one should we play?' she asks.

'You choose.'

'How about this one?'

THE GETAWAY. I say fine I say good I say you go first. She puts in 50p a big coin the machine gulps it down shudders throws up a little silver ball.

Praise be.

'What do I do now?'

'Pull that lever.' So she pulls so the spring jumps forward so the silver ball is on its way. MILLION! RPM DRIVE. GO! 'Hit the flippers.' Two little buttons on the side of the machine. Flip flip hit hit she goes. AGAIN AGAIN ... TURBO ... FREEWAY ... LANE CHANGE ... RED LINE ... RED YELLOW GREEN. It's about to fall into the gobble hole. No! I nudge with my stomach all the lights flash at once. DRIVE 65 STAY ALIVE ... SHERIFF 63 BUCKLE UP...

'I did it I did it I did it!' The only one of her mother jumps up and down.

OK UP AGAINST THE CAR BUDDY growls the machine then the whole Arcade goes dark and still. Whistles hoots, 'Hey, what's going on over there?' The attendant comes running.

GETAWAY GETAWAY GETAWAY!

I think we blew a fuse.

Pinball, is that you?

Sixty

By now the Prince had removed all traces of himself including Grandma Hoo Ha's nursing chair, Lord Hoo Ha's golf clubs and if you ask me it makes surprisingly little difference. The Chick's tent is her tent. Not that she knows it yet for she still believes without him she wanders in a wilderness.

Happy wandering!

She handed over his handsome red leather map case (empty). He took it in his arms he pressed it to his chest and I say unto you it was a dangerous moment. He looked down upon the Chick with an *omer* (which is the tenth part of an *epha*) of regret.

Just a minute.

The Prince felt with his hands which were feeling hands that something was wrong: it felt *thin*. So he opened it up and . . . 'What's all this?' The Chick said, 'No more. I tore them up.' He smiled his professional forgiver's smile saying, 'I suppose it's highly symbolic.' The empty book that was his wife also said, 'I suppose.'

Two weeks later he received notification of divorce proceedings against him.

'According to Jewish divorce law,' I tell the Chick, 'a woman has to write a *get*, deliver it to her husband, then he delivers it to her in accordance with the laws of divorce. She may think she is divorcing him but everybody knows he is divorcing her.'

In fact it's the reverse with the Chick. The Prince has left her and therefore 'divorced' her and everybody knows it. And yet if she divorces him legally maybe she will succeed in convincing herself she is getting rid of him.

'It's easy over here.' She holds up a piece of paper. 'All I do is charge him with adultery, get the two of them to sign my piece of paper and that's it.' Do-It-Yourself divorce, pih.

'Make him pay,' I tell.

'I did.'

Praise be no more I do's.

This is progress. A month ago she was on her belly she ate only dust. Now she breathes air, low air but air nevertheless. Peradventure she's on her way up. This I suspect she does not.

We are widows we are cast out we are in mourning. Arthur is no more the Prince is no more.

Another way of putting it is like this. Our lips are our own. No man is lord or prince or lawyer over us.

Haha haha!

Freedom from slavery!

Keziah. I look at her what do I see? An oriental type a head of frizzy reddish hair. One from column A one from column B an original combination. A little buck-toothed a little gap-toothed (thank me!) a little turned in at the toe. One day she will stand she will know she is standing, she will not fall over. Also she will know that no one lifted her up but she lifted herself up. And she will walk with her feet putting one in front of the other saying, it is reasonable.

When you know you resemble a giant clay flowerpot you expect nothing. This is me. If I get something I think Good! So I do not lose.

When you resemble a rose you expect everything. This was Pinball. When she did not get everything she said Not Good on all the somethings. So she lost. We got pricked.

The Chick resembles a flowerpot with graceful flowers stuck in it. Ugly beautiful she expected everything she expected nothing. She expected the Prince to love her she also expected him to leave her.

He co-operated in her expectations. With his big blue suitcase and his Chinese cowboy hat he fulfilled her expectations. A not-so graceful backing out.

Hold your horses. There was one thing she forgot to tell and it is an important telling and it is this.

THE PARTING WORDS OF A PRINCE: 'Just remember I didn't leave you because I didn't love you but because you didn't love me.' He put on his hat he tripped on his doormat which was now her doormat.

So it was her fault. So she was wrong.

Yet she was right (*You will leave me*).

So she won. Yet she lost.

A lot of so's a lot of yet's.

So what two things does she now know?

1. He didn't leave her because he didn't love her (in other words he *did* love her).

2. One day he would forget her name.

Men stupid men.

Sixty-one

Once upon a time a group of worshippers put the horn of the ram to their lips. They turned their faces to the rising sun and blew, *bhoo bhoo*. It was dawn it was Palestine. A long time ago. The call of the shofar was a call to peace. Come! Worship! Give thanks! it said. But the Roman occupation troops heard otherwise. They heard in the call of the shofar *Revolt! Revolt!* so they armed their arms, Let's go. And they felled the blowers, take that. The remnant stood and stood.

The Chick also stood. We stood together beside the shore which is beside her house, a nice spot nettles and brambles and thorn trees notwithstanding. A lot of birds.

'K-peek k-peek,' tells one called oystercatcher.

'Can you see its orange legs?' She shows.

'Also an orange nose.'

'Beak,' she corrects.

'Whatever. A nice outfit.'

K-peek k-peek.

'Which reminds me. You look like an Israeli soldier. What are you hiding from? If I had a shape like yours I'd dress myself up like an oystercatcher very chic.'

'What's the point?' she says. 'It's cold here. Nothing fits me.

I don't go anywhere. Who should I dress up for?'

I do not say k-peek. Instead I say, 'Get in the car.'

'Why? Where to?'

'Drive.'

So we drive to town we find a boutique. Slinky bimbo clothes shoulder pads buckles glitter, hoo ha.

'Here try this.' I smack her in the chest with a little red number a slit up the side.

'Don't be stupid where would I wear that?'

'To cook oatmeal in. OK try this.' A loose silk pantsuit with a long jacket, charcoal grey, soft soft (just like me!). This she tries on this she likes this we buy for her. Well it's an improvement on black.

'What about you?' she asks me.

'These clothes would fit on my nose.'

This she sees is true.

We go home she pushes me down into an archair she lifts my chublegs on to Lady Hoo Ha's embroidered swan hassock. 'You've been taking care of me for months now,' she says, 'it's time I took care of you.'

Taking care, pih.

'You were the one who was nearly burnt to death.'

'Skin grows back.' Skin is easy hearts not so easy, this I do not need to say. I see an unravelling of crimpy red wool piling up beside my rocker. You think you can take care of *me*?

Self-pity, feh.

She brings me a glass of sherry medium sweet just nice. I sit alone while she cooks in the kitchen I raise my pinkie to heaven. Outside I see a porch I see two rockers I see a lot of birdcages. It's time to see to my toilette.

I go upstairs I put on my black satin with the red rose (fabric) the size of a Findhorn cabbage. (That's the place where they say prayers to their vegetables, it shows.) I present myself in the kitchen her oven door drops open.

'Wow, where did you get *that*?'

'I brought it with me you never know when the occasion for celebration will arise.'

'Are we celebrating?'

'We are celebrating.'

She calls me fabulous she calls me extraordinary she calls me Larger Than Life. She tells me I look like a flamenco dancer. I say nothing because once in a while a person needs to believe a lie.

She goes upstairs she puts on her silk suit. Orange hair orange lips even orange socks on her feet. K-peek k-peek, no wonder she likes it here. So long as we don't have to eat oysters.

A real feast. I sit down she pours wine into glasses with stems. She lights candles. She puts the soufflé on the table it has risen up even over the rim of her baking dish. 'We have to eat it right away or it will sink.' She breaks the crust with her spoon I stick my face into the steam. 'Watch out you'll burn your new face.' She puts a dollop on my plate. My mouth is filled with such a yellowy softness it makes me want to cry.

We eat we drink we drink we eat.

Hoo ha, the feast of freedom.

'Kezie, did you ever see a squirrel fly?'

'What?'

'I was sitting in there before looking out your window and suddenly this squirrel took off up up up into the sky as if it grew wings I never saw it land, am I going out of my mind or what?'

'No,' she says, 'you're probably a little drunk.'

We eat pears for dessert also poached in wine. Soft and sweet just like us. She offers me a long bumpy crunchy biscuit to go with it. I take a bite I pretend it's the Prince's spinal column. I chew and chew until there's nothing left.

'Let's go for a stroll,' I say.

'Now?' asks the one who still misses.

'Now.'

'Can you walk?'

'Can a bird hop?'

She in her silk me in my rose. We turn left along her lane which is facing west which is where I'll be going soon. West West and more West. Jenny Brown's Point. 'Who was this Jenny Brown?' I ask. She says all anybody knows about her was she was an old woman who kept pigs two hundred and fifty years ago.

'*An old woman who kept pigs?* Wait a minute let me figure this out. Was she born an old woman? Once upon a time she must have been a *young woman*. When did she start keeping pigs? Nobody knows nobody cares. All they remember is an old woman. Isn't that funny!'

'Definitely drunk,' she pronounces.

'I could come and live here. Adolf the Pig Lady. It wouldn't be bad. We could grow old and smelly and hairy (hairier!) together.'

'You could,' she says, 'there's plenty of room.'

'Or you could come home. Pinball's part of the house is empty. You'd have plenty of room plenty of freedom.'

'I think we better get back,' she says. 'It's too dark for walking you'll break a leg.'

'What are those spiky things?' She says thorn trees or thorn bushes. Already they're losing their leaves they look nervous about it. And now I pose an important question.

ADOLF'S QUESTION TO HER NIECE KEZIAH: 'Why do you suppose God spoke to Moses out of a thorn bush?'

'I give up. Why?'

'To teach us that even an ugly thing like a thorn bush can be filled with beauty.'

'Like you,' she says.

This I like this is progress.

Sixty-two

'What are you looking at?'
'Nothing.'
'What are you doing?'
'Also nothing.' One hand on the door handle one hand on my wherewithal which is on my lap. We're on our way to the airport. A lot of trucks called lorries a lot of rain a lot of spray. Between us a stick with a knob on the end for shifting gears a radio a bunch of used tissues a shrivelled apple core.

'Why are you holding on like that?' Her vision is peripheral.

Because I am. Soon I fly now I hold.

'Relax, we're not going to crash.'

Annie, are you there?

'Look at you,' she says, 'all loaded up like a trolley. At least throw your bag in the back seat, there's plenty of room back there. You might as well get comfortable we have an hour's ride or so.'

'You like these little cars?'

'Shut up,' she says. More progress.

She switches on the radio we do not listen. Soon a big ugly ocean will roll between us. She holds on to her steering wheel I hold on to my stomach which is a rising-up stomach. We are rocked we are blown. Maybe it will rain so hard we'll go bobbing off the motorway a little red Ark with wheels. Who are the creatures of this Ark? Two women. One old one young one big one small, both quite strong. Wait a minute, you can't have an Ark without at least one man one woman, your basic pair. Who says so? It is Written. Poo to what is Written.

'Would you like me to send you Pinball's rocker?'

'What made you think of that all of a sudden?'

'I've been thinking.'

'I don't know. It doesn't sound right. The porch would look unbalanced. You would miss it.'

Missing, pih. No rocker no Pinball no Arthur no Keziah. A sad song but true. Everyone I enjoy is under the ground or at the other end of the earth.

(Will she be there when I get back? Rocking?)

'It doesn't smell too good. You could get it reupholstered. Some nice soft fabric embroidered flowers nice and English.'

'Nah. You keep it. Her ghost would hate it here.'

We stand at the place where you can't go any further without going too far. International departures. 'You'll have to say goodbye here,' they tell.

'Come with me,' I say. I can't move.

'What, now?'

'I'll buy you a ticket.' We're plucking at each other's coats.

'I can't, you know it.'

I know.

'I have to get on with my life. So do you.'

Rocking and sewing and feeding canaries. 'You wouldn't like looking out on a clothes-line full of giant old ladies' bloomers.'

'Don't be stupid. I'd love to spend more time with you but . . .'

But what, my Chick? It would be too easy too familiar we have to do this thing alone. This I know this we both know.

'You'd get bored,' she says. 'You'd probably drown.'

'I'd miss my birds, even my stupid job.'

'Yes.'

'What will you do?'

'I'll Do. I may apply to do a Ph.D.'

'Hoo ha, in what?'

'Coastal ecology.'

'Birds?'

'Among other things.'

'What about your house?'

'I may have to sell give him half.'

Half a house, pih.

'What about your Disaster Box?'

'What about it?'

'The one Pinball sent you.'

'What about it?'

'You've been collecting all these gems?'

She looks at her feet. Standing feet, hosannah!

I say, 'Throw it away. It's time.'

I am foot-looking too. I see jogging shoes with purple stripes. They're standing the feet are standing in them. She looks at mine. Also standing only broader Dr Scholl's triple-E width. The feet walk towards each other close close and then they walk away.

☐ The Wasp Factory	Iain Banks	£5.99
☐ Geek Love	Katherine Dunn	£6.99
☐ The Palace Thief	Ethan Canin	£6.99
☐ The Virgin Suicides	Jeffrey Eugenides	£6.99
☐ Samarkand	Amin Maalouf	£6.99
☐ Unsustainable Positions	Esther Selsdon	£5.99

Abacus now offers an exciting range of quality titles by both established and new authors which can be ordered from the following address:

Little, Brown & Company (UK),
P.O. Box 11,
Falmouth,
Cornwall TR10 9EN.

Alternatively you may fax your order to the above address.
Fax No. 01326 317444.

Payments can be made as follows: cheque, postal order (payable to Little, Brown and Company) or by credit cards, Visa/Access. Do not send cash or currency. UK customers and B.F.P.O. please allow £1.00 for postage and packing for the first book, plus 50p for the second book, plus 30p for each additional book up to a maximum charge of £3.00 (7 books plus). Overseas customers including Ireland, please allow £2.00 for the first book plus £1.00 for the second book, plus 50p for each additional book.

NAME (Block Letters)_____

ADDRESS _____

_____

_____

☐ I enclose my remittance for £_____
☐ I wish to pay by Access/Visa Card

Number ⬚⬚⬚⬚⬚⬚⬚⬚⬚⬚⬚⬚⬚⬚⬚⬚

Card Expiry Date _____